Rituals
of the
Season

20173449

Rituals
of the
Season

Margaret Maron

THORNDIKE
CHIVERS

This Large Print edition is published by Thorndike Press®, Waterville, Maine USA and by BBC Audiobooks Ltd, Bath, England.

Published in 2005 in the U.S. by arrangement with Warner Books, Inc.

Published in 2006 in the U.K. by arrangement with Robert Hale Ltd.

U.S. Hardcover 0-7862-8003-4   (Mystery)
U.K. Hardcover 1-4056-3524-X   (Chivers Large Print)
U.K. Softcover 1-4056-3525-8   (Camden Large Print)

The text of this Large Print edition is unabridged.
Other aspects of the book may vary from the original edition.

Set in 16 pt. Plantin by Elena Picard.

Printed in the United States on permanent paper.

British Library Cataloguing-in-Publication Data available

Library of Congress Cataloging-in-Publication Data

Maron, Margaret.
  Rituals of the season / by Margaret Maron.
    p. cm. — (Deborah Knott series) (Thorndike Press large print mystery)
    ISBN 0-7862-8003-4 (lg. print : hc : alk. paper)
    1. Knott, Deborah (Fictitious character) — Fiction. 2. North Carolina — Fiction. 3. Women judges — Fiction. 4. Weddings — Fiction. 5. Large type books. I. Title. II. Thorndike Press large print mystery series.
PS3563.A679R58 2005b
  813'.54—dc22   2005016802

For Natalie Jeanette Maron,
our longed-for, unexpected,
totally welcomed bonus

Acknowledgments

My thanks to Sheila Kay Adams for her cousin's definition of spinsters and old maids; to Louise Guardino of the A/B Afterburners for enlightening me about softball bats; to Aria and John McElhenny, who let me borrow a clever feature from their own wedding reception; and to Daniel "Chipp" Bailey, Chief Deputy Sheriff of Mecklenburg County, NC, for his technical expertise.

District Court Judges Shelly S. Holt and Rebecca W. Blackmore, of the 5th Judicial District Court (New Hanover and Pender Counties, NC), and Special Superior Court Judge John Smith continue to keep me updated on North Carolina law and court procedures. I owe them more than I can ever repay.

Margaret Maron
Johnston County, NC

Deborah Knott's Family Tree

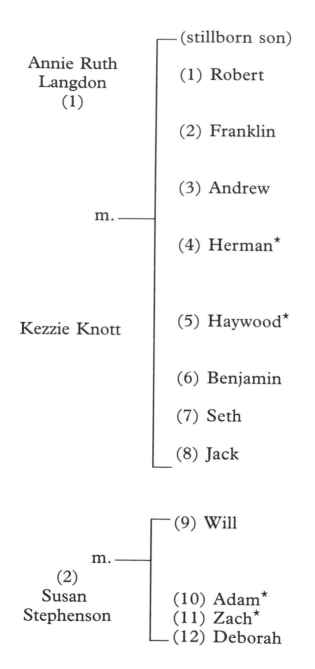

Annie Ruth
Langdon
(1)

m. ———

Kezzie Knott

— (stillborn son)

(1) Robert

(2) Franklin

(3) Andrew

(4) Herman*

(5) Haywood*

(6) Benjamin

(7) Seth

(8) Jack

m. ———

(2)
Susan
Stephenson

— (9) Will

(10) Adam*
(11) Zach*
(12) Deborah

*twins

m.———┤ 1) Ina Faye
       2) Doris > children > grandchildren

m.   Mae > children > grandchildren

m.———┤ 1) Carol > Olivia ("Tally")
       2) Lois
       3) April > A.K. & Ruth

m.   Nadine > *Reese, *Denise, Edward, Annie Sue

m.   Isabel > at least 3, including Valerie, Stephen, Jane Ann > g'children

m.

m.   Minnie > at least 3, including Jessica

m.

m.———┤ 1) Patricia ("Trish")
       2) Kathleen
       3) Amy > at least 2 children

m.   Karen > children
m.   Barbara > Lee, Emma

*twins

Many believe that politeness is but a mask worn in the world to conceal bad passions and impulses, and to make a show of possessing virtues not really existing in the heart; thus, that politeness is merely hypocrisy and dissimulation. Do not believe this; be certain that those who profess such a doctrine are themselves practising the deceit they condemn so much . . . True politeness is the language of a good heart.

Florence Hartley,
The Ladies' Book of Etiquette, 1873

Friday, December 10

The white sedan was later than expected, so late that the driver of the nondescript car parked on the shoulder was beginning to wonder if something had already happened to her. Then suddenly, there she was, zipping along in the fast lane of the interstate, her usual ten miles an hour over the speed limit, as if North Carolina's traffic laws did not apply to her.

You'd think somebody in her position would be a little more observant of the law, the driver thought wryly, pulling back onto the highway. *After all, she's sent people to jail for stuff not much more serious than speeding.*

In half an hour, the daily reverse flow from Raleigh would start to clog this stretch of highway, but right now traffic was still light, and in less than a minute both cars were side by side, traveling at the same speed.

The thirty-something woman appeared to be singing along with her radio when the second car pulled even. She glanced over casually, then her eyes widened in recognition and she smiled as she powered down her side window with a motion for the other to do the same.

"Hey!" she called cheerfully, her eyes flicking back and forth from the road ahead to the car beside her. "How's it going?"

"Going good right now."

The revolver came up to shoulder level and the woman's eyes widened in disbelief. Before she could flinch or dodge, a single shot pierced her jugular just above the small green-and-red cloisonné Christmas wreath pinned to the collar of her white cashmere sweater.

There was one quick glimpse of jetting blood, the sound of screeching brakes, then her car swerved away and crashed headlong into an overpass abutment.

The other driver touched the accelerator and sped on through the early twilight without a single look back in the rearview mirror.

Traveling north on the interstate in his

unmarked sedan, Colleton County Sheriff's Deputy Mike Castleman had his eye out for Judge Deborah Knott's car. Word had come through the dispatcher from Major Bryant that the judge was unaccountably late and not answering her cell phone, so if anyone should happen to spot her . . .

No sign of the judge's car, but up ahead Castleman did see one that matched the profile of the more brazen drug traffickers who frequented this stretch of interstate through North Carolina. Only one person in the car, so he didn't bother calling for the usual backup. He had just switched on the blue lights hidden behind his radiator grille when a second call came through that a white Lexus had crashed into the abutment where Possum Creek Road crossed over I-95.

He immediately thumbed his mike. "I'll catch it, Faye."

The suspect car ahead had obediently pulled over, but with his blue lights still flashing and his siren now wailing as well, Castleman gave a go-ahead wave to the sullen-looking Hispanic inside, made a U-turn across the grassy median, and headed south.

At the crash site, several civilian cars had

stopped. Their passengers milled around, trying to keep warm while they waited for professionals to arrive and take charge. A tall man strode forward when he spotted the badge on Castleman's heavy leather jacket.

"I was a medic in Iraq," he told the deputy. His warm breath made little puffs of steam in the chilled air. "The driver's dead but there's a baby girl in the backseat that looks to be hanging on by her toenails."

Baby girl? *Oh, Jeeze!* thought Castleman, who had not noticed the car seat until that moment. The bottom fell out of his stomach. His own daughter was nineteen, but he never came upon a situation like this without immediately thinking of her, and he was stricken by the sight of that lolling head.

More sirens and flashing lights lit up the darkening evening as an ambulance and a patrol car swerved to a stop. Red and blue strobes flashed over the car's bloody interior and made the white leather seats and steering wheel look as if they had been splashed with chocolate syrup then dusted with powdered sugar when the air bag popped open.

In the backseat, several gaily wrapped

Christmas packages lay jumbled by the impact. The medic pointed to a small one about six inches square.

"I don't know what's in it, but it's heavy as hell and it was on the kid's chest when I got here. Probably what knocked her out."

A large bruise had begun to darken the forehead of the baby girl buckled into the car seat. Otherwise, she did not move.

The driver's face was obscured by the deflated air bag and the front end of the car was so badly smashed that the baby was already on an ambulance to the hospital before they could get the car pried open enough to get her out.

"Oh dear God!" said one of the deputies when the dead driver's face came into view. "Y'all see who this is?"

"Christ almighty!" swore Castleman, peering over his shoulder. "I was in court with her just this morning."

Chapter 1

Punctuality is the mark of politeness.

Florence Hartley,
The Ladies' Book of Etiquette, 1873

I had adjourned court a little early that bleak December afternoon after taking care of everything I could without a prosecutor (the assistant DA had a late doctor's appointment), but I'd heard that the party outlet in Makely sold inexpensive wedding favors and, yeah, yeah, with less than two weeks till the big day, you'd think I would have already taken care of every detail worth mentioning.

Wrong.

Having avoided it for this long, I was now so hooked on this whole wedding thing that I was like a junkie who needs just one more fix. Although my sisters-in-law didn't know it, what I planned to wear was already hidden in an empty closet at Aunt Zell's house, along with my shoes, gloves, and the dark red velvet cloak that would ward off December's chilly winds going to and from the First Baptist Church over in Dobbs. (That the hooded cloak flattered the hell out of my dark blond coloring was purely incidental.) My bouquet had been ordered. The country club had been booked for a simple champagne reception, the gold band I would place on Dwight Bryant's finger had been engraved and entrusted to Portland Brewer, my matron of honor, and when I left home that morning, I was completely caught up on all my thank-you notes. (One good thing about a Christmas wedding is that greeting cards can do double duty.)

The only item lacking was the little bride and groom for the cake. And trust me, I do know they're tacky and not exactly cutting edge, but my bossy, opinionated family wouldn't feel it was a real wedding cake if I only had rosebuds and ribbon icing. I'd ordered a cake topper off the Internet — one in which the groom was dressed in a formal blue police uniform — but it still hadn't come. Kate Bryant, Dwight's artistic sister-in-law, had volunteered to paint the uniform brown like the one Dwight would be wearing and to change the bridal gown, too, but she was going to need a couple of days to work her magic and one of my own sisters-in-law had suggested I might find something suitable at the Makely store.

"Sorry," said the clerk. "You should have tried us back in the spring."

"Back in the spring, I didn't know I was going to need one," I told her.

At that point, I should have walked out of the store and headed straight back to Dobbs, but I saw so many cool stocking stuffers for my numerous nieces and nephews that I completely lost track of the time. It didn't help that traffic on the interstate was so backed up by an accident or something that I got off at the next exit and had to negotiate unfamiliar back roads.

"Dammit, Deb'rah, where've you been?" growled my groom-to-be when I pulled into a slot in front of his apartment well after dark and nearly ninety minutes later than I'd promised when we talked at noon.

Dwight Bryant and I first met on the day I was born — he remembers it; I don't — but until three months ago I'd always thought of him as just another of my

18

eleven older brothers. Surprised the hell out of me when pragmatic lust abruptly morphed into a romantic love as fiery and all-consuming as a Nora Roberts novel, especially when Dwight confessed that he'd been hiding his true feelings for me behind his honorary-brother role for years.

Doesn't stop him from still yelling at me like one of my brothers, though. Bareheaded, no jacket, he was pacing back and forth on the windswept landing in front of his second-floor apartment when I got there, and he made it down the steps before I could get my keys out of the ignition.

I tried to explain about court finishing early and how I then got sidetracked by Christmas shopping and after that, the traffic so that —

He didn't want to hear it. "And you couldn't call? Or remember to switch your phone on so I could call you?"

I admitted that I'd absentmindedly left my phone in the pocket of my robe, which was now hanging in an office at the Makely courthouse, but he caught me in his arms and held me tightly against him as if to make sure that I was whole and unharmed. For such a big guy, he can be surprisingly gentle. His hands and cheeks were like ice.

Felt good, though, and my body started to throb and buzz until I realized that part of the vibration came from the cell phone hooked on his belt.

With one arm still around me, he unclipped the phone, checked to see who it was, and said, "Yeah, Faye?"

I didn't hear what the dispatcher was saying, but there was nothing ambiguous about his reply. "Tell them to disregard that BOLO. She's here now."

I couldn't believe it. He'd done a be-on-the-lookout for me?

I twisted away from his arm, grabbed the small bag of groceries from the front seat of my car, and stormed up the stairs to his apartment.

"That was totally uncalled for," I said angrily, when Dwight finally followed me inside. I had flung my coat across the back of his couch and now I was slamming cupboard doors as I pulled out pots and pans.

"I haven't accounted to anyone since I was eighteen," I told him, "and I'll be damned if I'm going to start toeing some imaginary mark now just because we're getting married."

He closed the door quietly against the chill December night and stood there white-faced, staring at me, until I finally realized that he had probably spent the past hour remembering how close I came to dying the last time I didn't answer my cell phone for five hours.

I let go of my anger and went to him.

"Hey," I said softly, standing on tiptoe to brush his lips with mine. "Nothing's going to happen to me ever again. I'm going to be here safe and sound for the rest of your life, but not if you try to keep me in bubble wrap, okay?"

"I wish to God I could," he said and kissed me with such vehemence that I knew something bad had happened.

"What is it?" I asked. "What else did Faye tell you?"

"That traffic backup you ran into on the interstate just now? It was Tracy Johnson. She smashed into an overpass."

"*What?* Is she okay?"

He shook his head. "Sounds like she died instantly."

I stood there with my mouth open. Brisk, efficient Tracy Johnson? The tall and slender ADA who loves high heels as much as I do and who tries to hide her beauty and brains behind the ugliest pair of horn-rim glasses in eastern North Carolina?

Impossible!

"I just saw her," I protested. "She prosecuted today's calendar."

"I'm sorry, shug," he said.

"What about Mei?" I asked. "Tracy left court early because Mei had a doctor's appointment for an ear infection."

"She was in the car, too. They're going to air-vac her to Chapel Hill, but it doesn't sound good."

Three years ago, Tracy got tired of waiting around for a man who wasn't intimidated by her height or her mind and decided to adopt from China. It had taken her two years to complete all the paperwork, and she was utterly besotted by the baby, who was just beginning to walk and talk. Portland and I and some of the women from the DA's office had given her a shower once the adoption went through.

She was a few years younger and we were never hugely close, but I did respect her. She was an excellent prosecutor, efficient, prepared, and fairer than most who just want the win, no matter what.

"Does Doug know?" I asked. Doug Woodall is our district attorney and Tracy's boss.

"Doubt it," Dwight said. "They just ID'd her and family takes precedence. Did she have any?"

22

"I'm not sure. I know her parents are dead, but I think she has a sister or brother over in Widdington. Or maybe it was a cousin that came to her shower when she brought Mei home from China this spring."

Tears spilled down my cheeks and my heart was sore just thinking about that poor little baby. Unwanted by her birth mother, now she'd lost the adoptive mother who adored her. What would happen to her?

Dwight's cell phone buzzed again. "Yeah, Faye?"

His face went even grimmer as he listened, then he said, "Give me the coordinates again. And call Jamison and Denning. Tell them to meet me there."

Jack Jamison's one of the new detectives he's training and Percy Denning is Colleton County's crime scene specialist.

"What now?" I asked as he holstered his gun and reached for the heavy winter jacket hanging on a peg by the door.

"The wreck wasn't an accident," he said. "The EMTs say Tracy was shot."

"*Shot?*" All sorts of wild possibilities tumbled through my mind. I tried to think what was in season now. "Tracy died because some dumb hunter wasn't paying attention?"

Dwight shrugged. "The ROs say it looks like a deliberate act."

ROs — responding officers.

"Why?"

"Won't know till I get there, shug." He zipped his jacket, gave me a quick kiss and was gone.

Chapter 2

At these smaller dinner companies, avoid apologizing for anything, either in the viands or the arrangement of them. You have provided the best your purse will allow, prepared as faultlessly as possible; and you will only gain credit for mock modesty if you apologize for a well-prepared, well-spread dinner.

Florence Hartley,
The Ladies' Book of Etiquette, 1873

After Dwight left, I changed into jeans, pulled one of his old sweatshirts over my red silk turtleneck, and tuned the radio to a station playing Christmas carols. While the Mormon Tabernacle Choir sang of peace on earth, good will to men, I browned the chuck that I had picked up at a grocery store in Makely. I'll never be a gourmet cook, but I do okay with the basics and Dwight's not likely to starve to death, no matter what some people think.

The smells of well-browned onions and carrots soon filled the efficiency apartment. Beef stew is good cold-weather comfort food, and if Dwight was going to be late, prolonged simmering would only enhance the flavors.

The simple act of cooking usually mellows me out. Not tonight, though. Not even with the seasonal music and the stiff Jack Daniel's I had poured myself. As I sliced and browned and stirred, I kept picturing Tracy slumped over her steering wheel on some frozen stretch of I-95.

Not a hunting accident, the first officers on the scene had told Dwight. So who?

And why?

Back before I ran for the bench, Tracy and I had been natural antagonists — I as a defense attorney, she a brand-new prosecutor with a something-to-prove chip on her shoulder and the preponderance of the law on her side. But we hung with the same crowd, saw some of the same guys, and occasionally reached for the same pair of shoes when Fancy Footwork held their seasonal sales. She was way too tall for the high heels we both adored and she grumbled about how some male judges will subconsciously let their judgments be colored if a woman towers over them, but when three-inch apple green slingbacks call to you in the spring, it's hard to react logically.

A boy soprano sang "O Holy Night" in a high pure voice, and memories of Tracy crowded my mind: evenings at Miss Molly's on South Wilmington Street in Raleigh before she adopted Mei and quit dropping by smoke-filled cop bars on Friday nights. Trading war stories, the drinks, the laughter. I remembered how she'd bought a round for the house the first time she got a death threat from a felon she'd sent to prison. We'd even gone to a concert over in Greensboro together with a couple of SBI agents we'd met at Miss Molly's. She went out with the good-looking one several times and then he dropped her for a little five-foot-nothing blonde who made him feel big and strong in a way Tracy never could. In fact, now that I thought about it, he was probably the last straw before she decided to adopt.

Back in the spring, after I broke up with a game warden from down east, we sat next to each other at our local district bar association dinner and I was moaning to her about the dearth of good men. She had smiled and said, "But you know what? When you quit looking, suddenly they're right under your nose."

"Tell! Tell!" I'd demanded, but she'd just smiled again and kept her own counsel, which made me pretty certain that she was seeing someone. Mutual friends seemed to have the same impression, but since no one had a name and since Tracy always started talking about Mei the minute anybody asked about her love life, I hadn't pursued it.

Now I wondered. More women are killed by husbands or lovers than total strangers. Could this be a love affair gone horribly wrong? If she'd been in a relationship, though, why keep it secret?

Because he was married?

Not hardly likely, as my Aunt Sister would say. Yes, propinquity can sneak up on you and clobber you over the head when you're not looking, make you do things you never thought you would, but Tracy had been a levelheaded realist and I'd heard her speak scornfully of such couplings too many times to think she wouldn't have made propinquity zip its pants the minute it started breathing heavily.

On the other hand, between work and Mei, when would she have had time to get involved with a complete stranger? I thought of the other men in Doug Woodall's office. Chubby little Chester Nance, who'd run against me my first campaign? He's at least two inches shorter than Tracy and appears to be happily married.

Certainly not Doug himself. Even though he just turned forty, our DA has a no-nonsense wife who is famous for advising newlywed paralegals, "Sugar, you want to keep him on the straight and narrow, you keep him too dick-sore to even *think* about getting it up for another woman."

(Around the courthouse, it's a given that Mary Jess Woodall effectively practices what she preaches.)

Which brought us to Brandon Frazier. He left a mediocre private practice to work for Doug after Cyl DeGraffenried resigned. Now, he could be a possibility: divorced, no children, lean, intense, dark hair, smoldering navy blue eyes. Hairy as a shag rug, though, judging by his wrists and the back of his hands. Not my taste — except for a few stray hairs in the middle, Dwight's chest is fairly smooth — but maybe the caveman look was a turn-on for Tracy.

Or was her death something to do with her work as a prosecutor? Doug rotates his staff through both courts, the DWIs *and* the felony homicides. He's a political animal — it's an open secret that he has his eye on the governor's mansion in Raleigh — and it's his name on the ballot every four years, but he's comfortable sharing the spotlight as long as everyone remembers who the star is. Although Tracy often worked district court, she really shone in superior court's serious criminal cases, and after Cyl went to Washington, Tracy moved up from second chair and handled some of the big cases when Doug was stretched too thin. She enjoyed demolishing the defense and procuring stiff sentences for career felons.

The house phone rang.

"Deborah? How come you're not answering your cell? I've been calling all over for you."

"Hey, Portland," I said. Portland Brewer's an attorney here in Dobbs and we've been best friends since childhood. I explained about leaving my phone in the pocket of my robe, "and you don't have to yell at me about it. Dwight already did."

30

But Portland didn't want to natter about my absentmindedness. "You hear about Tracy Johnson?"

"I was here when Dwight got the call," I said. "You know anything more?"

"Other than that she and the baby were both killed?"

"No, Mei's still alive. They're airlifting her over to Chapel Hill."

"Really? I heard she died, too. And that Tracy crashed because someone shot her."

"Who told you that?"

"Avery. Is it true?"

Avery is Portland's husband and an attorney, too. A tax attorney. If he'd already heard that Tracy had been shot then it was all over the courthouse.

"It's true, but I don't know any details. Dwight doesn't think it's a hunter's stray bullet, though. I just hope we haven't suddenly acquired our own interstate sniper."

"A random shooter? Oh Lord! I drive back and forth on that stretch two or three times a week."

"Me too. But if it isn't random, who could she have angered so badly, Por?"

"Well, she did get another death threat a couple of weeks ago."

"She did? Who?"

"That manslaughter case over in

31

Widdington, where the guy shot his girl-friend's brother and claimed self-defense."

I only vaguely remembered it. "Last year? Where the brother tried to stop him from beating up his sister?"

"That's the one. It came to trial right before Thanksgiving and Tracy went for the maximum because he had a history of domestic violence."

"Wife-beaters don't usually have friends willing to kill for them," I said.

"No, but somebody else could maybe think she's the reason their man or woman's in prison."

"True."

Portland has more contact with the major violent felony cases than I do these days, but she couldn't think of any others that had generated a desire for revenge on Tracy. Most defendants pour their venom over prosecuting witnesses, not the prosecutors themselves.

Changing directions, I asked, "You ever hear who she was seeing these days?"

"Nope, but you know what a clam she could be. Getting disclosures out of her was like pulling stumps with a mule. She'd give you what you asked for, but you had to ask for every specific thing by its name, rank, and serial number. Wasn't she ADA down in Makely today?"

"Yeah," I said. "She left early, though. Mei had a doctor's appointment late this afternoon or she'd have been at daycare."

We talked about how unreal it was that Tracy should be dead so abruptly when everything had been so normal today. We kept going over the last times we'd seen her, which triggered a couple of odd memories. "Remember last week when you and she came in to see me about your motion to suppress some evidence against your client?" It was a motion I had denied.

"The Puckett business? I still think your reasoning was jesuitical on that."

"Give it a rest," I told her. "If anybody was arguing from arcane precedents, it was you."

Portland gave an unladylike snort. "So what happened?"

"After we dealt with your motion and you flounced off, she —"

"Hey! I did *not* flounce," Portland protested. "Waddled maybe, but big as this baby is, my flouncing days are over."

"You flounced," I told her firmly. "Anyhow, Tracy stayed behind a few minutes."

"What for?"

"I'm not sure."

It was only a few days ago, but between the wedding, Christmas, and having my house torn up six ways to Sunday, I can't seem to concentrate on anything else outside my courtroom unless someone practically grabs me by the shoulder and pushes my nose in it. And Tracy hadn't been that direct. Now that I thought about it, I realized that she might have been working herself up to discuss something important, but at the time, she'd been too circuitous for me to pursue it.

"She wondered if I thought the ends ever justified the means, then she looked at my ring and said something about the wedding, and one thing led to another till I almost forgot why she'd stayed. As she was leaving, though, I asked her if there was anything else she wanted to talk about and she said it was nothing important."

"So?" I could almost hear Portland's shrug.

"So here's the kicker, Por. She wanted to know if marrying Bo Poole's chief deputy wasn't going to compromise my impartiality, make me more inclined to believe police testimony over a defendant's witnesses. She's not the first one to ask that, but for some reason it really ticked me off this time. I told her that I'd just ruled against you and you were going to be my matron of honor. Anyhow, now that I look back on it, I can't help wondering if she decided not to ask me what she'd started to because of Dwight."

"If ends justify means?" Portland mused. "Are there any big cases coming up? Dwight arrested anybody that she was going to prosecute?"

"Not that I've heard. Just the usual run-of-the-mill stuff."

Major criminal cases don't wind up in my court. Oh, I might do an occasional probable cause hearing, but Dwight hadn't testified before me anytime recently and I really didn't have a clue as to the makeup of his caseload these days.

This is not due to a lack of communication on his side or a lack of interest on mine. No, it's part of the evolving ground rules we set up back in October. I've already told our clerk of court and my chief judge that I'd be recusing myself from any case that might require Dwight's testimony and that we've agreed not to discuss any district court cases arising from his department's investigations until after the case has been tried. Privately, Dwight and I had further agreed that I wouldn't bitch about frivolous charges and flimsy evidence if he wouldn't second-guess my rulings. The agreement's been in force for only two months, but so far it seems to be working.

Portland and I kicked it around some more before the baby kicked so hard that she couldn't concentrate. "See you tomorrow night," she said as we hung up.

Tomorrow night?

For a minute, my mind blanked; then I looked at the calendar hanging over Dwight's phone. There in the square for Saturday night was "Jerry's. 7 pm. Bar Ass'n," a reminder in my very own handwriting that our local bar association was hosting a dinner for Dwight and me. Almost every other square from now till Christmas had something scrawled on it. Amusingly, Sunday night was also "Jerry's. 7 pm. Bo." I had laughed when Dwight told me that Sheriff Bo Poole wanted to give us a dinner party at Jerry's, too.

"Want me to tell him to pick another place or time?" Dwight had asked.

"Not on my account," I'd said. Jerry's specialized in steak and catfish and I figured we could have steak one night and catfish the next. It was sweet that so many people wanted to celebrate our wedding, but I was beginning to feel as if we were running a marathon, with the twenty-second as our finish line. The day before the wedding, the twenty-first, was simply marked "Cal" and "rehearsal dinner." That's when we hoped to spend a quiet afternoon with Dwight's son. I'd seen him only once since the engagement and that was the last time he was down, back in late October. He seemed pretty cool with the situation, but it's hard to know what's going on in an eight-year-old's head.

Dwight's brother Rob had volunteered to drive up to Virginia to bring the child back as soon as his school let out for the holidays. For reasons still unknown, Dwight's ex-wife was actually cooperating with our plans and had agreed to let Cal spend Christmas with Dwight for the first time since their divorce.

Some of my sisters-in-law think it's weird that we're going to stay home after the wedding and celebrate Christmas out on the farm with the usual family get-togethers instead of taking an elaborate honeymoon trip somewhere, but Dwight and I both feel it's important to demonstrate to Cal as soon as possible that he's a welcome part of our new life.

I gave the stew another stir. It needed salt and a bay leaf. Salt was easy, but the only spices in Dwight's cabinets were pepper, a bottle of Texas Pete, a box of celery seeds, and a jar of garlic powder.

With the wedding less than two weeks away, his cupboards were getting down-right bare. Moving him out to the farm wasn't going to take much more than a couple of pickup trucks, his and maybe one of my brothers'. Cartons filled with CDs, videotapes, DVDs, books, and summer clothes lined one wall. He didn't want to dismantle his sound system or pack up his large flat-screen television until the last minute, but all his beer-making equipment — carboys, kegs, and four cartons of empty bottles — was already taking up a corner of my garage.

Dwight called shortly after ten to say he was on his way.

"Any word on Mei?" I asked.

His silence and then the long intake of breath told me all I needed to know.

"Oh no," I whispered.

"Looks like the impact bounced a heavy Christmas present off her head. Probably internal bleeding." In the background, I could hear staticky bursts from various car radios.

"Was the shooting really deliberate?"

" 'Fraid so."

"Come on home," I said.

"Fifteen minutes," he promised.

With tears streaming down my cheeks, I finished making up the dough for dumplings while children sang of Santa Claus and jingle bells. What kind of monster would deliberately shoot a woman with a sick child in her car? And why there and then — on the interstate where the speed limit was seventy miles an hour? Why not wait till she was alone, walking across a parking lot, say, or unloading groceries from her car?

I had just spooned the dumplings over the top of the stew and put the lid back on to steam them when there was a knock at the door.

"Dwight?" I hurried to unlock it, assuming that he'd left his keys in the truck.

"It's me," a familiar voice said. "Let me in."

I opened the door and there was my cousin Reid. Despite the raw December night, his overcoat was unbuttoned, his shirt had come untucked, and the odor of sourmash almost knocked me over. He was totally hammered.

"God, Deb'rah!" He swayed in the burst of cold air and his words were slurred. "I jus' heard. Tracy Johnson. Shot dead. And her li'l baby, too."

"Love and joy come to you . . ." sang the radio.

Chapter 3

Be careful in conversation to avoid topics which may be supposed to have any direct reference to events or circumstances which may be painful for your companion to hear discussed.

Florence Hartley,
The Ladies' Book of Etiquette, 1873

Reid took two steps toward the couch, then the smell of beef and onions hit his nose and he made an abrupt detour for the bathroom.

He was still pounding the porcelain when Dwight returned.

Dwight's lips were cold, but his kisses weren't.

When I could breathe again, I said, "You okay?"

"Now I am." He buried his face in my

hair. "You smell good enough to eat."

"You're just hungry," I said, turning toward the kitchen.

"Yeah," he said and pulled me back to him.

His chilled hands were busy warming themselves under my sweater when the sound of flushing stopped him. His eyebrows arched a question.

"Reid," I said. "Too much bourbon."

My cousin and former law partner swayed unsteadily in the doorway of the bathroom. His handsome face was a pasty green and his hair was still disheveled, but he'd tucked his white shirt back in and his speech was marginally clearer.

"Sorry," he said. "Client's Christmas party an' then somebody came in that'd heard — God! Tracy Johnson?" He caught himself on the doorjamb and looked at us in glassy-eyed confusion. "Don' know why I came here. I'll get out of y'all's way."

He patted his pockets for his car keys and started for the door, but Dwight put out a hand. "Not like this, ol' buddy. You can't drive off from here ready to blow a twelve."

I poured him a glass of tomato juice. "Drink this. You need food."

He protested and almost gagged again,

yet he let me lead him to the table, and once he'd swallowed some juice, his color improved.

Reid's a few years younger, but between my late start in law school and a year in the DA's office back before Doug Woodall was elected, we both joined the law firm about the same time. He became the current Stephenson of Lee and Stephenson, Attorneys at Law, when his father, Brix Junior, retired to play golf in Southern Pines. The current Lee is John Claude Lee, my mother's second cousin; Brix Junior was her first cousin on the Stephenson side. People new to the region (and still unfamiliar with our continuing penchant for genealogical linkage) tend to glaze over when I try to spell out how I'm related to both of my ex-partners even though they're no blood kin to each other, but old-timers nod sagely and work it out immediately that Reid's my second cousin.

"Good dumplings," said Dwight, helping himself to another one.

"Dotty made a beef stew you wouldn't believe," Reid said wistfully.

"Dotty never made a beef stew in her whole life. It's *boeuf bourguignonne,*" I reminded him, exaggerating the French pronunciation. I like Reid's ex-wife, but even her cookouts are haute cuisine. Everything has to be marinated in wine and *fines herbes.*

"*Cassoulet,*" Reid mourned. "*Coq au vin.*" He picked at a carrot but not much was getting to his mouth and he still seemed queasy. "Wish I never had to see another pizza or take-out box. Hate fast food."

"So quit complaining and get Aunt Zell to give you some cooking lessons." Over the last few years, I've learned that a touch of commonsense bitchiness can stave off the maudlin self-pity that overtakes Reid whenever he drinks too much and starts remembering what his philandering's cost him. Dotty was the love of his life and he's crazy about their son Tip, but she finally had enough. He came home early one morning to find all his personal belongings boxed up on the front porch. When she re-married last year, he disappeared down a Jameson bottle for a solid week.

As Reid stared moodily at his plate, I glanced over at Dwight, who had kept up his end of amiable table talk despite what he must have seen in the last few hours.

For their own mental stability, EMTs, trauma nurses and doctors, police officers, social workers, and yes, judges, too, learn

44

how to compartmentalize. I haven't experienced half the things Dwight has, but in my four years on the bench, I've seen men and women with eyes swollen shut in faces pounded into raw meat. I've seen infants whose tender little bodies have been used as ashtrays. I've seen children whose backs and buttocks are so scarred they look as if they've been flogged with barbed wire.

You do what you can to alleviate the suffering and to punish those responsible, and all the time you know you're just shoveling sand against the tide. "Vanity of vanities, all is vanity," says the pessimist of Ecclesiastes. "What profit hath a man of all his labor? . . . That which is crooked cannot be made straight."

And yet, what's the alternative? To sit above the fray and do nothing but wring our hands? Or to wade in and keep shoveling?

At the end of the day, though, we have to lay our shovels down and come back to friends and families who not only don't understand, but don't want to understand. So we try very hard to distance ourselves from the emotional assaults of our work and we tell ourselves that we've left it at the courthouse or hospital. Sometimes, if we're lucky, that's almost true.

Nevertheless, it helps to have someone you can share it with. Long before he became my lover, Dwight was my friend, my sounding board, my safety valve for venting; and whatever other changes marriage may bring, I'm hoping that this part won't change for either of us.

"She called me this morning," Reid said abruptly. "Wants to come by the office Monday."

"Dotty?" I asked.

"Tracy."

"Why?"

He stared at me blankly and I patiently rephrased the question. "Why was Tracy coming to the office, Reid?"

"Martha Hurst. See Dad's file."

"Who's Martha Hurst?" asked Dwight, who was still in the Army back then.

Truth to tell, the name wasn't much more familiar to me because Martha Hurst's trial took place the summer I was cramming for my bar exam. Except for the brutality of the crime and that a woman had killed a man instead of the other way around, it wasn't all that different from a dozen more where domestic disputes play out in violence. Brix Junior — Brixton Stephenson Senior died before I was born, but my family still can't remember to drop

46

the "Junior" from Reid's dad's name —
was Hurst's court-appointed attorney. I assume he mounted the best defense possible. What I mainly remembered is that a
jury found Hurst guilty and a judge sentenced her to death, and that's what I told
Dwight.

"Gonna strap her on that gurney in January," Reid said plaintively. "Give 'er the
big needle. Tracy said so."

Which must mean that all of Hurst's appeals had finally been exhausted.

"What was Tracy's interest?" I asked.
"She wasn't around when that woman was
tried and sentenced."

He shrugged. "S'posed to explain Monday." He yawned deeply and his eyes
unfocused. He pushed his plate away,
propped his elbows on the table, and
leaned his head on his hands.

"Come on, bo," Dwight said. "Time to
get you home. Deb'rah?"

I was already digging through my
cousin's pockets for his car keys.

Dwight half carried him downstairs and
put him in the truck and I followed them
to Reid's place, where we put him to bed.

I tried again to get him to speculate as to
why Tracy wanted to see Brix Junior's file
on Martha Hurst, but it was useless. He

just kept moaning, "Poor Tracy," so we pulled the covers up around him and left him to sleep it off.

On the drive back to Dwight's, with the heater warming my cold feet, I asked why he thought Tracy's death was personal and deliberate.

"And it wasn't any random sniper either, if that's what you're asking. Whoever pulled the trigger probably knew who he was shooting."

"How can you tell?"

"For starters, think how cold it is. Tracy wasn't wearing her coat or her gloves and she had a baby with an ear infection in the backseat, yet the passenger-side window was down."

"She was talking to whoever shot her?" For some reason, that made it more horrible. "I guess you won't know what kind of gun it was till you get the bullet back from the ME."

"No bullet," he said gloomily. "The shot came from such close range that it tore through her throat and smashed through the window on her side of the car. I've got guys out walking the median with metal detectors, but I'm not holding my breath."

I told him about the death threat Portland said Tracy had received recently. Like me, he thought it unlikely that someone convicted for domestic manslaughter could have arranged Tracy's death, "but we'll certainly check it out."

"Want me to call John Claude? Ask him to let me look at Brix Junior's files on Martha Hurst?"

"*I'll* get up with John Claude," he said. "You concentrate on the wedding and let me handle this investigation."

"Just trying to be a good helpmeet," I said innocently.

He looked down at me with a grin. "Oh yeah?"

"I won't meddle," I promised, "but I do know more legalese than you do and I might could pick up on something in the files that you'd miss."

"Don't bet on it. Besides, Tracy's death probably doesn't have a thing to do with Hurst's execution."

I meant it when I said I wouldn't meddle. On the other hand, Doug Woodall was bound to be at the bar association's dinner for us the next night. What could it hurt to ask Tracy's boss if he knew why she was interested in Martha Hurst?

Chapter 4

Sisters ought never to receive any little attention from their brothers without thanking them for it, never to ask a favor of them but in courteous terms.

Florence Hartley,
The Ladies' Book of Etiquette, 1873

Although some of my farm-bred brothers are better than others at reading a blueprint, every one of them has building skills; and back in October, as soon as they heard I was marrying their lifelong buddy, they put their heads together and decided that their wedding gift would be the new bedroom and bath we planned to add onto my house. If Dwight and I would buy the materials, they would do the work, and they'd get it finished well before the wedding.

Or so they promised.

The house had been torn up for two months now, and when I was there earlier in the week, it looked to be another full month before we could begin using the new space.

The good thing about family is that you can call up and yell at them if they get behind schedule. The bad thing about family is that they don't pay you one dab of attention, not when king mackerel and blues are running down at the coast or when deer season's in full swing. On a farm, there's always something that needs picking or baling or plowing, or else it's a big green piece of machinery that breaks down and takes five trips to the John Deere place before all the right parts can be found. To my pointed questions of when they planned to finish, it was, "Hey, chill, little sister. You ain't getting married till almost Christmas. Why you so antsy? It'll get done."

With their freezers now full of fish and venison and farm chores at low winter ebb, my brothers swore they really would have the additions finished before the twenty-second. Dwight and I had planned to spend Saturday working alongside them, but I wound up driving out alone because Sheriff Bo Poole had called a meeting about Tracy's death and Dwight wanted to check on the lines of investigation he'd set in motion the night before.

I got there expecting to sand Sheetrock. Instead, I found Robert just pulling off his face mask as he unplugged the sander after smoothing the final joint. His hair, forehead, and green denim coveralls were white with spackle dust.

"Herman and Nadine are coming over this morning to finish wiring all the boxes, so we might could be ready to start painting this evening iffn them boys can ever figure out how to cut the trim," he said.

Out in the two-car garage, someone had brought over a space heater so that they could work without the hindrance of heavy winter jackets. Will, Seth, and Andrew had lined up lengths of molding and baseboards on the sawhorses and were now arguing over how to set the angles on Andrew's miter box.

Will and Seth threw me welcoming grins, but Andrew had an exasperated look on his face. "I suppose you got an opinion on how we ought to be cutting 'em, too."

"Not me," I said. Spatial calculations always fox me. I can do verbal problems, but those visual problems where you're supposed to look at a figure and then match it to one rotated two turns? No way. "Last time I tried to cut some forty-five-degree angles for a doorway, I wound up with twenty feet of trim for firewood, so I've got no dog in y'all's fight."

"Humph," Will snorted. "That'd be a first."

"Hey, shug," said Seth, the least critical of my brothers. "You see what we fixed Dwight?"

I shook my head. I hadn't been out since Tuesday and for all I knew they could've ripped off half the walls and added an indoor pool.

"Was April's idea," said Andrew, with a touch of husbandly pride.

That didn't surprise me. April keeps coming up with new suggestions. She loves to move walls and windows and is the only one of my sisters-in-law to own her own table saw.

I looked around the garage and saw nothing different.

"No, it's in the house," said Seth.

They followed me in to watch my reaction and Robert came through the living room to join us. All four brothers beamed in anticipation.

When I first planned the house, I never expected to do much formal entertaining, so the kitchen and dining room are a single large space divided by a work counter. On the dining room side, one whole wall is nothing but a floor-to-ceiling china cabinet. Below are drawers and closed shelves that serve as a long buffet. Above are more closed shelves. Everything's painted white enamel with brass fittings. Together they hold all the china, silver, crystal, and table linens that my town-bred mother gave me before she died. The first time I came through the kitchen, I hadn't noticed April's new addition because it had been built into a corner wall and already had its first coat of matching white enamel. It looked like an armoire and they had boxed it in so that I was now missing about two feet of counter space. When I opened the armoire doors, I had to laugh. There sat a professional-looking beer tap. Opening the lower doors revealed a small refrigerator unit big enough to hold two five-gallon aluminum kegs.

"Daddy was over here the other night," said Will, "and he saw Dwight's beer-making stuff out in the garage."

"We got to talking 'bout how Dwight's always saying the worst part about making it is the bottling," said Seth.

"— so Daddy said he'd buy a tap for the

kegs if we could figure out where to put it," Robert said.

"And you know April," Andrew finished.

"Dwight will love it," I told them. "You guys are wonderful."

They put their aw-shucks faces on, but I hugged each of them anyhow. I couldn't wait for Dwight to see it. While stationed in Germany, he developed a taste for premium beers that his wallet couldn't afford once he was back in the States, and particularly not after he had to start paying hefty child support. A friend had suggested that he pick up some hops and malt at the American Brewmaster in Raleigh and try making his own. I'm more into bourbon and tequila than beers and ales, but I have to admit he gets delicious results, everything from heavy winter stouts to light summer lagers. I've helped him bottle a couple of five-gallon batches, though, and yes, it's tedious as hell siphoning the beer into individual bottles and then working that capper. This refrigerated tap would really please him, especially since it was a gift from Daddy.

After Dwight's own father was killed in a tractor accident, Daddy had treated him like another one of his boys, loading them up on the back of the pickup to go for ice cream in the summer, using a tractor to pull a train of their homemade sleds around icy lanes in the winter. If Will and the little twins got a switching for some over-the-top piece of mischief and Dwight was involved, his legs got switched, too. At report card time, he got a dime for every A, just like the others.

But what would tickle Dwight even more is that Daddy also used to be in the business of making his own drinking supply. Unfortunately, his recipes were never as legal as Dwight's.

While the boys went back to figuring out miter angles, I took the shop vac Seth had brought over and began to vacuum up the Sheetrock dust and small stuff that littered the floors. When I got to the new bathroom, I was delighted to see that the fixtures were fully plumbed in now. The shower stall itself still needed some tiles, as did parts of the floor and countertop, but the toilet and sink had water and things were looking good.

Seth's wife Minnie, Andrew's April, and Robert's Doris arrived while I was admiring the slope of the oversize walk-in stall. I thanked April again for suggesting that we build it like that so that no shower curtain would be needed. "And the beer tap's fantastic."

Herman's deep voice suddenly boomed from the living room. Everybody else usually comes in through the back porch into the kitchen, but he has to use the front door, which is flush with the ground and easier for his wheelchair.

His wife Nadine immediately came to find us, and the first words out of her mouth were, "Did your dress come in yet?"

For some reason, she and Doris were worried that I had ordered something totally inappropriate, and they had appointed themselves arbiters of family values. I know they mean well, but I can't resist teasing them. In truth, no one had seen what I planned to wear except Aunt Zell and Portland and they were pretending to be as worried as the others that I'd have to walk down the aisle in my judge's robe if the dress didn't come soon.

"I don't know why you can't at least tell us what color it is," Doris grumbled.

"Because if you say you hate it before you see it, I'll feel awful."

"Long as you don't get pure white, it'll be fine," Nadine said. "I mean, everybody in Colleton County knows Dwight's not the one that picked your cherry, though I do think you could be a little more careful about letting folks know y'all two are already keeping house. I remember how proud I was when Denise walked down the aisle dressed like a pure angel in that white silk dress. Didn't she look like an angel, Minnie?"

"She certainly did," Minnie agreed with a perfectly straight face. Not by the flicker of an eyelash would she nor April nor I ever hint that Nadine's older daughter had no more right to pure white than I did, even though Denise's baby weighed a full eight pounds when it was born "prematurely" seven months later.

"All the same, I have to say that I looked really good in the white satin version I tried on," I said innocently.

Doris pounced. "So it's satin?"

"There was also a red satin version."

"You wouldn't!"

I laughed. "You're always acting like I'm a scarlet woman. Wouldn't a scarlet dress be appropriate?"

"She's just teasing us," Nadine said. "Even Deb'rah wouldn't wear red satin when her own matron of honor's wearing red velvet."

"White velvet?" April asked, getting into the game.

"Maybe," I told her.

"Off-white velvet?" Doris considered off-white velvet and nodded approvingly. "What about the veil?"

"Well, I did see one with a twelve-foot train but then I'd've had to have trainbearers and I thought that'd be a little much."

"Oh, I don't know," said Nadine. "There's enough grandbabies in the family. That might've looked real cute."

Before she could get into just how cute the little ones would be pulling on a long veil, Will and Seth came in with lengths of cut molding and began nailing them in place. I was impressed by the precision with which Andrew's forty-five-degree angles met each other snugly at the corners.

Nadine and Doris went to help Herman finish wiring the wall switches and outlets, while April recruited Minnie and me to lay tile in the bathroom. For the first time, I began to feel optimistic that we might just bring it in on schedule.

At noon, we paused for lunch. My sisters-in-law had brought sandwiches and Dwight got there just as they were pouring the iced tea.

"Aw, y'all didn't have to go to all that trouble," he said when he saw the beer tap. "I'd've married y'all's ugly little sister anyhow."

"It's only fair," said Seth. "You're the one doing us a real big favor."

"Yeah," Will chimed in. "Daddy thought we were going to have this old maid on our hands forever."

Doris giggled. "Not an old maid. A spinster."

"There's a difference?" asked Dwight.

"Hold on, now," said Herman, who always gets red-faced whenever the talk turns the least bit bawdy in mixed company. He rolled his wheelchair back from the table. "We here to work or we gonna just sit around flapping our jaws?"

A few hours later, after the others had called it a day, Dwight and I were getting ready for the bar association's dinner.

We were running late and had told each other that it would save time to shower together. This was proving not quite accurate.

"So what *is* the difference between a spinster and an old maid?" Dwight asked, as he soaped my back.

"Well, as Doris would've said if Herman hadn't stopped her, a spinster ain't never been married. But an old maid ain't never been married ner *nothing*."

Chapter 5

Do not make any display of affection for even your dearest friend; kissing in public, or embracing, are in bad taste.

Florence Hartley,
The Ladies' Book of Etiquette, 1873

Jerry's Steak & Catfish House is popular with our district bar association. The food is good, the prices are reasonable, and, best of all, its location out in the country, heading for the county line, makes it fairly convenient for everyone in the two counties that comprise our judicial district.

As usual, Jerry had given us the large private room upstairs. The front glass wall lets us look out over the main pond where a lot of his catfish are raised. In the middle of the pond, a large Christmas tree cast colorful lights across the surface of the dark water. Inside the restaurant, three more trees shimmered in the softly lit rooms and were refracted by each windowpane and bit of glassware. The tree by the front door was decorated in cow ornaments of every description, from delicate hand-blown glass Holsteins to sturdy plastic Belted Galloways. The one at the foot of the staircase was devoted to fish ornaments, interspersed with an occasional clamshell angel or gilt-rimmed sand dollar that had been brought back from the coast by dedicated patrons. Those two trees were artificial, but the third was a real ten-foot fir decorated in hundreds of small clear lights and red velvet bows of varying sizes. It stood at the top of the stairs, where this year's president of the association, my cousin and former law partner John Claude Lee, waited to welcome us individually.

In honor of the season, the tables on the upper level were covered with dark red cloths. Each round table held a centerpiece of votive candles, holly, and cedar; and because Jerry's something of a romantic under his tough exterior and this dinner was, after all, to celebrate an impending wedding, clusters of fresh mistletoe hung above each table as well. The fat white berries gleamed translucently in the candle-light.

Jerry's place will never be mistaken for a trendy New York bistro, but stepping into its friendly, down-to-earth warmth after a chilly walk across the windswept parking lot was like slipping into a cozy hand-knitted sweater.

Our regular meetings usually throb with hearty laughter and boisterous talk, but to-night, even though Dwight and I were al-most the last to arrive, the room was subdued. Plenty of talk, not much laughter.

"Sad business about Tracy and her little girl," John Claude said in greeting us. His wife Julia, tall and patrician, presented a cool cheek for us to kiss, then clasped my arm more warmly than usual. "It *is* awful. Especially now, here at Christmas. I just hope it won't put a damper on the wed-ding. Everyone's so worried about that. You know how happy we've all been for both of you."

I took Julia Lee's words with a big block of cow salt as we headed for the open bar set up beyond the tree. Dwight might be a well-respected lawman among my peers, but for some of those peers, the respect was tinged with condescension, the respect an elitist might give to a good plumber or electrician — fine to share a beer and sandwich with in the kitchen while he fixes the thing you couldn't, fine to play the good ol' boy with at a ball game or when shooting a game of pool down at the local bar, but not someone you'd necessarily bring home for cocktails in the living room.

Even Tracy had alluded to Dwight's lack of formal degrees. Never mind that his Army intelligence tours overseas and in Washington probably equaled a college education. Attorneys and judges don't usually marry sheriff's deputies. They're supposed to marry another attorney, a doctor, a successful business owner, or a college professor. Dwight had a personal letter of appreciation from a former president of the United States hanging on his office wall, but he didn't have that piece of paper signed by the president of a medical or law school hanging right beside it.

Despite the glasses that were raised in our direction as we crossed the room, there were probably several who thought that this marriage was unsuitable, especially a couple of those who'd put the moves on me in years past. But hey, I've been raising eyebrows all my life. Why should my final choice of men be any different?

And yet . . . ? Here in this roomful of bar members, I suddenly realized that part of the vibes I attributed to them might actually derive from that last one-on-one with Tracy last week. She had annoyed me by asking whether Dwight's job wasn't going to compromise my courtroom objectivity, but before that, there had also been a throwaway remark about lawmen with only a high school education. Didn't the disparity bother me?

Distracted by all that was going on in my life at the moment, I had been much too full of love and joy to take offense. Instead, I'd laughed as I gathered up my papers to leave. "My daddy quit school in sixth grade to start making moonshine and most of my brothers are farmers or blue-collar tradesmen. Where's the disparity?"

"I guess you've never worried about public opinion anyhow, have you?" she'd said, and then came that question about whether I could stay fair when judging defendants arrested by Dwight's subordinates.

That's when I'd snapped at her. I might not sweat the white-glove upright-pillar-of-society stuff in my personal life, but I do take my job pretty damn seriously. I'd sworn an oath to that effect on my mother's Bible and I would bend over backwards not to break it.

Avery and Portland Brewer were tending bar when we got there. He was dapper in a black shirt and red tie; she was absolutely huge in a shapeless black suit brightened by a gold-and-silver Christmas scarf.

"If I can't drink it, I can at least play in it," she said.

"Hang in there," I told her. "By New Year's Eve, you can drink all the champagne you want."

She gave a long-suffering grimace. "No, I won't. I'm going to breast-feed, remember? So there goes another dry year."

Avery mixed me a bourbon and diet Pepsi while Portland poured Dwight a beer and said, "Tracy's baby. Did she suffer?"

"I really don't think so," he answered, and I hoped he wasn't just trying to spare Portland's feelings. "It looks like she was knocked out on impact and never regained consciousness."

Portland touched her swollen abdomen protectively. "The only good thing in this whole sorry business is that Tracy didn't know. She didn't, did she?"

"No way," Dwight assured her.

Tears glistened in Portland's eyes. "I've

never seen or held this baby, but I already love it so damn much that if anything happened to it —"

Avery put his arm around her. "Nothing's going to happen, honey."

She gave him a shaky smile. "I know that. I do know that. I said *if.*"

As we moved away from the bar, we were given hugs and handshakes by every other person, but Dwight was also questioned about what, if any, progress had been made on finding Tracy's killer.

"Don't let this one get away," said Doug Woodall when he and Mary Jess intercepted us.

"Not if I can help it," Dwight said. "I'm going to need to talk to you Monday, see what cases she was working on. And I hear she got a death threat recently."

"That was just some loser mouthing off. But anytime, Bryant. My office is at your disposal."

"Come on, sugar," Mary Jess told my groom. "I see some mistletoe over there and I intend to get me a big ol' kiss. You don't mind, do you, Deborah?"

"Would it matter if I did?"

"Not a bit," she said cheerfully as she hauled Dwight away. "You can kiss Doug, if you want."

He cocked his head at me and we both laughed. Before I could ask him anything, though, two of my fellow judges came up to wish me well and to rehash the elections just past. Now that judges in North Carolina run on a nonpartisan ticket, politics is marginally less divisive, although all of us know who's liberal and who's conservative, who's for the death penalty and who would be happy to have it abolished.

The jury was still out for me on that point. Putting a killer to death winds up costing the state more than giving him life imprisonment, and only the most naive think of it as a deterrent anymore. Too, I'm beginning to get a little uneasy with the idea of my state acting purely for revenge, especially when it doesn't administer the death penalty fairly. On the other hand, every time I start thinking it should be abolished completely, along will come the murder of a child or an old woman that's so flat-out brutal that the details can't be printed in a family newspaper, and I'm right there with the old eye-for-an-eye and a-life-for-a-life attitude.

My subliminal thoughts on the death penalty were suddenly interrupted when, through a sober-suited group of attorneys, I spotted a smiling brown face. She came straight to me and I stared in disbelief. *"Cyl?"*

"Hey, girl," she said, laughing at my total surprise.

I gave her a hug. "What are you doing here?"

"Well, I heard it was a party, and since you won't come to Washington, I decided Washington better come to you."

Cyl DeGraffenried is all things black and beautiful. Top five percent in her law class at Duke, too. Doug really hated it when she left his office a year ago last fall and joined a prestigious black lobbyist firm in D.C.

"You came all this way for me?" Our friendship had gotten off to a rocky start, but we'd since shared so much that I knew we'd always be tight.

"Well, you and Grandma. She threatened to disown me if I didn't come visit now, since I can't be here for Christmas."

Cyl wore a deep purple silk pantsuit, nipped to accentuate her tiny waist. White silk scarf, chunky gold jewelry, and a haircut to die for. I knew I looked just fine in my own caramel-colored wool dress, knee-high brown boots, and a great-aunt's topaz brooch and earrings, but she was so polished and urban that I felt just a touch of country dowdiness.

"How long are you down for?" I asked.

"Only for the weekend. I fly back after church tomorrow."

"What do you mean you can't be here for Christmas? Are you telling me you can't come to our wedding either?"

She shook her pretty head. "Sorry, but I think I'm going to be in Wisconsin."

"Wisconsin? You 'think'?"

"It's a long story."

"Then come for breakfast tomorrow morning. We can't talk here and it sounds like we've got some serious catching up to do."

We'd barely set the time before someone came up behind me and put his hands over my eyes.

"Guess who, darlin'?"

For a moment, my mind blanked and then I laughed. "Brix Junior?"

I turned around to see for sure and was caught up in a warm hug by my mother's first cousin. Reid's dad was Stephenson tall, with a rangy athletic build and snow white hair. Handsome as ever. Reid will look just like him at that age.

"I don't believe it," I said. "They still letting you into these dinners?"

"Don't be pert, darlin'," he said. "I may

be retired but I've kept up my membership and soon as I heard they were throwing this thing for you tonight, I told Jane we had to come."

"Is she with you?"

Brix Junior nodded toward a clump of women over near the windows and yes, there was Jane with Julia Lee.

"You both look marvelous," I said honestly.

"Retirement agrees with us," he said complacently. "Course, Jane sits on as many boards and foundations as she ever did, but it's a poor week I don't get in at least five rounds of golf."

Brix Junior had always been popular with his colleagues, and they came crowding around to see him. As he turned to hold court, he said, "We're staying with Zell and Ash tonight, so we'll see you for lunch tomorrow."

Tomorrow? Stricken, I remembered that Aunt Zell had extracted a promise that Dwight and I would come for Sunday lunch tomorrow, a date I had forgotten to calendar. Breakfast with Cyl, lunch with Aunt Zell and Uncle Ash, supper here at Jerry's again tomorrow night? With all this social eating, I was going to have to let out some seams if I wasn't careful.

★ ★ ★

John Claude took his place at the head table and rapped his empty glass with a fork to get our attention. "If everyone will be seated, our waiters are ready to take your orders."

I looked around for Dwight and found him rubbing lipstick from his face. "How many women have you been kissing?" I asked him.

"Not me," he protested. "I was ambushed."

"Yeah, yeah." I reached for his handkerchief and took care of a spot he'd missed, then smoothed his brown hair where someone had ruffled it.

We were directed to the head table and I made sure I wound up on Doug Woodall's left. I figured that if Julia Lee kept Dwight occupied on my other side, I might could sneak in a few questions.

Someone had gone to the trouble of creating little individual menu cards with wedding bells, my name and Dwight's, and tonight's date printed across the top.

Across the room, I saw Reid seated with Jane and Brix Junior. He looked awful, and when our eyes met, he gave a shamefaced nod.

After the waiters had taken our orders,

John Claude again called for our attention.

"This is not a regular business meeting," he said, "but before we get into the festivities, let's take a moment to acknowledge the tragic death of one of our own. As you all know, Tracy Johnson, one of our assistant district attorneys, was shot last night by an unknown assailant as she drove home with her daughter, Mei. Let us close our eyes and observe a moment of silence for those two lives that are lost to us forever."

Again, brief images of Tracy tumbled through my mind from the years I had known her — her clear intelligent eyes, her frown when I ruled against her, her quick nod of satisfaction when I found for the State, the time I bought a pair of black high heels she'd wanted but regretfully opted not to buy because of her height, her delight when we surprised her with that baby shower, her tenderness when strapping Mei into the car seat, her dismay when she realized that her favorite white silk blouse had a pureed-spinach stain that wouldn't come out.

"Judge Parker, would you lead us in prayer?" John Claude said softly.

Luther Parker rose to oblige. He had run against me and won in my first election to become our district's first black judge. Reared up in an AME church down in Makely, he knew all the words and phrases, and from him they sounded genuine and sincere as he prayed for Tracy and Mei, then for Dwight and me, and finally for all of us gathered together in this place.

"Amen," he said and whispered amens rustled around the room.

John Claude rose with his wineglass in hand. "There will be time for speeches after dinner," he said, "but for now, let's lift our glasses to Deborah and Dwight and to many long years together."

Everyone smiled and lifted their glasses.

"Hear! Hear!"

"Cheers!"

"Much happiness, guys!"

The waiters returned with our food and soon we were cutting into perfectly grilled steaks and baked potatoes. The tables gradually became lively with talk and laughter, and when Julia Lee started telling Dwight about something that her poodle CoCo had done, I took a sip of my Merlot and turned to Doug Woodall.

"Refresh my memory," I said. "Who prosecuted the Martha Hurst case?"

Doug frowned. "Martha Hurst?"

"Brix Junior defended her a few years

back. She's on death row, scheduled to die next month unless the legislature imposes a moratorium. At least that's what Tracy told Reid when she asked to see Brix Junior's case file on Hurst. Why would she be interested in a case that happened before she joined your staff?"

"I didn't know she was."

"She didn't ask you about it?"

He shook his head, and for the first time I noticed tiny flecks of silver in his thick dark hair.

"That was back when Wendell Barham was still DA, right?" I said.

"Right." Doug's hand strayed to the collar of his jacket, where his thumb and index finger slowly rubbed the left collar point. "But Barham didn't work the case. I did. It was my first death penalty win. First and only woman, too."

My own hand started for his collar. "May I?"

He hesitated, then shrugged. "Sure."

I lifted it and saw the row of tiny gold nooses pinned there near the seam line.

"How many now?" I asked. Doug had just won his third term of office and part of his appeal was his strong advocacy of the death penalty for particularly heinous crimes.

75

"Six." His face turned grim. "And when Bryant arrests whoever did Tracy, I'll put in my order for number seven."

Chapter 6

You can, in a pleasant chat with a friend at home, have more real enjoyment in her society than in a dozen meetings in large companies, with all the formality and restraint of a party thrown around you. There are many subjects of conversation which are pleasant in a parlor, tête-à-tête with a friend, which you would not care to discuss in a crowded salon, or in the street. Personal inquiries and private affairs can be cosily chatted over.

Florence Hartley,
The Ladies' Book of Etiquette, 1873

Dwight and I were so tired when we got home from Jerry's that we just dumped the gifts we'd been given on the dining table and fell into bed, too exhausted to do more than snuggle next to each other to keep warm under the quilts before falling asleep.

Next morning, we were up by seven-thirty. I've never met Dwight's ex-wife and he won't badmouth the mother of his son, but from things his mother and sisters have let drop and from the way he's so handy around the kitchen, it's clear that she never waited on him. He automatically started the coffee while I cleared the table for breakfast.

Because the bar association had put Portland in charge of getting something suitable for us, we now owned a wonderful hand-thrown greenish gray bowl about eighteen inches in diameter and six inches deep. She had commissioned it from Jugtown Pottery over in Moore County and it was signed on the bottom by Vernon Owens. In the future, it would hold nuts or fruit or maybe even enough coleslaw to feed all my brothers and their families at our next pig-picking. Right now, it was piled high with Christmas ornaments.

Portland had asked each attendee to bring something for our first tree together, and my colleagues had responded so enthusiastically that the bowl couldn't hold them all. A few of them were merely fancy glass balls; the rest were figurals that were meant to bring a laugh or to zing us. Judge Longmire had used a permanent marker on a shiny gold star so that it now looked like a deputy's badge and was labeled "Colleton County Sheriff's Department." Kaye Barley, an attorney from Makely, had contributed a sleek little black sports car that was meant to evoke the Firebird I'd wrecked up in the mountains this past October, and Julie Walsh, an ADA in Doug's office, gave us a comic Justice peeking from under her blindfold. A sorrowful-looking plastic beagle might have started life in its natural brown-and-white coat, but an ardent Republican judge had sprayed it yellow. An equally ardent Democrat gave us a donkey wearing a Santa Claus hat.

A particularly elegant gold-and-white angel came with a gift card signed by John Claude and Reid. John Claude may have chosen the angel, but I'm sure he never noticed Reid's embellishments. At least, I assume it was Reid who had doctored the tiny open hymnal the angel was singing from. In almost microscopic lettering, the hymnal was now titled *Kama Sutra* and was open to pages sixty-eight and sixty-nine.

Yeah, that would definitely be Reid.

I'd about strangled on my coffee when Dwight pointed it out to me last night.

"Want me to build us a tree?" Dwight asked now, pouring us each a mug of fragrant coffee as I shifted the fragile ornaments over to the buffet counter next to his new beer tap.

"My goodness, Major Bryant." I fluttered my eyelashes at him in my best Scarlett O'Hara manner. "You can build trees?"

"Yeah, well, I'm not crazy about those bought ones. I'd rather just go out and cut us a pine. You mind?"

"A pine?" I quit fluttering and looked at him dubiously. A thick and bushy cedar I could understand, but our scrub pines aren't very thick and I do like a full tree.

"That's what we used to have when I was a kid after Dad died and Mama went back to school to get her teaching certificate."

I knew things had been tight for Miss Emily. Widowed. Four young children. Of course there wouldn't have been money for store-bought trees, and so many people used to go out foraging for Christmas trees back then that wild cedars were just about eradicated in our area. I remember hearing my own mother complain that there were no decent-shaped ones left on the farm. Nowadays, between artificial trees from Kmart and picture-perfect fresh firs at every grocery store, cedars are making a comeback along our hedgerows.

Daddy used to grumble about the foolishness of paying good money for a tree that was going to wind up on a New Year's Eve bonfire, but Mother could argue him down every time. Her store-bought trees always filled the front corner of the living room, nearly touching the ten-foot ceiling of the old farmhouse, ablaze with lights and shimmering with strands of silvery tinsel.

I hadn't realized that Dwight's childhood trees were different from mine, but if a skimpy Charlie Brown pine was what he wanted, I could certainly play Linus.

"Why don't you wait and let Cal help you cut it?" I suggested.

His brown eyes lit up with pure happiness. "Good idea."

"And we'll need a stand that holds water."

"No problem. I'll ask Mama if she still has our old iron one. She only puts up a little artificial tree these days."

He glanced at his watch. "What time's Cyl coming?"

"I told her eight-thirty. That'll give us a couple of hours before she has to make preaching services at Mount Zion."

"I'm going to clear out for a while, then. You don't want me here if y'all are going to do catch-up. I've scheduled a briefing this morning anyhow, so I'll go in early. Start on Tracy's office. See what they've got for me so far."

I reminded him that we were due to take lunch with Aunt Zell and Uncle Ash at one o'clock. "Jane and Brix Junior will be there, too."

He scowled. "Does that mean a jacket and tie?"

" 'Fraid so."

I set a cast-iron skillet on one of the burners, turned the flame on under it, and took out several pieces of the link sausage Maidie had sent over from hog-killing the week before. Dwight went off to get dressed but came back almost immediately, wearing nothing except shorts and socks, with a dark wool shirt in one hand and two knitted ties in the other. "Which tie you like better with this shirt?"

When I hesitated, I got another scowl. "You saying I've got to wear a white shirt, too?"

"It doesn't have to be white, but dress

shirts are really sexy," I murmured.

He grinned. "Yeah?"

"Yeah."

"Too bad, shug. My only clean ones are back in my apartment."

"Which is only a few blocks from the courthouse," I said sweetly as I stood on tiptoes to nuzzle his ear.

"I'm still going to look like a cop," he warned, doing a little nuzzling of his own.

"But a handsome, well-dressed cop who —"

The sausage popped before I could complete that thought.

He looked down at me with a speculative eye. "Who what?"

"Who makes me forget I'm supposed to be fixing breakfast for an old friend who's due here any minute." I rescued the sausages just before they began to burn and gently rolled them over without piercing their casings.

"Not for another half-hour." He put his arms around me from behind.

I tried to concentrate on browning the sausages. "Would you like for me to wrap toast around a piece of this for you to take with you?"

"Actually," he said huskily, "what I'd really like . . ."

Okay. I admit it. I'm easily distracted. So what else is new?

Praying that Cyl would be late, I turned off the stove.

Cyl was on time, but it turned out not to matter. By the time she drove up in her rental car, Dwight was finally dressed and walking toward his truck.

He waved to Cyl, said he'd see me at Aunt Zell's, and then headed back out the way Cyl had come.

The mercury must have been rising all night because it was a little warmer this morning than the night before. I was comfortable enough in my dark blue zip-up cardigan and gray wool slacks, although I could feel the cold porch floor through my wool socks as I held the screen door open for Cyl.

I hadn't seen her to actually talk to since back in early summer, three months before Dwight proposed, so even while we were busy hugging, we were also taking a quick inventory of each other. I wasn't consciously eating less these days; nevertheless, my scale and my clothes both told me that I was thinner than I'd been in years, probably because I seemed to be riding a perpetual roller coaster of happiness and exhilaration. Being in love apparently burns up a lot of calories. I knew I looked okay, but next to Cyl?

She was drop-dead gorgeous again this Sunday morning, in a fitted tan leather jacket and a slim tan leather skirt that was topped by a russet turtleneck in silk jersey. A vaguely African-looking necklace of polished brass and beaten copper disks flashed in the thin December sunlight beneath her open jacket and echoed the radiance of her face.

"Atkins or South Beach?" I demanded.

She shook her head with smug smile. "Neither. I eat anything and everything, but nothing seems to stick to my ribs. Or my hips. And what about you, girlfriend? I was noticing last night that you're getting downright skinny." Her smile became a mischievous grin. "Dwight giving you plenty of exercise?"

At that instant, something else caught the sun and I grabbed her left hand. There on her third finger was a gold ring set with the largest emerald I'd ever seen outside of Fitch's Jewelers in Raleigh.

"Wisconsin?" I asked.

She blushed. "We're flying out to meet his parents and spend Christmas there."

"When's the wedding?"

"We haven't set a date yet, but probably in the spring."

Over sausages and blueberry pancakes — we figured we might as well enjoy our immunity while it lasted — I heard all about Taylor Hamilton Youngblood and how they'd met outside a Senate subcommittee's chambers, both of them there to lobby for a bill to improve workplace conditions for pink-collar workers. He was Northwestern Law, followed by a fellowship at Harvard's Kennedy School of Government. More important, he was also tall, good-looking, with skin as dark as hers (the rest of Cyl's family are so light that she and her favorite uncle used to call themselves the only real Africans in the family), and totally smitten.

"Smitten's good," I said, passing the maple syrup.

"Smitten's great," she agreed. "I was so envious when you told me about you and Dwight. I thought it was never going to happen to me again, and then three weeks ago, bang!"

It had been a hard year for Cyl, getting over her doomed affair with a married minister.

"You were wasted here in Colleton

County," I said. "You're meant for bigger things."

"You think?" But a shadow had fallen over her lovely face. "Do you ever see Ralph and the children?"

"Occasionally. He's always going to be a little in love with you. Oddly enough, though, I get the impression that things are better between him and his wife these days. She'll need crutches the rest of her life, but she can drive again and she seems to have undergone something of a sea change since the wreck. She's not as hostile to whites and Stan says they're even allowed to watch television now. I gather she's eased up a lot. Finally realized what she came so close to losing."

"I hope so." Her large brown eyes misted over for a moment. "He deserves that."

By which I knew that she was always going to be a little bit in love with him, too.

Inevitably, talk soon wound around to Tracy Johnson's death.

"That poor baby!" Cyl exclaimed. "It's wicked that she had to die, too."

I told Cyl everything I'd heard. She was appalled to realize that Tracy might have been shot while talking to her killer and could have had a split second's awareness that she was going to die.

"Did y'all keep in touch?" I asked. "Do you know if she was seeing someone?"

"Sorry. We weren't close at all. Never did the girl-talk thing. I didn't even know the adoption had gone through till you told me, remember? She and I joined Doug's staff about the same time and I think she resented it when I got to lead some big cases while she was still sitting second chair. I had the feeling that she thought it was a matter of reverse discrimination, not because I might have been more competent than she."

I laughed and speared a stray blueberry with a tine of my fork. "Certainly not more modest."

Cyl laughed, too. "Well you know what they say — if it's true, it's not bragging. I *was* more competent. I looked at my cases with more objectivity, and I didn't automatically assume that everything a police officer said about a perp was necessarily true." She cut her eyes at me. "Not even when it was Major Dwight Bryant saying it."

"I never noticed you not going for the kill," I objected.

"That's because dubious cases never got to court." She took a sip of coffee and touched her napkin to her lips. "I either cut them loose because there wasn't enough solid evidence to support a prosecution or I let their attorneys bargain down the charges."

"And Tracy?"

"Tracy Johnson was a middle-class white girl who grew up believing that police officers are there to serve and protect people like her and her kind."

"Tracy was no racist," I protested.

"I'm not saying she was. I'm just saying that her innate assumptions about police probity were shaped by a set of life experiences somewhat different from mine. Different from yours, too, probably."

Well, yes. With a bootlegging daddy and a couple of brothers who'd sowed acres of wild oats before they finally settled down? Not to mention some nieces and nephews who have played with pot, found ways to buy beer before they were twenty-one, and been arrested for vandalism? And yes, a few cases have made the paper lately where it's clear that if law officers or prosecutors hadn't withheld a key piece of exonerating evidence, the nonwhite, non-middle-class defendant might have walked.

"Did you like her?" I asked.

Cyl turned her coffee cup slowly around

and around in her slender brown fingers as she thought about my question. "I didn't *dis*like her," she said at last. "She tried a little too hard for Doug's approval, and if she ever disagreed with him, I never heard it. She was too politically ambitious to get on his wrong side."

"Huh?"

"Oh, she didn't talk about it openly, but she was keeping tabs on Doug's game plan. When he runs for governor, I'm pretty sure she planned to run herself — become Colleton County's first female DA."

"I didn't realize," I said, "but now that you say it . . . she never missed a political luncheon and she was active in the precinct. Always ready to speak to any civic group. She really was positioning herself, wasn't she?"

"It wasn't all politics," Cyl said, trying to be fair. "I do think she was totally ethical. At least by her own lights. And I don't believe she ever consciously cut corners, but when she was convinced that the bad guys were bad, she certainly went for the slam dunk."

"Like Doug."

Cyl wrinkled her nose in distaste. "I saw you checking out his row of trophy pins last night."

"Did you ever ask for the death penalty?"

"No. Doug always took those cases."

I realized that we'd never actually discussed the question before. "You for it or against it?"

She seemed surprised that I'd ask. "For it. Aren't you?"

"I don't know, Cyl. It bothers me that there are guys sitting on North Carolina's death row for murders they committed when they were seventeen. I guess I go back and forth."

"Why? When you've got a mad dog ravaging through the flock, you don't hope you can train it not to kill. You put it down. Don't you?"

"Maybe. If you're sure it's really mad and that it's the one that did the killing."

"It's never been shown that North Carolina's put someone innocent to death."

"Maybe not, but a lot of death penalties have been reversed or commuted on solid grounds."

"Which only proves that the system works."

"We don't know that it's always worked. And you're not going to sit there and tell me it's administered fairly."

"I'll give you that," she conceded. "Money, race, and class do make a difference, but just because some killers don't have to pay with their lives doesn't mean that the ones who do get death don't deserve it."

"Reid says Tracy was looking into the Martha Hurst conviction."

"Who's Martha Hurst?"

"One of Doug's little gold nooses. Before your time," I said. "Doug prosecuted back when he was an ADA under Wendell Barham. Martha Hurst was a woman who beat her stepson to death with her own softball bat."

"Black or white?"

"White. It was Doug's first capital case. His first death penalty. She's supposedly scheduled to die in January."

Cyl frowned. "And Tracy was questioning it?"

"Who knows? Reid's dad defended the woman and Tracy asked to see his files. She was going to say why tomorrow."

Cyl set her coffee cup down softly on its saucer. "I told you Tracy and I weren't close and that we didn't talk all that much? One thing we did talk about, though — we hated those stupid pins. We both thought that asking for the death penalty and getting it was too serious to be treated like another macho contest."

"My cock's bigger than yours?" I murmured.

"Exactly," she said.

Chapter 7

The real charity is to keep servants steadily to their duties. Their work should be measured out with a just hand; but it should be regularly exacted in as much perfection as can be expected in variable and erring human nature.

Florence Hartley,
The Ladies' Book of Etiquette, 1873

Sunday, December 12

When Dwight got to the DA's office on the second floor of the courthouse, one of Doug Woodall's assistants, Brandon Frazier, was waiting for him with a stack of manila file folders. "So far as I know, these are all the cases she was working on as of Friday," he said.

"Which was her desk?" Dwight asked.

"There," said Frazier, pointing to the one under a window that overlooked the courthouse parking lot.

The huge oaks that would shade cars in the summer were stripped bare of leaves this mild December morning. Only a few cars in the lot today. He watched as one of his detectives, Mayleen Richards, drove in, parked, and crossed the street, where she passed from his view. He made a mental note to get Richards to use her computer expertise to pull the records on Tracy Johnson's computer. He knew how to use the machines for day-to-day tasks, but that was as far as it went.

He switched Tracy's on, but her files were password-protected and Frazier couldn't tell him what it was, so he shut it down again.

Like everyone else to whom Dwight had spoken so far, Brandon Frazier claimed to know little about his colleague's personal life.

"Hell, man — I don't know if she even *had* a personal life, you know what I mean? Some of us were talking last night at Jerry's, wondering if Tracy had anything going on the weekends or evenings. Nobody knew. I mean, she was friendly and all. She'd go out for drinks after work before she adopted Mei, but she was still in her new-mom mode."

Something bitter in the tone of his voice made Dwight remember that Frazier and his wife had split a couple of months after the birth of their own baby. Too much attention to the baby on the wife's part? Jealousy on his? His own wife had been like that when Cal was born, but by then he'd known the marriage was a mistake, so it didn't matter to him that Jonna gave all her attention to their son. Took enough pressure off him that, for a while there, he thought they could make a go of it, that both of them loving Cal would make up for not loving each other.

"She'd talk about the baby," Frazier said, "or if somebody brought up a television program or a basketball game she'd seen, she'd join in, but mostly it was about work."

"Good-looking woman like her, you not married — y'all never hooked up?"

Frazier shrugged. "Wasn't for me not trying. When I was still in private practice, she wouldn't go out with me because it might be a conflict of interest, her prosecuting my clients, you know? And then when I came over here, she still wouldn't go out with me. Said she wanted to keep her professional life separate from her personal. Well, she sure did that, didn't she? She was a damn good prosecutor, though. I hope Doug finds somebody else right away because it's going to be rough taking up her slack."

"Who was tight with her here in the courthouse?" Dwight asked as he opened the desk drawers.

Frazier watched him poke through paper clips, rulers, pens, staples — the usual office supplies that clutter everyone's desk. Except for an envelope of baby pictures, some cosmetics, a box of tampons, and a stash of foil-wrapped butterscotch candies, it could be his own desk.

"I don't know that anybody was particularly tight with her, but I think she and Julie usually wound up eating lunch together most days when they were both in the building."

Julie would be Julie Walsh, another ADA.

"Enemies?" asked Dwight, holding to the light a silver-framed picture of Mei in a little ruffled bathing suit and matching chartreuse sunglasses. He and Deborah had never discussed children. Did she want one of her own? For that matter, did he want another? He set the picture down gently. "We heard she got a death threat recently."

Frazier obligingly looked up the name and present location of the prisoner who had recently threatened her and was now serving time at a prison farm in the next county.

"Nobody took him seriously, though. He was just pissed that Tracy gave the jury a solid case and wouldn't cut a deal."

"What about Martha Hurst?" Dwight asked.

"Who?"

Dwight explained and Frazier just shook his head. "Sorry. I was still living in Tennessee back then."

As Dwight opened the top files and began to scan through Tracy's current workload, Frazier said, "What about her Palm Pilot?"

"Her what?" Dwight said absently, already absorbed in the case against some dumbass who had robbed a Wendy's as one of his deputies was ordering a hamburger at the drive-through and then shot and wounded a customer.

"Her electronic scheduler and address book."

"Oh, right. Y'all find it?"

"It's not here at the office. Everybody says she carried it in her purse. She would've had it with her when she was killed."

Sitting at her desk in the Colleton County Sheriff's Department shortly before eleven this Sunday morning, Deputy Mayleen Richards looked over her notes for the briefing session Major Bryant had scheduled, and wished she had more to give him.

A tall and sturdily built woman who had just turned thirty-three, Richards had cinnamon brown hair and a prominent nose set in the middle of a face full of freckles. She had grown up on a tobacco farm near Makely, and after finishing a two-year course in computer programming at Colleton Community College, she had tried to sit at a desk in the Research Triangle, but the work was too sedentary for her muscular frame and she had hated the petty office politics. After six years of it, she abruptly quit, divorced the white-collar husband who was on a slow track to middle management, and talked Sheriff Bo Poole into hiring her to update the department's computer system while she trained to become a sworn officer. Uniformed patrol was a step in the right direction, but the detective squad was her ultimate goal, and now that she had her chance, she wanted desperately to prove herself to Major Bryant.

Not for one single minute would Richards ever admit to having a crush on her boss, not even to herself. The only emotion she would consciously acknowledge was gratitude that he had approved her promotion to his command in October. All the same, he had delegated primary responsibility for uncovering details about Tracy Johnson's personal life to her, and she was frustrated by how little there was to report.

Yesterday morning, Johnson's brother and his wife had driven over from Widdington with a key to the house, a two-bedroom condo at the western edge of Dobbs. Dr. Johnson, a history professor at Eastern U., was several years older than his sister, and while the two were fond of each other, they hadn't shared much in common beyond their parents, who were both long dead. "We usually got together for birthdays and holidays," said Mrs. Johnson, "and we were always there for each other in emergencies, but you know how it is."

Yes, the detectives were told, Dr. Johnson was executor of Tracy's will and would have been Mei's guardian, had the child survived. Tears glistened in the eyes of both when he said that. "We never had children either. She would have been more like a granddaughter than a niece."

They wished they could say who might have wanted to kill Tracy, but they were clueless. "You'll let us know when you've finished with the house?" asked Mrs. Johnson. "We'll need to clean out the refrigerator before everything spoils."

Mayleen Richards and her colleague, Detective Jack Jamison, spent the next few hours interviewing neighbors and searching the house. Unfortunately, it was not a Norman Rockwell development with block parties, potluck suppers, and neighbors running in and out of one another's kitchens. Here on a Saturday morning, they were able to find a lot of people home. On the other hand, most of the residents were young professionals who worked and played in Raleigh and had little interest in cultivating close ties in a place where they didn't expect to live more than four or five years before moving up to something larger. Johnson's condo was an end unit, and the unit next door was owned by a retired doctor who had closed the place in November before leaving to spend the winter in Florida. The next nearest neighbors were childless work-aholics, who claimed nothing beyond a nodding acquaintance.

A quick canvass of the street gave them three more who thought they might recognize Tracy if she had the baby with her, but the general response was either a blank stare or a momentary curiosity about the tragedy. "Oh, yeah, I saw that on the news this morning. You mean that was the woman who lives at one-thirty-eight? Jeez Louise! Who you think did it?"

The inside of the condo was only slightly more revealing. For starters, it was much tidier than Jamison would have expected for the home of a toddler, and it smelled of a woodsy air freshener augmented by the live Christmas tree that stood in front of the living room window. At the base of the slender tree were four or five brightly wrapped presents.

The two detectives pulled on latex gloves, and while Jamison searched the office area for the Palm Pilot Tracy Johnson was known to use, Richards went straight to the dead woman's bedroom and bath.

Paydirt.

In the medicine cabinet, amid three different over-the-counter cold remedies for infants, were an opened packet of condoms and a wheel of birth control pills with five empty slots. Lace-trimmed teddies and satin thongs were in the lingerie drawer of a bedroom bureau, but utilitarian cotton briefs and simple, no-nonsense bras made up the bulk of Johnson's underwear.

Mayleen Richards thought of her own lingerie drawer. Since her divorce, she hadn't been in a relationship serious enough to warrant going out and buying new frills. Unbidden came an image of herself wearing peach-colored bra and panties and Major Bryant running his finger along the elastic waistband. She instantly flushed so hotly that her face was one large orange freckle when her guilty eyes looked back from the mirror above the bureau.

Where the dickens did that come from? she wondered, then flushed even deeper as she suddenly remembered the erotic dream she'd had last night. A dream that had left her wet and throbbing.

Major Bryant was going to marry Judge Knott week after next. She was going to a party in their honor tonight, for pete's sake. Dreams were nothing, she told herself. Hell, she'd dreamed about half the guys in the department. All it meant was that her subconscious wanted a man in her life. Any man. Not necessarily Major Dwight Bryant, who was totally off-limits.

Giving herself a mental shake, she willed herself to forget about dreams and focus on reality.

Indications were good that Johnson was probably sexually involved with someone, but the bathroom was spotless. Ditto the rest of the condo. The hamper was empty and folded laundry lay in neat piles on the washer. Fresh towels hung on the racks, clean sheets were on the bed, and the tracks of a vacuum cleaner could be seen on all the carpets. On the kitchen counter was a note: "You need more bleach and scouring powder."

The evidence was unmistakable. "Her cleaning woman must have been here yesterday," she told Jamison.

"No Palm Pilot or Rolodex on her desk or in the drawers," Jamison reported. "You want to check out her computer?"

"Sure."

Easier said than done. Richards pressed the power button and nothing happened. No lights, no familiar hum. She pulled out the CPU tower from beneath the desk.

Well, there was the problem. It wasn't plugged in. The cover felt loose to her, though, and it needed only a slight tug to come off because the screws were right there on the floor. She took one look and realized that the inside had been gutted. Everything that made this personal computer personal was gone.

"Damn!" she said. She would process the CPU inside and out for prints, but whoever did this was not only savvy enough to know that deleted data could be retrieved but had probably worn gloves, too. "Damn, damn, damn!" she swore again.

"What?" asked Jamison.

When she told him, they checked the entrances and discovered that someone had simply shoved through the flimsy lock on the back door, ripping the keeper from the doorjamb, and then had pushed the keeper back into place so that the break-in would not be immediately noticed.

"Clean, neat job," Richards said. No smudges, no visible shoe tracks across the recently mopped kitchen floor. When they dusted for prints, it was as they pessimistically expected: *nada*.

They continued searching.

In the entry closet, stuck down behind

some coats and scarves, Jamison came across a box with a baby doll, doll carriage, and some stuffed animals, a box very similar to the one in a closet in his own house except that his box held little-boy toys.

"It's the baby's Santa Claus presents," he said sadly.

In the end, the only thing they had found with immediate possibilities was a short list of phone numbers posted by the kitchen phone.

Back in the office that afternoon, Mayleen Richards dialed the first number on that list — "Dr. T" — and listened to a recorded message from Mei Johnson's pediatrician's office. She jotted down the name of the practice and found it listed in the phone book. First thing Monday morning, she'd check out this Dr. Trogden. See what he could add.

Second on the list was Johnson's own number in the DA's office, followed by young Mei's daycare center and two women, who said, when called, that they occasionally babysat for Ms. Johnson.

"What?" shrieked Nettie Surles, who answered a Makely number. "The baby's dead? That's impossible! They were just here."

"When?" asked Richards.

106

"Friday afternoon. Little Mei had an ear infection so she couldn't go to daycare. Tracy dropped her off here in the morning and then came back for her that afternoon after she finished in court. Babies don't die from an ear infection. Not in this day and age. Who did you say you were? What happened?"

Richards explained as gently as she could and heard the woman begin to cry. She took down Mrs. Surles's address and asked if she could be interviewed the next morning.

"Well, now, I do go to church at ten . . ."

They agreed on nine o'clock and Richards dialed the next number.

"Such a shame," said Marsha Frye, who lived there in Dobbs, only minutes away from Tracy Johnson's condo. "She was a nice woman and the baby was just precious. Who could imagine such a thing happening to them?"

She readily agreed to an interview, "but could you come now? The children are about to have their afternoon snacks."

When Mayleen Richards drove out to the Frye home, Marsha Frye proved to be a young woman about her own age, with a warm and easygoing temperament. The house was a fifties-style brick ranch and was now surrounded by mature trees and overgrown foundation plantings. Inside, the living room was almost bare of furniture except for a shabby couch, shelves jammed with picture books, plastic bins full of toys, and a couple of low tables and small chairs. Colorful fingerpainted pictures of Christmas trees were thumbtacked to the plasterboard walls, and drying on a windowsill were a dozen or more sweetgum balls and English walnuts that had been dipped in silver or gold paint and tied with red ribbons, ready to hang on a real tree.

Four small tots, each holding a sippy cup of juice, lounged on the couch watching a Frosty the Snowman video.

"The three blondies are mine," she told Richards. "Triplets. Three years old in February. We childproofed the house and turned this room into a playroom. I figure two more years, then they're off to kindergarten, we redo the place, and I get my life back."

"And you babysit for others, too?"

"Four or five aren't much more trouble than three," Marsha Frye assured her. "But I didn't take Mei on a regular basis. I've kept her overnight once in a while when Tracy had to be out of town, but normally Mei goes to a daycare center near the courthouse. I was just the backup when Tracy had to work late or when Mei was sick. I'm a registered nurse and I can tend a sick baby without infecting the others."

"She was sick Friday," said Richards.

"I know. I kept her Thursday because she was just starting with her earache again. But Tracy has — I'm sorry, *had* someone down in Makely for when she worked there. Nettie somebody-or-other. I'm afraid I don't know her full name."

"Nettie Surles?"

"That's probably it," Mrs. Frye said. "I do have the daycare number, if you need it."

But when Richards pressed her for more information about Tracy Johnson, Marsha Frye had shrugged her shoulders helplessly. "I'm sorry. It was pretty much a business arrangement, not a personal friendship. I haven't had time to make new friends since the triplets came, and she wasn't one for a lot of small talk either. The kids keep me on the run. I know she was an assistant district attorney and I gather that she liked her work and I also know she was crazy about Mei. Just the way she smiled when she came to pick her up."

One of the sippy cups hit the floor with a thump.

"Mama, can we have more crackers?"

"And I want more juice."

"I hate this stupid Frosty," said the dark-haired child from the end of the couch. Can't we watch *Harry Potter*?"

"How do we ask?" Mrs. Frye said automatically.

"Pleeease!" came the chorus in four-part bedlam.

"Sorry," Mrs. Frye said to Richards.

"That's okay," said the deputy. "I can see myself out."

Until this Sunday morning, Jack Jamison had attended only three autopsies since his promotion to full-time detective, and all three had been on middle-aged men with whom he'd had no personal connection. The first time, he had expected to be queasy and was modestly proud of himself when the experience proved no more gory than the hog-killings he helped with every winter after the weather turned cold enough to slaughter and process the meat before it could spoil. Once a chest and belly are sliced open, entrails are entrails, whether human or pig.

The third one, a victim who hadn't been found until at least a week after his death, was pretty bad, but the smell of rotting flesh is part of farm life, too, where dogs and possums occasionally crawl up under a house or barn to die and have to be fished out piece by piece.

Disgusting, but bearable.

Today's session was the roughest yet, though. This was the first woman and the first time he had actually known the victim. He had briefed her about an ongoing investigation just last Wednesday. He had even held the baby girl once, a gurgling little charmer who was only a few months older than his own son. Now her tiny form lay on the next gurney, a small still mound that barely lifted the sheet. And no matter how much he told himself that the baby was beyond any pain or suffering, he'd nevertheless had to look away when those first cuts were made with scalpel and electric saw.

"No surprises here," the ME had said. "Blunt trauma to the head, resulting in intercranial hemorrhage and transtentorial herniation."

Now Jamison stood impassively as the ME finished his external examination of Tracy Johnson's naked body and then nodded to the diener, whose job it was to open her up.

The daycare center had proved just as

fruitless as the interview with Marsha Frye, and Mayleen Richards's Sunday morning drive to interview Nettie Surles down in Makely had not added much more.

Mrs. Surles was slightly hard of hearing, but it was clear that Tracy Johnson had entrusted Mei to her care because she looked like everybody's dream grandmother: white hair, merry eyes, a comfortable bosom made for cuddling babies, and a house that smelled of cinnamon and vanilla.

"Are you sure you won't have another sugar cookie," she urged Richards.

"No, ma'am, thank you."

"I hope you're not doing that no-carbs thing they keep talking about. I'm sure so much meat and fat can't be healthy. These are just made from good pure sugar, flour, and butter. Couldn't hurt a flea."

"No, really," Richards murmured. "I had a big breakfast."

"Oh, that's good. Breakfast is the most important meal of the day. That's what I always tell Tracy. You make sure that baby gets her milk and fruit and oatmeal and she'll grow up healthy as a horse."

The sudden memory that, no, little Mei was not going to grow up had Mrs. Surles in tears again.

Between sniffles, she described how

Tracy had called her on Friday morning. Mei had an earache. The doctor could see them late that afternoon if Tracy could get there before five, so could Mrs. Surles look after her that day? That way Tracy could drive straight to Raleigh without having to swing over to Dobbs to pick up Mei.

"She gave me pain syrup for the baby, and after she was gone I put some warm sweet oil in Mei's ear. I know it's old-fashioned, but it does seem to help, and then I let her sleep on my heating pad. That's what the poor little thing did most of the day. Just slept or watched television. Tracy came for her a little before four and bundled her up and took her out to the car. She cried when Tracy strapped her into the car seat. I know they save lives, but honestly! So uncomfortable for the little ones. Tracy said she'd probably go back to sleep the minute she started driving, but I can never help thinking they'd be better off if they could just stretch out across the seat the way my children used to do."

Eventually, Richards worked the conversation around to Tracy Johnson's personal life.

"Well, now, you know, I do think she might've had a fellow. Right before Halloween, she had on a pair of new earbobs.

113

Not dimestore stuff either — real pretty gold and turquoise. Looked like Mexican or Southwest. Said a friend gave them to her and I said, 'Friend? Or boyfriend?' and the way she laughed, I could tell it was a boyfriend. 'Just make sure he can love Mei as much as he says he loves you,' I told her. 'Oh, it's nowhere close to that,' she says. 'Not yet anyhow.' "

" 'Not yet'?" asked Richards.

" 'Not yet,' " Nettie Surles said, giving a significant nod of her head.

Now, as the hands of the clock on the office wall edged closer to eleven, Mayleen Richards began thumbing through the bank records they had taken from Tracy Johnson's desk. So far, the only thing of interest were checks made out to Johnson's cleaning woman, and she sighed as she added that name to her notes.

Across the hall, Don Whitley, one of the department's drug patrol, looked up from his own report at the sound of her sigh.

"Tough morning?" he asked sympathetically.

"Not really. Just coming up empty." Richards crossed to stand in the open doorway of the deputies' squad room and nodded to two uniformed officers who had just come from the magistrate's office, where they had booked two DWIs.

Whitley was mid-thirties and an inch or so taller than her own five-eight. He wasn't movie star handsome, but he did possess a certain boyish appeal and Richards found herself giving him a second look. He had come on to her when she joined the department until she made it clear she wasn't interested. Now, though . . . ? She wondered if maybe she'd been too hasty. Whitley was pretty solid. He was taking courses this fall at the community college. Going for an associate degree in criminal justice.

Divorced, of course, and what else was new? More than half the people in the department had been divorced. The job was notoriously hard on marriages. The constantly changing shifts, the opportunities to fool around, the difficulty of leaving the work at work. Jack Jamison seemed to be handling it okay, but he'd only been married what? Two years?

So maybe Major Bryant's second marriage wouldn't last either.

Appalled by where her thoughts had once again strayed, Richards said, "Is Castleman around?"

Mike Castleman, also on the drug interdiction squad, had been one of the responding officers in Friday night's crash.

"Comes on at four," Whitley said.

"I wanted to ask him if he saw a Palm Pilot lying around at the scene Friday night."

"You missing one?"

"Not me. We can't find Tracy Johnson's."

"You know for a fact she had one?"

"That's what they tell us in Woodall's office. We haven't found it yet. Sure will help if she interfaced it with her office computer." She glanced across the room to the heavier of the uniforms. "Hey, Greene? Weren't you one of the ROs Friday night?"

Tub Greene looked up from his paperwork. "Got there right behind Castleman."

"You happen to see her Palm Pilot?"

"Sorry. A bunch of people were milling around, though. We took their names. Y'all contacted all of them yet?"

"Not yet."

Whitley leaned back in his chair and Richards noticed the dark circles under his eyes and the thick textbook on his desk. Between shift work and college, he was probably carrying a killer schedule.

"What about her house?" he asked. "You check it out to see if she had a computer there?"

"Yeah, but somebody beat us to it. Pulled all the memory."

"The hell you say!" he said, sitting upright. "When?"

Richards shrugged. "Probably sometime between when she left on Friday morning and when we got there yesterday morning."

"Denning check it out?" he asked, referring to their crime scene specialist.

She shook her head and described the ease with which the break-in had occurred. "Didn't seem worth calling him for a full workup."

Don Whitley jerked his head toward Major Bryant's office further along the hall. "He know about her computer yet?"

Before she could answer, she heard voices and turned to see Bryant and Jamison. Bryant gestured for her to join them and held the door of his office till she was inside, then took his chair behind the wide desk.

"So what do y'all have?" he asked.

Richards started to speak, but Jamison interrupted her.

"I just got back from Chapel Hill," he said, his voice urgent with excitement. "The autopsy. She was pregnant, Major. The ME estimates about six weeks."

117

Chapter 8

Professional or business men, when
with ladies, generally wish for miscel-
laneous subjects of conversation, and,
as their visits are for recreation, they
will feel excessively annoyed if obliged
to "talk shop."

Florence Hartley,
The Ladies' Book of Etiquette, 1873

I walked out to the car with Cyl a few minutes before eleven. We both hated to say
good-bye, but duty's always out there, isn't
it? Standing with its hands on its hips,
yelling at us to get over here right this
minute and tend to business? Cyl was due
at her grandmother's church. I was due at
Aunt Zell's. All the same, we lingered for a
long moment in the mild December sunshine with clasped hands.

"Next time I see you, you'll be a married lady," Cyl said.

"And you won't be far behind me. Knock 'em dead in Wisconsin, okay?"

"I'll try. And you be happy, you hear?"

"I hear."

We hugged again, then she looked at her watch, yelped like the White Rabbit, and was gone.

I walked back into the house, loaded the dishwasher, wiped down the stove and countertops, then went into the bedroom to change into Sundayish clothes — pantyhose, heels, and something with a skirt — which would imply that I'd attended church even if I hadn't. Not that Aunt Zell and Uncle Ash would care, nor Brix Junior either for that matter. But Jane was a separate case. Even though she's not particularly religious, Reid's mother always does the correct thing, and unless one is sick enough for a doctor, that means church on Sunday. I'm cowardly enough not to risk her raised eyebrow by arriving at Aunt Zell's looking as if I'd obviously skipped.

Instead, I struggled into opaque black tights, a black turtleneck jersey dress with a short skirt that showed off my legs, two-inch heels (ditto), and a red cardigan banded in narrow black velvet. Gold earrings and a thin gold chain. All I needed was a halo of tinsel to look like an ornament on a Sunday School Christmas tree.

By now it was well past twelve and I was running on automatic. I pulled out clothes to wear to court next day and wondered if I would need to get gas before driving back to Makely. My overnight case was nearly packed before I remembered that it was dinner at Jerry's again, which meant we'd be sleeping here tonight. Hard to keep it all straight.

Only a few days ago, Dwight had said, "You know what's gonna happen before it's all over, don't you? You're gonna be in my apartment, wondering where the hell I am, and I'm gonna be out here thinking the same thing."

Ten more days, I told myself, as I returned my toiletries to the bathroom cabinet and my lingerie to the dresser drawer.

Ten more days.

Shortly before one o'clock, I let myself into Aunt Zell's kitchen over in Dobbs. She had the oven door open to check on the rolls, and the smell of hot yeast mingled with the aroma of caramelized onions and a well-browned pork roast. The heat of the oven had left her with pink cheeks, and

120

damp white curls wreathed her sweet face.

As soon as she saw me, she smiled. "Oh, good. You're just in time to help me bring everything to the table. Hang your coat on the back of that chair, honey, and fix the tea, would you?"

Aunt Zell is my mother with the edges knocked off. She even looks like Mother — a slender erect build, blue eyes, firm jawline. But her tongue was never as tart and she suffers fools a little more willingly. God knows, she suffered me willingly enough. After I came back to Dobbs, before Daddy and I made up and before I moved back to the farm, I had lived upstairs in the apartment that they'd originally built for Uncle Ash's mother. Until he retired last year, Uncle Ash's job had kept him traveling all over the western hemisphere and both of them professed themselves so pleased that I was there to keep Aunt Zell company while he was gone that they wouldn't let me pay rent.

I filled the glasses with ice, poured warm sugared tea over the ice, and carried the tray through the swinging door into the dining room. Through the arches of the front entry hall, I saw Jane and Brix Junior in the living room. Reid was there. Dwight, too.

He hadn't changed into a white shirt, but he looked fine in a dark blue one that harmonized nicely with a blue-and-gray tie and his charcoal gray jacket. Our eyes met and my heart turned a somersault. I still wasn't used to it. How could a man I've known forever, a man I'd taken as much for granted as air and water, suddenly turn into someone whose smile could make my knees go weak? His smile was as familiar as my own face in the mirror, so why should it now flush me with hot desire?

"Ah, Deborah," said Uncle Ash. "Is it time for me to carve the roast?"

"I think so," I told him.

He gave me a welcoming hug before going out into the kitchen, and Jane followed to see if she could help, so I left them to it and joined the others in the living room.

Much as I wanted to go put my arms around Dwight, I restrained myself and smiled at Brix Junior. "Dwight ask you about Martha Hurst yet?"

Dwight shook his head and grinned at my cousins. "What did I tell you?"

"What?" I asked when Brix Junior nodded in amused agreement.

"Dwight said you'd probably ask about her before we sat down to dinner."

I refused to be embarrassed. "Does that mean you've already discussed it?"

"And I've told Reid to give him all the files. There's nothing in them that wasn't said at the trial. She fired me immediately afterwards and petitioned the court for a different attorney."

"Was she guilty, Brix?"

"All my clients were innocent," he said. "Except those who told me to bargain for a deal."

"Did Martha Hurst want a deal?"

"One was never offered. Doug Woodall had enough to convict and Judge Corwin was bad for giving the death penalty. It was his last one before he retired."

"But was she guilty?" I asked again.

He shrugged. "Who knows?"

"*You* should," I said tartly. "It was a capital case. Did you let Doug roll over you without a fight?"

Brix Junior drew himself up and frowned at me. "Are you implying that I gave that woman a less than adequate defense?"

That woman. I heard the distaste in his patrician tones.

"She qualified for a court-appointed attorney and that was you, right?"

He gave a frosty nod.

"So it wasn't as if you could go out and

hire enough expert witnesses to confuse the jury."

"Expert witnesses would have been irrelevant. It was open and shut, Deborah. The victim was her stepson. They fought constantly. It was her baseball bat that viciously mutilated his genitals after she split his head open and left him so battered and bloody that his own mother couldn't identify him at first."

I had forgotten the details of the murder, but now it was coming back. "Didn't Doug claim that they'd been lovers and that she killed him because he dumped her and was seeing someone else?"

"That was part of the case against her. My client did admit that they'd once had a relationship, but she swore that she was the one who broke it off because he was dealing drugs and was violent towards her. When she married his father, he continued to cause trouble. He lived with them off and on and witnesses heard her threaten to beat his brains out because he was stealing from them."

"He sounds like a real piece of work," I said.

"Exactly," Brix Junior agreed.

"Someone who would have made a lot of enemies?"

"I was told he had a rough sort of charm that could defuse anger," he said, neatly rebutting the argument I hadn't yet made.

"So once they had Martha Hurst, they didn't bother to look for anyone else?"

Until then, Dwight and Reid had listened in silence. Now Dwight said, "Didn't Bo look to put anybody else in the picture?"

"There were, of course, others with whom he'd fought, and we did put that fact before the jury, but the two most probable had alibis and the rest were tangential."

Brix Junior left the partnership shortly after I joined it, and we didn't work together long enough for me to be familiar with his courtroom procedures. I myself always wanted to know if my clients did what they were accused of. Some attorneys, though, feel they do a better job if they can maintain at least a pro forma belief in their client's innocence, so unless said client insists on pleading guilty, they don't want to be told differently. I hadn't realized that Brix Junior fell into that category.

Dwight was looking skeptical. "So you never asked her?"

"About other suspects?"

"No. About whether or not she killed him?"

"That's not the way I worked."

"But you thought she did it," I said.

"Her guilt or innocence was irrelevant to the defense we presented."

"Oh come off it, Brix," I said impatiently. "You're not in practice any longer, but she was your client and she got death. The execution's scheduled for next month. If she really was guilty, what was Tracy Johnson's interest and why the hell won't you give us a straight answer?"

"Good luck," Reid muttered from behind me.

Making sure that I was aware that he was totally annoyed with me, Brix Junior swallowed the last of his pre-lunch sherry and set his glass firmly down on the buffet tray. "I though we were up this weekend to celebrate your forthcoming wedding, Deborah. I was not aware that I'd be facing an inquisition."

"And Tracy wasn't aware that she was going to be killed," I retorted.

"Do you seriously think the two are related?" His question wasn't for me, but for Dwight, who shrugged and said, "Too early to tell. It might be coincidence, but then again —"

"Oh, very well," said my cousin, turning back to me with a petulant air. "Do I think that Martha Hurst did, with malice aforethought, take her baseball bat to Clarence Hurst and beat him to a pulp fore and aft? Damn straight. Never once — during the trial or before — did she show any remorse or regret. No, she didn't confess, but she did say more than once that he needed killing and that whoever did it did the world a service. Unfortunately, 'needed killing' quit being a defense in this state around the turn of the last century."

As Jane, Aunt Zell, and Uncle Ash brought in bowls and platters of steaming food, Brix Junior said, "And now could we please drop this subject and talk about more pleasant things? Do you play golf, Dwight?"

Sunday dinner proceeded decorously and cordially after that. Butter wouldn't have melted in my mouth when I told Aunt Zell that the minister out at Sweetwater Church had asked after them. And so he had when I ran into him at a gas station in Cotton Grove two days earlier. Dwight kept a straight face while Jane gave me an approving smile and inquired about the arrangements for our champagne reception at the Dobbs country club. The check she and Brix Junior had given us as a wedding gift had been specifically earmarked for decent French champagne instead of the sparkling California wine Dwight and I had originally budgeted for, and wedding talk carried us safely through coffee and Aunt Zell's warm apple crisp.

Chapter 9

Avoid exclamations; they are in excessively bad taste and are apt to be vulgar words. A lady may express as much polite surprise or concern by a few simple, earnest words, as she can by exclaiming "good Gracious!" "Mercy!" or "Dear me!"

Florence Hartley,
The Ladies' Book of Etiquette, 1873

Sunday's thin sunlight had disappeared beneath dreary gray clouds and the temperature had begun to drop again by the time we gathered on Aunt Zell's back porch to wave good-bye to Jane and Brix Junior. We were only a few days away from the winter solstice, so here at three o'clock, it was already beginning to feel like twilight.

"We should get moving, too," I said,

giving Aunt Zell a thank-you hug.

Dwight's known Aunt Zell even longer than I have, and as he bent to kiss the cheek she offered, she reached up and patted his. "Have I told you how happy Ash and I are about you and Deborah?"

"No, ma'am," he said. "Not exactly."

"Well, we are. And I know Sue would be, too. She thought the world of you, Dwight, didn't she Ash?"

"She did," Uncle Ash said solemnly, laying his hand on Dwight's shoulder. "Miss Zell and I were talking about it last night. You won't remember this, son, but we were out at the farm one day and you young'uns — you boys anyhow — had a dodgeball game going and Deborah wanted to play. The others said she was too little, but Seth went ahead and picked her for y'all's team and every time one of the others aimed the ball at her, you or Seth would snatch her out of the way. Sue said you had a kind heart."

"Awww," I said, slipping my hand into Dwight's. "My hero!"

He, of course, had gone beet red as he always does when he's complimented to his face.

Reid grinned. "Even then he knew."

He, too, kissed Aunt Zell good-bye, then

said to us, "If y'all want to follow me over to the office, I'll see if I can find Dad's files on that Hurst woman."

"Well —" said Dwight.

"Okay," I said.

The partnership of John Claude Lee and Reid Stephenson, Attorneys at Law, occupies a white clapboard house half a block from the courthouse. According to the historical plaque on the front, it was built in 1867 by my mother's great-grandfather, who was also John Claude's great-grandfather; and when the family built a larger house away from the center of town, it eventually passed to John Claude's father, who started the partnership with Brix Junior's father. Although the exterior is an authentic example of nineteenth-century vernacular architecture, right down to the original wavy glass, black wooden shutters, and gingerbread porch trim, most of the interior has been remodeled completely out of the period. Some of the moldings are original, as are the hardwood floors, but the walls and staircases have been moved several times over the last hundred years.

There's a large, airy bedroom suite upstairs that can accommodate out-of-town witnesses and which Reid still uses as his personal cathouse whenever he can sneak the woman of the moment past John Claude's suspicious eyes.

Downstairs, John Claude uses the double parlor on the front left and Reid has what was once the formal dining room. The old kitchen and pantries have been converted into a high-tech center for business machines and for the paralegals who assist Sherry Cobb, the office manager, whose own area was carved out of the formal entrance hall when the staircase was relocated to the back.

My former office on the front right now houses the firm's law library and my desk has been replaced by a conference table. It's been four years since I left the firm, but they still haven't replaced me. I'm not sure if that's because they can't agree on a new associate or because John Claude's holding my space in case I lose the next election.

While Reid hunted for the Hurst files in the storage room that had been fitted out with steel shelving, Dwight and I went straight on through to the sunroom at the back of the house. With the ease of old familiarity, I opened a set of louvered doors that hid a sink, refrigerator, and microwave. There was a bottle of good white wine in the refrigerator but Dwight passed when I offered it to him, so I made a pot of coffee instead. Julia Lee has always stocked the freezer with gourmet coffee from a grocery in Cameron Village, and we had our choice of several different packets. Soon the rich aroma of Jamaica Blue Mountain filled the sunroom.

"Smells good," said Reid as he deposited two heavy archival file boxes on the long deal table. "Just a little milk for me, okay?"

Normally I would have told him to get it himself. When I worked here, the only people I ever fixed coffee for were my own clients, but since this was technically his coffee, not mine, I found some of those little plastic cups of non-dairy creamers in the refrigerator and handed him a couple, along with a full mug.

I pulled the lids off the boxes and both were full of manila folders wedged in so tightly that it was difficult to pull one out. No matter what his private thoughts on his client's guilt or innocence, if the sheer amount of paper was any indication, Brix Junior had certainly gone through all the motions on her behalf.

I wanted to start reading immediately, but Dwight put the lids back on the boxes

I'd opened. "Do I need to sign something for this?" he asked.

"We might as well do it up right," Reid said. "Technically, it's a privilege issue, but this close to her execution date, I really doubt if Martha Hurst would object."

He printed off a receipt form and took it back to lay on the shelf after Dwight signed and dated it.

"You sure Tracy Johnson didn't say anything to explain why she wanted to see these records?" Dwight asked when Reid returned.

My cousin rinsed the dust of the storeroom from his hands and dried them on some paper towels. "Sorry, not a clue."

"I still don't understand why she came to you on this," I said. "You weren't even out of law school when the trial took place. Why didn't she ask John Claude?"

Again he shrugged, but this time there was something else in his eye. Something sheepish?

"Oh for God's sake," I said, slamming my hand so hard on the table that our coffee mugs rattled on the tabletop. "Have you slept with every available woman in this whole damn county?"

"You were hooked up with Tracy?" Dwight asked, instantly alert.

Reid held his hands up defensively. "No!"

I glared at him.

"Not recently anyhow. Not since last spring. April maybe. Or May. And don't look at me like that. It was never serious. For either of us. It was just — well, hell, Deborah, don't tell me you've never been there. She didn't have anyone and I didn't either. We played by her rules. She wanted to keep it strictly physical — no emotional entanglement — and that was fine with me."

I bit back the sarcastic remark on the tip of my tongue and washed it down with a swallow of coffee instead.

"Not since spring?" Dwight asked. "Who was she with now?"

"Nobody, far as I know."

"Oh please," I said. "She hadn't slept with you since May and you didn't ask why? What? You thought you needed to buy fresh deodorant? Get a different mouthwash? Change the sheets?"

Dwight laughed and Reid bristled. "Believe it or not, dear cousin, Tracy wasn't the only woman in Dobbs who —"

I held up my hand. "Spare me the list. Just tell us who Tracy was seeing now."

"I don't know," he answered sulkily.

"She wouldn't say. Pissed me a little, though. Telling me she didn't want any serious entanglements till the baby was older and then giving him an exclusive?"

"Was he local? Another attorney? Someone from the DA's office?"

"Jesus, Deborah! How many ways are there to say 'I don't know'? We had sex. Damn good sex, but it came to a crashing halt more than six months ago. She didn't say then, and for all I know, she's had six more guys since then, okay?"

"You don't know either?" Dwight asked me.

I shook my head. "But Portland and I are pretty sure she was seeing someone seriously." I described Tracy's kitten-in-cream look from last spring and repeated her comment about finding someone right under her nose.

"You think that's who shot her?" asked Reid.

"Too soon to say, but I'm gonna need a DNA sample from you. I'll send somebody over tomorrow."

Reid and I both stared at him in bewilderment.

"DNA sample?" asked Reid. "But I told you. We hadn't been together in months."

I thought of bedsheets and maybe someone's toothbrush or shaver in Tracy's bathroom. Whoever she'd been sleeping with, if she'd had him there in her own place, he would surely have left fingerprints, hair, and God knows what else. "It's just to eliminate you," I told Reid. "Right, Dwight?"

"Right," he said, but he didn't quite meet my eyes.

Chapter 10

A courteous manner, and graceful offer of service are valued highly when offered, and the giver loses nothing by her civility.

Florence Hartley,
The Ladies' Book of Etiquette, 1873

Dwight and I had driven over to Dobbs separately, and since I would be holding court in Makely again the next day, that meant we also had to drive back to the farm separately. For once, I didn't mind. Dwight drives so slowly, I figured I could be halfway through the files that we'd put in the trunk of my car before he turned in to the yard.

I could have, too, if I hadn't found April there, sitting cross-legged on the floor as she put a second coat of white enamel on the beer tap's cabinet doors. The clean cool smell of latex paint filled the room.

"You didn't have to do that today." I set the first of the storage boxes on the dining table. Although Andrew's nine brothers up from me, April is his third wife and halfway between us in age. In addition to keeping Andrew and their kids in line, she's also a sixth grade teacher with lesson plans to fill out and theme papers to grade before school recessed for the holidays next week. "It's Sunday. You should be home with your feet up."

Her face was dotted with tiny flecks of white enamel. "No problem. The others will be over tomorrow to put up the rest of the molding, then all that's left is finishing up the bathroom and painting." Her tone was innocent but she was having trouble suppressing a grin. "You haven't heard from Nadine or Doris today, have you?"

"No, why? What's going on?"

Mischief danced in her hazel eyes. "Promise not to tell anyone?"

"I promise."

"Doris got some books from the library yesterday on wedding etiquette."

"Oh no," I groaned.

She laughed. "Don't worry. It's not about you this time. I mean, okay, it might've started out that way because Doris wanted to be able to cite chapter and verse if you tried to do something Miss Manners might not approve of." She stroked her brush across the final door panel and rose gracefully to her feet. "You're safe, though. She's been sand-bagged by a section on wedding symbols."

"Which ones?"

"Veils."

"I'm not wearing a veil."

"Good! You know what it symbolizes?"

I shook my head. "More fairytale princess nonsense? I never gave it much thought."

"Well, think about this," April said. "According to the book, the veil's supposed to cover the bride's face until after the vows, when the groom is told he may then kiss his bride. And, of course, he has to first lift off the veil."

I followed that train of thought to where it naturally led and then started laughing, too. No wonder April said it was good I didn't plan to wear one. "You're kidding," I said.

April was shaking her head gleefully. "No, I'm not."

"Lifting the veil is symbolic of taking the bride's virginity?"

"You got it, sweetie! It's a stand-in for the hymen. Nadine was mortified when Doris read her that."

And then I realized why she was so amused.

When Nadine's older daughter got married, Nadine had dressed that — and I quote — "pure white angel" in a full veil and Herman had escorted her down the aisle — this was before he needed a wheelchair. Upon being asked, "Who gives this woman to be married?" he had, as coached by Nadine, replied, "Her mother and I do." Then he carefully lifted Denise's veil and folded it back across her head like a halo, kissed her cheek, gave her hand to the groom, and took his place in the front pew next to Nadine, just as they'd rehearsed it all week.

"So symbolically speaking, Doris made my brother deflower their own daughter right there in church?"

"Don't you love it?"

"Can I please murmur 'incest' the next time Nadine gets on my case?"

"Only if you don't tell them I was the one told you. Doris swore me to secrecy." April put the lid back on the paint can and gathered up the newspapers she'd put down to catch any drips. One of her short brown curls was feathered white where it had brushed against the door. "She's almost as embarrassed as Nadine, because remember when Betsy got married six months later? Doris thought Denise and Herman looked so sweet that she tried her best to talk Betsy and Robert into doing it, too, only Betsy didn't want to walk down the aisle with a veil covering her face and Robert said he was sure his rough hands would get caught in it and he'd wind up pulling it off her head."

We were still giggling when Dwight came through the door, carrying the other file box, the ends of his tie trailing from his jacket pocket.

"What's so funny?" he asked.

"I'll tell you later," I said.

"No, you won't," said April. "You promised."

"I thought it doesn't count if you tell secrets to your mate."

"He's not officially your mate. Not till the veil is pushed away," she said, which only set us off again.

Dwight just shook his head at us and hung his jacket on the back of one of the ladderback chairs.

"Y'all want to come for supper?" April said as she slipped on her coat and pulled car keys from the pocket. "Andrew and A.K. are cooking a fresh ham on the gas grill."

"Thanks, but we've got another dinner at Jerry's tonight," I told her.

As she started out the door, April remembered that she'd stopped by the mailbox yesterday and picked up my mail, but had then forgotten to give it to me, so I walked out to the car with her. She slid into the driver's seat and handed me a stack of envelopes, junk mail, and catalogs through the open window.

"You're getting circles under your eyes," she said, giving me a critical look. "Don't let yourself get so tired you wind up at the altar too exhausted to give a straight answer."

"I won't," I promised.

"You and Dwight need to get to bed early tonight." She thought about what she was saying and grinned. "Or is that part of the problem?"

I drew myself up in mock indignation. "Why, Miz April, I don't know what on earth you're talking about."

"Yeah, and if we believe that, Denise has a veil she'll lend you."

Back in the house, Dwight had lit a fire

in the hearth and was now stretched out on the couch to watch the end of a ball game. Suffused with happiness and feeling domestic as hell, I sat down on a nearby lounge chair to open my mail. Among the Christmas cards was one from Judge Bill Neely and his wife, Anne-Kemp, from over in Asheboro. Across the bottom of the card, he'd written, "I hear the Barrister Boys got to play at one of the parties for you. I demand equal time. How about I pipe you down the aisle?"

The Barrister Boys (a.k.a. "Fast Eddie and the Scumbags") are a band of attorneys in Bill's district. I'm very fond of Bill and I'm told he's actually as competent on the Irish pipes as his friends are on guitar and banjo, but the only time I want to hear bagpipes is outdoors.

From a distance.

Like maybe two or three miles.

Dwight smiled sleepily when I read him Bill's mock offer. "I want to be there when you run that one past Nadine and Doris."

There were cards from friends I hadn't seen since law school, and cards from my West Coast brothers, who had promised to come east for the wedding and stay on for Christmas.

"It'll be good to see the whole family together again," Frank's wife Mae wrote. She enclosed pictures of their grandchildren.

One card showered a cascade of silver confetti in my lap when I opened it. It was from my carny niece, who was sorry their schedule wouldn't permit them to come up from Florida in time, "but we're playing a Shriner's Christmas festival then."

I slit open another envelope and caught my breath when I saw the picture inside. Mei Johnson was dressed in a red velvet dress, white tights, and a fur-trimmed Santa hat, and she held a white plush dog in her pudgy little hands. "Hope you and Dwight have a good one, too," Tracy had written.

Too?

I studied the picture through a glaze of tears. Here I was with my life still opening up before me like a stocking full of Christmas surprises while Mei's and Tracy's were both finished. No more surprises. No more Christmases.

The envelope was postmarked Thursday. I turned to show it to Dwight, but he was sound asleep.

I hadn't yet found a casual way to ask him what his detectives found in Tracy's house, but if it was evidence of a lover, where was he? Why wasn't he camped out in Dwight's office demanding action and results?

"More women are killed by their mates than by strangers," said the worldly pragmatist who lurks in the back of my head and always sees the dark lining of every silver cloud.

"Maybe he's out of town and doesn't yet know," soothed the preacher who shares head space and believes in the power of positive thinking.

I left Dwight sleeping and went out to the kitchen to pour myself a glass of wine. Brix Junior's file boxes were on the counter where Dwight had put them. Why had Tracy asked to see them? And what exactly had been going on in her head these last few days?

I lifted the lids and looked at the notations on the file tabs. They were in roughly chronological order, so I took the earliest box over to the kitchen table, got out a legal pad and pen for making notes, took a sip of wine, and began reading.

As is often the case, a lot of the papers were duplicates. Nevertheless, it took me nearly two hours and a second glass of wine to skim through Brix Junior's preliminary notes, the warrant for Martha Hurst's arrest, her first appearance and probable cause hearing, and all the witness statements, search warrants, ME's report, investigating officers' reports, etc., etc.

In clear English, it boiled down to a simple set of facts. On a hot Friday in August, sheriff's deputies had been summoned to the Sandy Grove Mobile Estates, lot #81. It was not their first visit to this particular house trailer. This time, however, it wasn't to put an end to a loud three-way domestic argument between husband and wife and the husband's adult son. This visit was triggered by an anonymous call — "Somebody's got hisself kilt," said an indeterminate female voice.

When deputies arrived, the somebody proved to be Roy Hurst, a white male, age twenty-six. From the smells percolating through the trailers when they opened the unlocked door, he had been dead for at least a day and probably longer. Beside the body lay a bloody aluminum softball bat, its handle wiped clean of fingerprints.

According to the medical examiner's straightforward report, death came from massive trauma to the victim's skull with a blunt instrument consistent with the bat. The first blow had probably come from the front while he was either sitting or standing. The others were to the back of his head after he was prone. He had then been turned over and his genitals pounded to a pulp, probably immediately postmortem and probably with the end of the same blunt instrument. Based on the ambient temperature as recorded by the detectives who arrived soon after the first responding officer and on the deterioration of the body, death had occurred three to six days earlier. In other words, sometime between the preceding Saturday and Tuesday.

The trailer belonged to a Gene and Martha Hurst. Gene Hurst, age forty-nine, was a long-distance van driver for a national moving company. Although family members are the usual suspects, he was meticulously alibied. He had left Raleigh on Friday morning, picked up the rest of his load in Nashville on Saturday morning, and headed west for Tucson and Phoenix.

I studied photocopies of the time-stamped tickets that plotted Gene Hurst's drive from one weigh station to another across the width of the country. They showed that he'd pulled out of Nashville around the time his son was last seen on Saturday morning.

Martha Hurst was a different matter. A thirty-four-year-old hospital aide, she claimed that she had only briefly seen her stepson that morning and never again. Okay, yes, they'd had a violent argument and she'd threatened to break his head, but that was because he'd come over and let himself in while she was taking a shower after he swore he'd given back all the keys from when he used to share the trailer with his dad before they were married.

"How would you feel if you walked out of the shower buck naked and there was a man standing in your bedroom?" she'd asked Brix Junior.

When Brix Junior delicately reminded her that she and the younger Hurst had been lovers before she married his father and that he might possibly have seen her buck naked before, Martha Hurst had said yes, and that was all the more reason for him to get the hell out of her house and out of her life.

As for the rest of Saturday, she had come home from her ball game around six, stood her bats and glove in a rack by the front door, and then taken another shower before going out to celebrate the win. And yes, she might've had too much to drink, especially after she discovered that the rings she'd left on her dresser before the game had gone missing; and yes, she might have told her teammates that she wanted to bust his head like a ripe watermelon, but she certainly hadn't gone home and done it, because he wasn't there and she couldn't run him down by telephone. Next morning, she had left for a week at the beach with friends.

No, she had most certainly *not* left him to rot on her living room floor. "I'd have my rings on my fingers right now if I'd done that."

That was one bit of evidence in her favor, and I added it to the notes on my legal pad because Martha Hurst certainly sounded like a woman who wouldn't hesitate to go through a man's pockets looking for her missing rings. The rings weren't there, but a pawn ticket was.

The photos of the crime scene were extremely detailed. Every angle of the room had been covered and the body was so well-documented that I could see the maggots on his head and pants and almost read the pawn ticket. There was even a clear print of a bloody dent in the wall, beneath the light switch and thermostat, where the bat had evidently glanced off Hurst's head on the first swing.

With such an uncertain time of death — Saturday till Tuesday — it was hard for everyone to prove conclusively where they were, but of the other two strong candidates, one was in jail from Friday night till noon on Monday, when he was conveyed to Buxton for a full mental health evaluation, and the other could prove he was in Charlotte from Saturday morning till Wednesday.

It was hard to think of killing your stepson and ex-lover and then going blithely off to the beach for a week, but murderers have done weirder things and Martha Hurst did have a history of violence. She had quit high school when she punched out a teacher she said was hassling her; and after completing a GED, she'd lost her first job at a private nursing home because she'd hit her supervisor over the head with a metal bedpan.

A full metal bedpan.

From all the reports and witness statements, it would appear that Martha Hurst had been accused because of her angry threats against her stepson, even though she swore she hadn't seen him again after her admitted run-in with him around midday on that Saturday.

I was leafing through a final sheaf of Brix Junior's handwritten notes when Dwight came into the kitchen, rumpled and yawning.

"Couldn't resist it, could you, shug?" he said.

I smiled up at him. "If you really didn't want me to read these files, you wouldn't have brought them in the house, would you?"

He gave me a quizzical glance. "I thought we agreed that we were going to keep our work separate?"

"We are," I promised. "You know well and good that nothing about Tracy's death is ever going to come up in district court."

He took a pilsner glass from the cabinet. "So you can meddle in my work, but I can't meddle in yours?"

"That's different," I said. "Your department generates a lot of my cases."

Taking care not to touch where April had so recently painted, Dwight opened the armoire doors to the beer tap Daddy had given him, drew himself a foaming glassful, and held it up to the light in critical appraisal as he always does. Dwight takes the craft of beer-making seriously and keeps a notebook filled with observations about each batch. Some of the recipes he's developed are as complicated as any chemical formula, with their eighth of an ounce of this and a half-teaspoon of that. The color on this one was a dark golden brown and the head was so thick and creamy that after his first swallow, the rim of the glass was edged in an inch-wide band of foam.

"Brussels lace?" I asked, having picked up some of the terminology.

"Pretty, isn't it?" he said with a touch of pride as he pulled out a chair opposite me. A sweet malty aroma drifted across the table. He took another swallow of the ale and leaned back in his chair so that his muscular, six-three body was almost horizontal and only the back legs touched the floor.

"So tell me about Martha Hurst."

"Could I first tell you how much I love you?" I asked softly.

The chair came down with a bang and he leaned across with his big hands braced on the table to steady himself so our lips could meet. Barley malt, shaving cream, and soap mingled together with something indefinable that could only be the essence of his skin. His kisses are as slow and deliberate as his driving and I never want them to end.

"Okay," he said at last, settling back in his chair again. "Tell me about Martha Hurst."

* * *

When I finished telling Dwight all I'd gleaned from the files about Martha Hurst's arrest and trial, he said, "Sounds pretty open and shut to me. Any idea why Tracy would want to take another look at it?"

"Not really," I admitted. "The only thing I can think of in Martha Hurst's favor besides the pawn ticket still in his pocket is that I don't see anything about bloody clothes in the list of items that the deputies removed from the trailer."

"Who worked the case?" Dwight asked.

I looked at the signature on the report. "Silas Lee Jones."

Dwight made a face. I'd heard his opinion on Jones before. Not sloppy enough to fire for cause, not one to bust his bustle either.

"Look at these pictures," I said. "See all that blood? Whoever did this, you know they had to have blood on their hands, their shoes, their clothes, and yet there's nothing here about it or those items."

"Well, there wouldn't be if he came in on her again while she was still buck naked from her second shower," said Dwight. "Did that point come up at the trial?"

"Who knows? This isn't a transcript,

154

only Brix Junior's notes. He did put her on the stand, though."

"So?"

"Against his will. Which means he really did think she was guilty. But she insisted on testifying and he let her. According to his notes — not to mention the verdict — she didn't make a very good impression on the jury. I gather that Doug Woodall got her to contradict herself about her whereabouts at the time of death, but I'd have to read the transcript to see exactly how she screwed up."

"You got time to do that?" he asked.

I sighed. "Probably not, but I'll make time if you want me to."

"That's okay. I'll get one of my detectives to do it if we don't find out why Tracy was interested in Hurst by the time we finish questioning everyone in Woodall's office."

I was dying to know what they'd found at Tracy's house, but a pact is a pact and I'd already pushed it with the files.

Chapter 11

Many men can converse on no other subject than their every day employment. In this case, listen politely, and show your interest. You will probably gain useful information in such conversation.

Florence Hartley,
The Ladies' Book of Etiquette, 1873

Dinner at Jerry's that night was, in many ways, a rerun of the night before except that this time, we were on Dwight's turf instead of mine. Just as he knows many of the attorneys and judges by sight if not always by name, so too do I know a lot of the deputies and clerks who work out of the Colleton County Sheriff's Department. Several of them have testified in my court and are familiar faces in the courthouse corridors or around Dwight's office, but I had met very few of their spouses.

Bowman Poole, of course, I've known for ages because he and Daddy are good friends and he often comes out to the farm to hunt or fish. Of course, he wasn't elected till after Daddy gave up messing with moonshine, but that probably wouldn't have mattered. Bo would've arrested him, given the chance; and Daddy would've still voted for him and contributed to his campaign fund. They appreciate each other. I noticed a long time ago that successful lawmen and successful old reprobates are often just two sides of a single coin. It's the same with brutal cops and thuggish crooks.

Fate and circumstances.

Flip the coin.

Call it while it's in the air.

What makes a Bo Poole good at catching lawbreakers is the same foxy intelligence that makes men like my daddy hard to catch. (For what it's worth, the only thing Daddy was ever charged with was evasion of income taxes, back when a couple of the little crossroads stores he fronted bought a lot more wholesale sugar than the records showed they'd actually sold. I don't say that's good, I just state the facts.)

Bo's about my height, late fifties, with thin broomstraw hair, a trim build he carries like a gamecock, and a colorful folksy style that will probably keep getting him elected as long as he wants the job. Of course, colorful and folksy won't cut it at the ballot box if people don't feel their sheriff's competent, and Bo makes sure the department's clearance rate of violent crimes stays high. He also hound-dogs our county commissioners, always trying for a bigger slice of the budget pie so that he can afford the modern equipment and decent salaries that keep his good officers from being lured off to richer, more urbanized counties.

The quid pro quo is that he requires his people to keep their skills updated through community college courses and the various seminars the SBI or FBI regularly offer.

I respect him for his professionalism, but I love him for lazy summer afternoons out on one of the ponds, dabbling my hand in the still water while he and Daddy cast for bass and regale each other with war stories from their checkered pasts.

Like Daddy, Bo's a widower, too, so he stood alone at the head of the steps to welcome us where John Claude and Julia had welcomed us the night before.

"Kezzie Knott's daughter marrying a sheriff's chief deputy," he said, with a kiss for me and a warm handshake for Dwight. "I'd've never believed it if it was anybody besides Dwight."

"Anybody besides Dwight and I wouldn't believe it either," I assured him.

Deputy Jack Jamison arrived right behind us and introduced me to his wife, Cindy. I knew they'd become parents back in late summer, but for the life of me I couldn't remember if it was a boy or a girl.

"How's that baby?" I asked, hoping they'd give me a hint.

"Fine," said Jamison, both of them beaming. His wife was pretty, fair-haired, and, like her husband, a little on the tubby side, but a cuddlesome armful if the way Jamison was looking at her meant anything.

"This is only the third time we've both left him," she said shyly.

"We're honored, then," I said. "Is he sleeping through yet?" (From listening to some of my friends bitch about it, sleeping through the night seems to be the first big thing in a newborn's development.)

"Finally!" said the proud papa, and she added, "In fact, we may have to leave early so I can feed him before he goes down for the night."

Which naturally meant that we all immediately cast discreet glances toward her generous bustline. Cindy Jamison seemed like a nice person and I hoped no one else would notice the faint milk stain on the nipple area of her Christmassy gold satin blouse.

"Well, hey, hey, hey!" called several voices as we passed to the bar area, and glasses were raised to us.

Tonight, the bar was stocked with beer and wine only, and it was strictly cash. "But," said the bartender Jerry had provided, "I was told your money's no good here tonight, Major Bryant."

Dwight ordered a glass of Chardonnay for me and, after looking over the selection of beers, settled for a Michelob and added a bill to the tip glass.

"Hey, girl!" said a familiar voice and there was K. C. Massengill, whom I hadn't seen since Dwight and I announced our engagement. Her hair was still sun-bleached from the summer — she has a place out on Lake Jordan — but she's always worn it long and now it was cut in a short, sleek style that flattered her slender neck and sparkly chandelier earrings. More surprising than her haircut was her escort — fellow SBI agent Terry Wilson.

Once upon a time several years ago, for about twenty minutes between his second and third wives, I actually considered hooking up with Terry. Then I came to my senses and faced the fact that I would always come third behind his young son and his job as head of the SBI's unsolved murders team. Somehow we had the good sense to stay friends — probably because he's another lawman who likes to fish with Daddy. He and Dwight have gotten tight since Dwight came back to Colleton County, so we run into each other fairly often. He swears that he's known for at least a year that Dwight and I were on a collision course for marriage.

"And another one bites the dust," said K.C., giving me a hug.

"I like the haircut," I told her, "but I thought you needed it long so that you could change your looks on stakeouts."

She smiled. "No more stakeouts. Got promoted last month and now I sit at a desk most of the time."

"Really? Congratulations!"

Buffing her nails against the tunic of her black velvet pantsuit, she murmured with mock modesty, "Thank you, thank you."

"Yeah, we're gonna get old and fat together," Terry said, referring to the fact that he himself spends more time behind a desk these days than out in the field.

Together? It occurred to me that Terry's son is a sophomore at NC State and no longer a child. And maybe the job's not quite as all-consuming now that Terry does more supervising than active investigating.

As for getting old and fat, he might be carrying an extra five or six pounds around his waist, but K.C. was as slim and sexy as ever.

"So what's going on here?" I asked her later when we were in the ladies' room, freshening up our lipstick. "Y'all just ride out from Garner together or are you two seeing each other?"

"Well, our offices are in the same wing so, yeah, we do see more of each other these days."

"C'mon, K.C. This is me. Give."

"He makes me laugh," she said.

"And?"

"He's like that camel that gets his nose under the tent flap, and the next thing you know, the camel's sleeping in your bed."

"Y'all are living together?"

"It started out with fishing." She capped her lipstick and slipped the case back into her black velvet clutch. "I let him put his boat in the water at my landing this summer and one thing sorta led to another. I'm still not completely sure that he's not in it for the bass."

"Oh, right," I said.

She shook her head in bemusement. "I never intended to tie up with somebody on the job."

"Me either."

"Oh well, those roads to hell — they do keep getting themselves paved, don't they?" she said, and we smiled at each other in the mirror.

Tonight, Jerry's red tablecloths had been replaced by snowy white ones with alternating red and green napkins. The centerpieces were pots of red poinsettias wrapped in green foil.

Although Tracy's death was again the main topic of conversation around the room, for most of them it was more a matter of professional interest than a sense of personal loss. Yes, Tracy had conferred with many of these officers about various cases under investigation, but that was business. She had not socialized with them.

Among the ones who did have a personal connection were Mike Castleman and Don

Whitley, both white, and Eddie Lloyd, black, the three deputies who worked drug interdiction. According to Dwight, out on the interstate, they were like bird dogs in a covey of bobwhites, especially Castleman. "Going sixty-five miles an hour, he can look at two cars you'd swear were identical and point out the one that's carrying drugs while the other one's clean as a whistle."

Indeed, he'd even been in my court before lunch on Friday to testify at a probable cause hearing for a couple of Haitian mules who were being bound over for trial in superior court. Coincidentally, he was on duty Friday evening and was one of the first responding officers, but when he repeated the story again for the group, it was Mei's death that seemed to bother him more.

"When we talked about my testimony that morning, Ms. Johnson did say she was taking off early, but you never expect it to be somebody you know," he said. "But the baby. God! I didn't even see her at first. You automatically go for the driver or a front-seat passenger. Check for vitals, you know? When they told me there was a baby in the backseat —" He shook his head and took a deep breath. "Man, all I could think about was Heidi."

Heidi? I raised my eyebrows at Dwight.

"His daughter," Dwight murmured in my ear. "Grown now, but she hung the moon for him."

I knew he was divorced and I had him pegged more for a good-timing lover than a doting daddy. Early forties with thick curly black hair and dark flashing eyes, Castleman had even cast one of those eyes my way back while I was still in private practice and he testified against one of my clients, but I was involved with someone else at the time and wasn't interested.

He was personable and funny as a rule, but there was nothing funny about his story of coming up on Tracy's wrecked car. Eddie Lloyd had been off duty that night and listened without his usual hip-hop flippancy. When standing on a street corner in the seedier parts of Makely or Widdington, Lloyd could look like a strung-out user in bad need of a hit. Tonight he was sharp in a black turtleneck and dark gray jacket.

Don Whitley sat off at the end of the table and he didn't have much to say either.

"That's right," Dwight said to Don. "You and Tracy worked pretty closely on that carjacking case, back in the spring, didn't you?"

Whitley nodded sadly. "She was one smart lady."

The case had come to trial last month, and although I hadn't followed it closely, I knew that Tracy had gotten stiff sentences for all the perps involved, thanks to the meticulous case Whitley had built for her. He was mid-thirties and nowhere near as flashy as Castleman or Lloyd. In fact, I barely knew him except by sight, but Dwight had given him a commendation for that piece of work, and whenever he talked about the productive members of the department, Whitley, Lloyd, and Castleman were always mentioned. Between them, they were responsible for confiscating close to a hundred thousand dollars in drug money last year, which was partly why the department got a new crime scene van and was able to provide Kevlar vests for everyone.

Lloyd and Castleman seemed stone-cold sober but Whitley had clearly had more than one. He wasn't drunk, but he didn't seem in control of his emotions either. "She's the reason I'm going for my associate degree," he said mournfully. "She encouraged me to do it."

We were joined by Deputy Mayleen Richards, recently promoted to detective and one of those investigating Tracy's death. She's four or five years younger, a few inches taller, and always reminds me of a half-grown filly that still has moments of coltish, lurching awkwardness. For some reason, she often gets tongue-tied around me, and tonight was worse than usual. With shoulder-length hair the color of cinnamon and thick freckles, she turned brick red and only briefly met my eyes when she shook my hand and wished us happiness. It was with visible relief that she turned to Castleman and asked if he'd noticed a Palm Pilot in Tracy's car. "We know she owned one, but we haven't been able to locate it."

Castleman shook his head. "The window was open on the passenger side. Maybe it bounced out and one of the gawkers grabbed it."

"That's what I'm afraid of." Richards sighed and glanced up at Dwight. "We have a list of the bystanders, though, and we'll check it out. Maybe we'll find an honest person who'll give it back."

I've never used one of those electronic schedulers, but I remembered Tracy singing their praises when she first got hers.

"I can see why you'd want it," I said. "She used it for everything: address book, calendar, notes. She told me she'd thrown her old Rolodex in the trash. Everything was computerized."

Since Dwight was distracted by something another deputy was telling him, I sneaked in a question of my own. "Do you know who she was seeing?"

"Not yet. Didn't she tell you?"

"Sorry. Maybe he's just a figment of our imagination."

"Figments don't get you pregnant," Richards blurted just as Dwight turned back to us. She flushed an even brighter red and looked at him like a guilty kid with her hand in the cookie jar. "Oh gosh! That was really dumb of me."

"Yes, it was," said Dwight, and his face was as stern as I'd ever seen it. He looked around the small circle of officers, fixing each of them with his eyes. "This goes no further. Understood? If I hear even a whisper of this before we get the ME's official findings, I'll put every one of you on report. Is that clear?"

There were murmurs of "Yessir" and uncomfortable glances towards Richards, who stood there looking as if she could burst into tears.

Stunned as I was by hearing that Tracy had been pregnant, I nevertheless put my hand on Dwight's arm. "You'd put me on report, too?"

He relaxed enough to grin down at me. "Damn straight."

I made a face and that broke the tension. Except for Richards, the others laughed, and talk moved on to a series of break-ins in the Cotton Grove area that had them baffled.

Since Thanksgiving, there had been a systematic looting of houses around Cotton Grove and nobody had a clue who was doing it. In each incident, the owners had been gone for at least three or four days, either on vacation or traveling for business or pleasure during this holiday season. All the houses were without burglar alarms, in middle-class neighborhoods, and entry was always by breaking through a rear door or window. The only items taken were money, jewelry, and small electronics that were easily fenced. From their talk, I gathered that there were no fingerprints and nothing to indicate whether it was the work of a single person or a whole gang. The biggest puzzle was trying to figure out how the perps knew which houses would be empty, especially since all the victims had taken sensible precautions. They had stopped delivery of mail and newspapers, they had used timers to turn lamps on and off at normal hours, they had even alerted neighbors to keep an eye out. Unfortunately, nothing seemed to be working.

"What about the post office?" Mike Castleman asked. "Loose lips? The mail carrier?"

"We're talking two separate postal zones," said Raeford McLamb, the black deputy in charge of the investigation.

"Newspapers?"

"Three papers and at least four or five carriers."

Before others could offer suggestions, Bo Poole asked us to be seated so the waiters could take our orders. I wound up between Bo and Terry with Dwight across the table from us, next to K.C.

I chose broiled catfish and Dwight ordered fried oysters, then Terry caught us up on news of Stanton. Sounded as if his son was breaking hearts rather than breaking a sweat over his grades, "But hell, I never averaged better than a low B or a high C myself, so I can't cuss at him too bad. Besides, he found my old grade cards up in the attic and every time I say something about whether or not he's hitting the books hard enough, he reminds me of that D in calculus."

Dwight laughed and turned to answer a question Bo had about work, so I quickly asked Terry if he knew anything about Martha Hurst. He gave me a puzzled look. "Naw, like I told Dwight just now, when she called me this week, I had to go look up our records."

Now it was my turn to look puzzled. "Martha Hurst called you?"

"No, Tracy Johnson. Didn't you hear me tell Dwight?"

"Tell Dwight what?"

"Aw, no, that's right. That must've been when you and K.C. went to powder y'all's noses. Tracy called me about some other stuff this week, and before we hung up, she asked me, same as you, if I worked the Roy Hurst homicide."

"Did you?"

He shook his head. "I might've interviewed some of the witnesses, but the only reason I remembered the case even after I looked it up is because of how that woman took her bat to his balls. Scotty Underwood was our point man on that one. I don't know if Tracy ever got in touch with him or not."

It was a good thing we'd driven over to Jerry's in Dwight's truck. When all the

171

after-dinner toasts to wish us a long and happy marriage were finished, Jack Jamison and Raeford McLamb carried in the gift everyone had chipped in on. Wrapped in a green plastic tarp and tied with a huge red satin ribbon, it was clearly heavy and quite large — six feet long, eighteen inches wide, and a couple of feet tall — and it clanked when they set it down.

They made Dwight and me unwrap it right there and then, and I was delighted to see it was a bench swing, complete with long chains and sturdy hooks.

Beaming, Bo explained to those unfamiliar with the farm that there were two large trees on the bank of the pond below the house. "If they hang it there, then next summer they can sit and swing and fish from the shade."

"Or," said K.C. with a mischievous smile, "they could pad it with a few cushions and forget about fish."

I kept my mouth shut and let Dwight respond to that one.

Chapter 12

Say all that is necessary, in plain, distinct language, and say no more. State, in forcible words, every point that it is desirable for your correspondent to be made acquainted with, that your designs and prospects upon the subject may be perfectly well understood.

Florence Hartley,
The Ladies' Book of Etiquette, 1873

Sunday night, December 12

On the drive home that night, their new swing lashed down in the back of his truck, Dwight said, "I really appreciate you not asking any questions back there about Tracy being pregnant."

"Nice try," Deborah told him, "but if you're hoping to guilt me into not asking questions now that we're alone, that mule won't pull."

He glanced across at her with an amused shake of his head. "You want to tell me again how we need to stay out of each other's business?"

"C'mon, Dwight, be fair. We all knew Tracy. You can't expect me to pretend I didn't hear what Mayleen Richards said."

"Yeah, well, first thing tomorrow morning, Richards and me, we're gonna have a little come-to-Jesus talk," he said grimly.

She laid a placating hand on his thigh. "Don't be too rough on her, okay? It was partly my fault. I mean, you're her boss and I'm your — your —"

"Yes, you are," he said as she hesitated, searching for the right term.

She smiled in the glow of the dash lights. "Yes, I are what?"

"Mine," he said simply.

It was still a thing of wonder that she was there beside him, that in ten days she was actually going to stand up in church before God and the world — not to mention her whole family — and promise to be with him forever. He had loved her and wanted her for more than half his lifetime and now here she was. In his life. In his truck. In his bed. As the warmth of her hand passed through the fabric of his trousers, he felt himself begin to harden. To neutralize the moment, he told her about Tracy's autopsy.

"All the same," he said, "Richards knows better than to give out information like that in an ongoing investigation, I don't care who's doing the asking. This is precisely why we don't push the ME's office to give us the written report right away."

Next morning, Dwight found himself ramming home those same facts to Deputy Mayleen Richards, who stood before him contrite, apprehensive, and so humiliated that her face was a dull brick red from the hairline of her forehead all the way down her neck to her collar as he blasted her for last night's indiscretion. "You know the first forty-eight hours are the most critical, and that the longer we can truthfully say we don't have an official cause of death or any other findings, the better for developing leads. When it gets out that she was pregnant — and yeah, dammit, thanks to you, it's probably all over the whole county by now — you think any man's going to admit he even had a cup of coffee with her?"

"Sir, I don't think any of our people will talk," she said tremulously.

"You think not, huh? And what about their spouses or dates? You trusting enough to think they're going to sit on something this juicy?"

"I — No, sir."

Her eyes met his steadily. He'd give her points for that. And she didn't make excuses or cry. More points.

"Okay, Richards. That's it. Now get over to her computer and get me some names before the innards of that machine go missing, too."

Her eyes widened. "I'm still on the case? You're not going to bust me back to uniform?"

"If I was going to bust you over one screwup, you'd be sitting in a patrol car doing speed checks out on the bypass right now," he told her. "Just don't expect me to go this easy if you mess up again."

"No, sir."

Out in the squad room, Jack Jamison gave her a sympathetic look. "You okay?"

Her smile was radiant. "I'm fine."

Raeford McLamb glanced up from his computer screen where he was checking pawnshop records for any of the items stolen in the past week's break-ins and grinned at Jamison. "Getting married must be making him soft."

"Oh, he took me to the woodshed, all right," Richards assured them, "but he didn't fire me." She picked up a notepad from her desk and tucked it in the pocket of her black wool jacket. She never carried a purse if she could help it and all her jackets and slacks had as many pockets as a man's suit "Anybody wants me, I'll be in the DA's office."

"While you're there, ask them for her cell phone number," said Jamison, turning back to the pile of paper in the box on his desk. "That wasn't in the car either and I bet you a dozen Krispy Kreme doughnuts she had her boyfriend on speed dial. Oh, wait a minute. Never mind. Here's her bill with the itemized calls."

He pulled up a reverse directory on his computer screen and keyed in the first number. It was immediately identified as a daycare facility here in Dobbs.

Across the hall, Mike Castleman, with his hand over the mouthpiece of his phone, rolled his chair over to the doorway and said, "Y'all seen Whitley this morning? DA's office is on the phone. He's supposed to testify on Thursday, but he hasn't shown up for the briefing and Woodall's pissed."

When the others shook their heads, he spoke into the mouthpiece: "Sorry, ma'am, but nobody's seen him today. Did you try his pager? . . . Aw, now, Miss Helen, I wasn't implying you're dumb. No, ma'am. Honest. I was just trying to be helpful."

He was still using all his considerable charm to placate Woodall's testy secretary as Richards headed upstairs to the DA's offices on the far side of the courthouse.

Minutes later, Dwight Bryant emerged from his office and nodded approvingly as Jamison explained that he was going down the list of the most frequently called numbers on Tracy Johnson's phone bill and trying to put a name to each of them.

"I don't have this month's bill, but I'll put in a request for it."

"Where's Jones?" Dwight asked. Deputy Silas Lee Jones was old and lazy and had never been worth a damn so far as he'd ever heard, but the man would do to check out bystanders at the crash site and see if anyone had picked up Tracy's Palm Pilot.

"Must be with Whitley," Raeford Mc-Lamb said, cracking wise. "He's missing, too."

"I'm sorry," said Julie Walsh as she

watched Mayleen Richards's fingers flash across the keys of Tracy's computer. "Whenever she had to give me her password, she'd change it as soon as she got back to the office."

"She told you her passwords?"

"Sure. She'd call and have me pull up a file or something, but the next time, it'd be a different code."

"Like what?" asked Richards, knowing that most people don't bother to get too complicated.

"It was all to do with her daughter and numbers. Last time, I think it was M-E-I-six-eight-ten. Another time, it was one-two-three-four-M-E-I."

A deceptively fragile-looking young white woman, Julie Walsh was eager to help, but she had not worked there long. She had passed the bar exam last spring and only joined the DA's staff the past summer. "Tracy sort of mentored me here, but we weren't real close. I mean, we ate lunch together if we were both here at the courthouse, but she was older and what with the baby and all . . ."

Her voice trailed off. She tucked a strand of light brown hair behind her ear. Beneath her watchband, a tendril of tattooed flowers encircled her wrist so daintily that it was almost unnoticeable. On this chilly day, she wore brown corduroy gauchos, high-heeled brown leather boots, a man-styled white shirt, and a bright yellow zip-front sweater. There was a simple gold stud in one earlobe, a cluster of small gold bells cascaded from the other.

"Boyfriends?" asked Richards.

"Well, there's an attorney over in Widdington that I've gone out with a time or two, but —"

"Not you. Her."

"Oh. Well, yes. I guess. Don't ask me who, though, because she never talked to me about him, but I think they might've been having a fight because last Monday we came in and there was this jeweler's box on her desk and when she opened it, it was a gold-and-turquoise bracelet that matched some earrings someone — maybe him? — gave her for her birthday in October. She went ballistic about it. I mean, if it'd been a dishwasher or something, I could under-stand. My dad gave my mom a dishwasher for one of their anniversaries and she didn't speak to him for like six weeks. But this was jewelry, for pete's sake. In her colors. She really liked turquoise, you know?"

"She got mad because he gave her jew-elry?"

"Yeah." Walsh grinned. "Maybe she really wanted a dishwasher."

"Wait a minute. You said the box was here on her desk? How did it get here?"

The young ADA looked blank. "I never thought about that. It was just there. Gee. Somebody in our office?"

Richards could almost see her brain working as it ran through her colleagues here in the DA's office.

"No, I don't think so. Somebody would've said something. Maybe one of the attorneys in town? They're in and out all the time."

"I don't suppose you noticed the box? What store it came from?"

"Sorry. It's not like she passed it around. The only reason I saw it at all was because I was standing right here when she found it."

Richards shoved a pad and pen toward her. "Can you draw what it looked like?"

"I don't know."

Hesitantly, Julie Walsh sketched a wide silver cuff. "And there were like little rectangles of turquoise spaced along the edge." She indicated the stones with small dashes. "It might've had more but I didn't get a good look. She barely looked at it herself before she snapped the lid closed again.

She didn't put it on then and I never saw her wearing it. Maybe she gave it back?"

All during this time, Richards had been trying variations of the previous passwords. She jotted down yet another sequence of numbers after M-E-I, keyed them in, hit the enter key, and suddenly an alphabetized directory of files filled the screen.

"Oh wow!" said Walsh. "You did it."

Richards ran the cursor up and down the rows. She opened Johnson's computerized address book and skimmed through it, but nothing leaped out at her. It read like the courthouse directory: names, addresses, phone numbers, and e-mail addresses of attorneys, ADAs, deputies, and highway patrol officers that she'd worked with. Richards's own name was there. So was Major Bryant's.

And Judge Knott's.

Some of the names had personal data entered in the notes section — birthdays, children's names, alternate phone numbers. Judge Knott's had "marrying DB 12/22."

Unbidden came the fresh memory of the way the two had looked at each other last night. Richards's heart wrenched as she recalled the easy familiarity with which the judge had touched the major's hair, had held his hand, had fitted herself into the crook of his arm as they left Jerry's.

Nothing to do with you, she scolded herself silently and set the computer's parameters to print out the whole address book, notes and all, then went back to scanning the folders.

In a file labeled "Medical," she found the names and addresses of Johnson's ob-gyn and Mei's pediatrician along with a log of office visits, copayments, and reasons for the visits. Nothing unusual for either of them.

Nor was her e-mail account for this computer difficult to open. Again, all the messages seemed to pertain to her job here.

Going up one level, she discovered one more folder lurking among the system files. It was labeled "Personal." To her dismay, it was protected by a different password and none of the MEI variations seemed to work.

"Maybe she used her own name," suggested Julie Walsh, who had been watching over her shoulder.

Richards tried the usual combinations. Nothing.

Frustrated, she pushed back in the chair and looked up at the younger woman. "Did she ever mention Martha Hurst to you?"

"Not really. I heard her ask one of the clerks to pull the files on it, though."

Nearing retirement, gray-haired, and carrying seventy pounds over what he'd weighed when he first joined the department right before Bo Poole got himself elected, Deputy Silas Lee Jones reflected that it was a fine howdy-do when you had to ask witnesses if they'd seen something you couldn't rightly describe yourself.

Cell phones he understood, but Palm Pilots?

"What the hell's a Palm Pilot?" he asked plaintively after Major Bryant tracked him down at the coffee machine and gave him the assignment.

Castleman and Jamison explained all the things one could do with it.

Jones gave a disgusted snort. "Sounds like more trouble than it's worth," he said as he dialed the first name on the list collected at the crash site Friday night.

"No," said the witness. "I didn't notice a Palm Pilot, just her cell phone. It was in a holder on the dash, right next to that poor woman's head. Front end smashed to hell and gone and the light was still on in the charger."

"Oh crap," Jones said to the others.

"One of those bastards stole her cell phone, too."

The clerk was forty-four and fighting it. She was rail thin, her hair an artful strawberry blond, and her pink eye shadow matched the pink of the long-sleeved silk blouse she wore with formfitting black slacks and stacked shoes.

"Martha Hurst? Oh, yes. She asked me to pull the files last week. Some third-year law student at Eastern was reviewing the case for his law clinic."

"You know his name?" asked Richards.

The clerk frowned in concentration. "Norman? Newton? No, that's not right. Something like that, though."

Richards sighed. Well, how many third-year law students at Eastern with a name like Norman or Newton could there be?

Jack Jamison stood to stretch his arms over his head and flex his shoulders after two hours hunched over the phone bills and his computer screen. Jones had finished talking to everyone who answered the phone and had gone out for a smoke. Jamison looked through the windows to the opposite squad room where Castleman labored over his own computer screen. He started to call to him, then vetoed the idea. Instead he gathered up the bills and notes he'd made and walked down to Major Bryant's office. The door was ajar and when he cleared his throat, Bryant looked up.

"Talk to you a minute, sir?"

"Sure, Jack. What you got?"

"Well, it might not mean anything. I mean, there was a logical reason for them to talk, but this much?"

He laid Tracy Johnson's cell phone bills on the desk before his boss and pointed to the lines he'd highlighted. "Look at the times, sir. Some of these calls are pretty late at night."

At that moment, Bo Poole stuck his head in the door. "What's up with Whitley? He's not answering his pager and Doug Woodall's all over my ass about him."

"I'll put out an APB right away," said Dwight.

"APB?" The sheriff started to laugh, then realized Dwight wasn't joking. "A little extreme, don't you think? We don't need to treat him like a criminal just because he flubbed a briefing."

"Yeah, I think we do," Dwight told him. "Hey, Major?"

Mike Castleman spoke over Bo Poole's

shoulder. His jaw was clenched and his voice was tight.

"Later," said Dwight.

"No, sir. I'm sorry, sir, but you need to come look at my computer right now."

They followed him to his desk in the empty squad room.

"I was catching up on my messages and there's one from Whitley."

He moved the mouse, clicked it, and a message dated the night before appeared on the screen.

Sorry, pal, but I can't do this anymore. Wish there was another solution, but there isn't. Don

Grim-faced, Bo Poole turned to Dwight. "Do it," he said. "Now."

Chapter 13

We must work for our heavenly peace on earth. The mental discipline, to prosper, must be aided by divine grace, but it must spring from our own hearts.

Florence Hartley,
The Ladies' Book of Etiquette, 1873

Here in eastern North Carolina weather forecasters get downright giddy at the faintest possibility of snow; and the closer we get to Christmas, the more they massage their satellite photos to show how a system that could maybe — *maybe* — bring possible flurries might actually hang around long enough to blanket us by the twenty-fifth. Despite the hopeful chatter on television last night, we almost never get snow in December, but freezing rains were a distinct possibility. In the belief that the tires of rush-hour traffic would help keep the main roads from turning into sheets of greased glass, Dwight made me promise before I left home Monday morning that I'd head on back as soon as I adjourned court.

On the drive down to Makely, my mood was almost as bleak as the cold gray clouds that filled the sky. It wasn't just gloomy thoughts about Tracy, Mei, and the unborn baby either.

I was due to testify in superior court sometime today in the trial of a former colleague. I usually have reliable instincts about people, but Russell Moore had foxed a lot of people besides me. He was a big, good-natured country boy who'd pulled himself up by his own bootstraps, worked his way through college, went to law school at night, then, spurred on by the grinding poverty of his childhood, opened a one-man practice in Makely, determined to succeed. He played hard, but he worked hard, too, and was particularly good with juries, who tended to trust him implicitly. Hell, we all did. And why not? He was just like an overgrown Saint Bernard puppy, still something of a farmboy, awed by how far he'd come from the tobacco fields. But then he did an out-of-court settlement with an insurance company on behalf of a client.

A hundred-thousand-dollar settlement.

Only he didn't tell his client.

By the time he was indicted, he'd made at least three more similar settlements. That wasn't how he got caught, though. He got caught because he forged my name on a DWI judgment that allowed his middle-class client to get a restricted license. Said client was so happy that he could continue driving himself back and forth to work that he bragged about it in the wrong place, and when another attorney asked for something similar for one of his clients, I pulled the record to refresh my memory and immediately realized that it wasn't my signature on the form. My courtroom clerk said that wasn't her signature either.

Once Russell had drawn attention to himself like that, it took only a cursory examination of his records to discover the embezzlements.

Disbarred and disgraced, he was now on trial and I was a witness for the State. And yeah, I know that there are very few attorneys up for sainthood — there's a reason for all those crooked-lawyer jokes — and yes, they're expected to argue a client's innocence when, in their heart of hearts, they suspect he's guilty as hell. They may not be held to the spirit of the law, but they're damned well supposed to uphold the letter of it.

There had been little mention of Russell Moore at Saturday night's dinner. His acts shamed us all, but he'd been arrested back in June, so the nine-days-wonder element had long since dissipated.

When I got to my own courtroom, I was dismayed to find another white officer of the court and his wife standing before me, red-faced and repentant. Marvin Pittman was a town of Makely policeman, but the SBI had accidently discovered that he was fighting cocks out on his farm. An undercover agent on the trail of some illegal Mexicans suspected of running drugs through the area had gotten himself accepted enough to go along for a drug buy out in the country.

In addition to rounding up six men dealing the drugs, they had stumbled across the social aspects of the buy — one of the largest cockfighting arenas they'd ever seen. Inside Pittman's barn were four pens, bleachers, and an announcer's booth. Pittman's wife and fourteen-year-old son were even running a snack bar on the side, selling hot burritos and cold beers. Some forty people were arrested there that night and issued criminal summonses.

In addition to dozens of razor-sharp spurs, leather thongs, and other cockfighting accessories, the SBI had confiscated a half-kilo of coke, eighty-nine hundred dollars in betting money, solid gold prize jewelry worth another couple of thousand, and twenty-six gamecocks.

The gamecocks were currently residing at the county animal shelter.

The SBI conceded that the Pittmans had nothing to do with drugs and were technically unaware of the side action. All the same, cockfighting is illegal and they were charged with animal cruelty, selling beer and food without a license, and contributing to the delinquency of a minor.

Unfortunately, cruelty to chickens is only a Class 2 misdemeanor in North Carolina. Dogfighting is a felony, but not cockfighting. And just for the record, a second offense of animal cruelty other than chickens is a felony, but a second offense of chicken cruelty is still a misdemeanor. Where are North Carolina's chicken lovers on this? Why aren't they up in arms?

Even after all the charges were combined, a thousand-dollar fine and a suspended sentence were about the most I could give him since he didn't have any prior convictions.

The wife had a prior DWI, but feeling sorry for their teenage son I suspended any jail time for her on condition that she contribute one hundred hours of work at the county animal shelter and take her son with her for at least fifty of those hours.

After that, it was almost a relief to be presented with Bullard Morris, a fifty-year-old black man who had appeared before me more than once since I came to the bench. Bull Morris might have been shiftless, but he was usually amiable and philosophical when arrested for shoplifting or public drunkenness. This time, though, he'd been charged with disorderly conduct, and the police officer who testified against him said he'd been loud and profane and belligerently ready to fight when the officer was arresting Morris's roommate for possession of stolen property.

After he'd pleaded guilty as charged, I said, "That's not like you, Mr. Morris. What happened?"

"I'm sorry, Your Honor. Usually I wake up sober. I reckon I'm not real good at waking up drunk."

I gave him court costs and a suspended sentence on condition that he go for yet another alcohol assessment at Mental Health. "You don't get your drinking under control, you're liable to wake up shot some morning," I lectured him.

He earnestly agreed, but we both knew we'd be meeting like this again.

A bailiff approached the bench and told me that they were ready for my testimony in superior court, so I recessed for an hour, left my robe hanging in chambers and slipped into a deep green cropped jacket, and hurried down to the larger courtroom, adjusting the collar of my white shirt as I went.

Zack Young, the best criminal defense attorney in our district and certainly the one I'd retain if I were ever in serious trouble, had agreed to defend Russell Moore. According to courthouse gossip, Zack planned to argue mitigating circumstances — that the embezzlement began as an oversight error in bookkeeping and then escalated when Russell's widowed mother developed a leaky heart valve and had no insurance for the needed operation. As for the forgery, well, that was just Russell's well-known empathy for people in embarrassing situations, an empathy developed when he was a gawky hayseed who was jeered at because he drove back and forth to his night classes at law school in an old rattletrap that was held together with duct tape and baling wire.

According to Zack, he couldn't bear to see his client humiliated and reduced to commuting to his white-collar job by motorbike.

As I entered the courtroom by the side door, I took the nearest seat on a bench directly behind the defense table. I couldn't see Russell's face as Zack Young finished up with the witness ahead of me, but he seemed to be staring straight ahead. Zack is good, but I had a feeling that Russell knew he was staring at a few years of hard time. Juries aren't particularly sympathetic to attorneys who bilk their clients.

My testimony seemed to be part of the prosecution's clearing out of the underbrush before they got into the embezzlement part. Brandon Frazier was ADA and his questions were straightforward when I took the stand.

"Did you remember this case, Judge Knott?"

"Not specifically."

"When did it come to your attention?"

195

"When the attorney of another DWI with a similar suspended sentence petitioned for the same judgment as I'd supposedly given Mr. Moore's client."

"What did you do then?"

"I had a clerk pull the record."

"Why was that?"

"When someone to whom I've given a suspended sentence comes up again on the same charge, the original sentence is automatically activated. It would have been improper for me to give him limited privileges. I couldn't and I wouldn't. That's why I had the record pulled to see what was going on."

"And yet your signature was on the form?"

"It had been signed with my name, but that wasn't my signature."

"No further questions," said Frazier.

"Mr. Young?" said Judge O'Donnell, who was presiding that day.

Zack Young looked over the top of his glasses and thanked me for coming, as if I were doing his client a favor rather than helping to build the case of dishonesty against him. "Judge Knott, you said that was not your signature on the order. Do you know for a fact who signed your name?"

"No, sir."

"Could it have been a clerk or a —"

"Objection. Supposition," said Frazier.

"Sustained," said O'Donnell.

"In fact," said Zack, "you do not know that my client signed it, do you?"

"No, sir." Mine not to add that it really didn't matter who did the actual forgery. It was last in Russell's hands before it was filed with the clerk of court's office.

"Now, when you said you normally activate the original sentence, what does that mean?"

"It means that the more severe punishments that the original offense carried would now be put into effect."

"And in the case of Mr. Moore's client?"

"It would have meant that all of his driving privileges would have been revoked."

"So that he couldn't operate a motor vehicle under any circumstances?"

"That's correct."

"How was he supposed to get to work?"

"I'm afraid that's not the State's problem, Mr. Young."

"It didn't bother you that he might lose his job if he couldn't drive to work?"

"It did bother me. That's why I didn't take away his license the first time he appeared before me. But I explained very thoroughly that he would lose it if he were charged with a second DWI."

"I'm sorry," Zack said with an air of innocent bewilderment. "I thought you didn't remember this case. How can you know you explained it so thoroughly?"

"You're quite right," I conceded. "Spelling out the consequences of a second DWI is what I normally do, but I can't say with certainty that I did so in this particular case."

"No further questions," said Zack.

I'm sure he hoped that some members of the jury would be so befuddled by my less than absolute memory about something irrelevant to begin with that they might think I'd somehow been lacking in my rulings that day.

"You may step down," said Judge O'Donnell.

As I walked back to my own courtroom, I was dispirited to think of how hard Russell had worked, only to throw it away for that quick dollar.

If his secretary had been the one to open that unexpected insurance check, if his client hadn't assumed his claim had been denied, would Russell be sitting there as a defendant now?

Because even though he hadn't confessed, I was sure that his downfall must have began with that first sudden temptation, coupled with the knowledge that he could probably get away with it.

"What if you were tempted like that?" whispered the preacher.

"By money?" the pragmatist jeered. *"Give me a break."*

"It's a dark night. You're driving too fast. You're not drunk, but you have had a glass or two of wine. You feel a sickening thump off your bumper and realize that you've hit something. Maybe it's a deer. Maybe it's a person. Do you stop or do you keep driving?"

The pragmatist hesitated, weighing his options.

"I thought so," said the preacher.

It's my worst nightmare: that I will be faced with a choice like that and will come up wanting in that split-second decision that separates principle from self-interest.

Some judges, those who know they've driven with a blood alcohol level over .08, are apt to give middle-aged DWIs the benefit of any doubt. Judges with teenage kids tend to go a little easier on the teenagers who show up in their courts. Me? I can't help empathizing with defendants who are there because they yielded to that first self-serving impulse, especially if they make me believe that they're totally appalled by that yielding.

Grown men and women have stood before me with tears running down their faces, practically begging me to give them the maximum, anything to help ease the load of guilt they carry for doing something they'd always thought themselves incapable of doing.

O God, be merciful to me, a sinner.

In chambers, I hung my jacket on a peg and put back on my heavy black robe.

"All rise," said the bailiff as I took my seat at the bar of justice.

We moved methodically through the calendared cases. Plaintiffs and defendants had their minutes before me, then left, as did their supporters and accusers. By mid-afternoon the whole courtroom had turned over at least three times except for a wiry young black man. Eventually I realized that he had been there since shortly after I convened court this morning. I hadn't seen him confer with any of the attorneys and he didn't seem to be connected with any of the cases. He was neatly dressed in faded straight-legged jeans, a cranberry turtleneck, and a heavy black wool jacket that he'd removed and laid in his lap to act as a desktop for a spiral-bound notebook.

A new reporter for the local paper?

He was back after lunch and was still there when the last case of the day was disposed of.

As I stood to leave, he closed his notebook, hooked his jacket over his shoulder, and came forward.

"Judge Knott? May I speak to you?"

The white bailiff started to put himself between the young man and the bench, but I waved him back.

"Can I help you?"

"I hope so. I'm Nolan Capps."

He paused as if that would mean something to me.

"Yes?"

"Mr. Stephenson didn't call you about me?"

Call? Oh, Lord! I fumbled in the pocket of my robe. My phone. Still switched off.

"Sorry," I said. "My phone's been off all day. What can I do for you?"

"I was wondering if I could talk to you about Martha Hurst?"

"Martha Hurst?"

"Yes, ma'am. Mr. Stephenson thought you could help me."

I didn't see how, but I invited young Mr.

Capps back to chambers so I could pick up my briefcase and coat. Mindful of my promise to Dwight, I warned him that I could give him only a few minutes.

"That's okay," he said, looking around with interest at the behind-the-scenes hallways where so many plea bargains are worked out between DAs and attorneys. The halls were pretty much deserted now, although I was waylaid by a white police officer who wanted me to sign a search warrant for him. I skimmed through it and noticed that he'd neglected to fill in the house number on the street address.

"If you aren't specific, a good attorney will probably get the results thrown out if you do find the drugs and it comes to trial," I told him. "And in that neighborhood, you can bet it won't be a court-appointed one either."

"Oh, shit!" he said without thinking, and immediately apologized. "Sorry, ma'am. If you'll excuse me, I'll be right back."

"So how can I help you?" I asked Nolan Capps as I unzipped my robe and hung it behind the door.

"It's sort of complicated," he said. "I believe you know Bessie Stewart?"

Now there was a question straight out of left field.

Bessie Stewart was to Dwight's nosy, gregarious mother what Maidie Holt had been to mine — technically a domestic employee: cleaning woman, cook, baby-sitter, yet at the same time a friend as well, a friendship rooted in mutual need and mutual dependence. Like Maidie's husband on our farm, Willy Stewart was a tenant on the Bryant farm. When Miss Emily married Calvin Bryant and went to live there, she discovered that a childhood friend was there before her, eight years' married and already the mother of four children. I've heard Miss Emily speak more than once about how Bessie was the one who taught her the practical side of running a farmhouse and how to grass to-bacco and cotton without chopping up all the money plants. She actually helped de-liver Dwight when he arrived in the middle of a hurricane that blocked the roads with downed power lines and fallen trees. And when Calvin Bryant was killed in a farm accident three more children later, it was Bessie Stewart who pushed her to upgrade her certificate and go back to teaching, " 'cause you never gonna be no farmer, I don't care how long you live on one."

Miss Emily is principal at Zachary Taylor High School these days and Bessie

Stewart is still running the domestic side of the farm for her, so yes indeed, I certainly do know her. In fact, she intimidates me a little because I'm not quite sure that she approves of me as a proper wife for Dwight.

"How do you know her?" I asked.

"Her granddaughter's in one of my law classes."

"You're a law student at Eastern?"

"Third-year."

He was aiming for nonchalance, but I heard the pride in his voice, a well-deserved pride because Eastern's law school is making a name for itself in the ranks of smaller universities. Located over in Widdington, it was one of the first Negro colleges in the state after the Civil War; and while it opened its doors to all after segregation ended, the student body is still mainly black. At least it is in the science and liberal arts programs. For some reason, though, Eastern's law school attracted some top names in the field from the moment it opened and there has always been a good racial balance in its classrooms.

"You won't remember me," he said, "but we've met before. You did a symposium at Eastern last year. 'The View from the Bench'?"

"You came to that?" Luther Parker and I were there to represent North Carolina's district courts. Ned O'Donnell represented superior courts, and Frances Tripp, who administered my oath of office when I came to the bench, spoke about her work on the Court of Appeals.

"Yes, ma'am. It was great. Made me want to run for judge someday."

"Hold that thought," I said as my phone rang. One of Dwight's numbers appeared on the little screen.

"You on the road yet?" he asked.

"Just leaving," I assured him. "But I don't have a window here. What's the weather like?"

"Rough and getting rougher. It's raining and the temperature's dropping fast, so be careful, okay?"

"I will. See you in about an hour."

"We don't have anything on for tonight, do we?"

"Nothing on my calendar that I know of."

"I'll bring pizza."

"A man after my own heart."

"That's what I'm aiming for."

"Sorry," I said to Nolan Capps as I rang off.

"That's okay. I know you need to go, so

I'll be quick. See, our criminal law clinic is connected with the Actual Innocence project. We've already taken on our limit for the year, and besides, we don't do death penalty cases because they have access to a lot of legal reviews. But when I was telling my mother about it, she got all excited and wanted us to stop Martha Hurst's execution. You know about Martha Hurst?"

"A little," I said cautiously.

"Then you know that she's never confessed to killing her stepson. That's one of the criteria for taking on a case. Usually a prisoner can get a lesser sentence if they confess. Of course in Hurst's case, she wasn't offered a deal, so she had no incentive to confess. But she's still maintaining her innocence after all this time even though most killers eventually admit that, yeah, they did it."

As he spoke, the police officer returned with all the i's dotted and the t's crossed on his search warrant. I signed it and picked up my heavy coat.

"I'm sorry, Mr. Capps. I have to leave now, but walk out with me and tell me why your mother's interested in Martha Hurst."

He slid on his own jacket, tucked the notebook into an inner pocket, and held the door for me.

"They used to be on a team together when I was a kid and we lived in Cotton Grove. Fastpitch softball. Mom played third and Martha Hurst played short. I think I saw her hit two home runs in the same game once. Then we moved to Widdington and Mom started playing with a team there. They kept in sort of loose touch since sometimes their teams would be in the same tournament, and when the murder happened, Mom heard all the talk about it. Nobody on her team thought Ms. Hurst had done it, and Mom went to see her in prison a couple of times. She swears she would have known if Ms. Hurst was lying."

We walked down a double flight of marble stairs that led to the main rotunda of the old courthouse. It was a few minutes past five and most of the offices were dark. Our footsteps echoed off the marble-clad walls as we passed through the rotunda and continued down a long gloomy hall to the side entrance nearest the parking lot.

"So where do I come in?" I asked.

"First I tried the DA's office. Mr. Woodall said that as far as he was concerned, the case was over and done with. That she'd had all the benefits of the law, that she was guilty and now the law could take its course. But Ms. Johnson was prosecuting over in Widdington week before last. I got her to talk to me and she finally said she'd take a look at the records. I think she found something because she said she was going to ask to see the first defense lawyer's case file. That would be Mr. Stephenson's father, right?"

"Right."

"And now she's been shot?"

"You think there's a causal link?"

"Not necessarily. But it sure does complicate things."

I pushed open the door. A cold wet wind smacked us in the face, but the portico above sheltered us from the rain itself. The steps already looked slick, though.

"Anyhow, Kayra — Kayra Stewart — she said her grandmother knew just about everybody in this end of the county and that she worked for the mother of the chief deputy and she'd put in a word with him. And Kayra said she'd help while we're on Christmas break. Then, when I called Mr. Stephenson this morning to tell him we had Martha's permission to see all her records, he said he wouldn't mind if I looked at his, but he'd given them to the deputy. He said he had a feeling that you'd probably read them and that he'd call you and —"

"I'm sorry," I said, "but I really do need to go. Maybe we could talk tomorrow?"

"Martha Hurst only has a month to live," he said, giving me a soulful look.

It was too cold to argue. I opened my umbrella and started down the steps. He offered me his arm so I wouldn't slip.

Young, idealistic, and polite, too? He reminded me of my nephew Stevie. I sighed.

"You like pizza?"

"Yes, ma'am."

"Then follow me," I told him. "It's about a forty-minute drive, so keep up."

"Yes, ma'am!"

Chapter 14

Never, when advancing an opinion, assert positively that a thing "is so," but give your opinion as an opinion . . . your companion may be better informed upon the subject under discussion.

Florence Hartley,
The Ladies' Book of Etiquette, 1873

I expected Dwight to be annoyed when I called to say I was bringing a law student home with me, but I hadn't factored in his affection for Bessie Stewart. Not only was he not annoyed, he was actually pleased because Bessie had called him earlier that afternoon and asked him to help her granddaughter and "her young gentleman friend."

"Kayra's over at Bessie's right now," he

said, "so I'll tell her to meet us at the house and I'll pick up an extra pizza."

"Don't forget my anchovies."

"How you can eat those disgusting things, I'll never understand."

That's what he says every time I ask for them. "Yours not to reason why," I said.

"Yeah, well mine not to kiss you either."

"Hey, what about for better or for worse and all that?"

"In sickness and in health, yes. In anchovies, no."

I laughed, told him what landmark I was passing at the moment, and clicked off. Rain fell in slower, thicker drops, but so far the interstate was ice-free and I was able to keep it up to the speed limit. Nolan Capps's headlights stayed right with me.

We passed the cutoff I'd taken Friday evening to get away from the backed-up traffic and, a few miles later, the overpass where Tracy had crashed. The lights from the cars around me picked up shards of broken glass, which twinkled briefly in the darkness. By the time we got to my usual exit, the wipers were clearing icy slush from the windshield. Driving became more iffy on the back roads and there was a definite fishtail effect when I cornered too sharply at Possum Creek. It was a relief to turn off the hardtop into the dirt lane that led to the house.

An unfamiliar car sat next to Dwight's truck and both were sheeted with a thin glaze of ice. Dwight met us in the doorway. There might not be any post-anchovy kisses in my immediate future, but the pre-one would hold me for the moment.

I introduced Nolan Capps and he, in turn, introduced me to the young woman seated at the table in front of two large flat boxes that had filled the dining area with the entrancing aroma of tomato sauce, cheese, and oregano.

Kayra Stewart appeared to be in her early twenties. She wasn't exactly beautiful, but she had good bones that would probably age well. I looked for a resemblance to Bessie but couldn't see any beyond her yardstick-straight posture and her level appraisal of me as we shook hands. Her smooth skin was the color of mellow oak, her dark eyes were widely spaced and flashed with good-humored intelligence when she greeted Nolan. Her hair curled even more tightly than my friend Portland's and she wore it clipped short like Portland, so that her shapely head sat elegantly on a long slender neck. She was dressed in formfitting jeans and a slouchy

212

old red crewneck sweater over a white jersey turtleneck. No jewelry beyond a mannish-looking square-faced wristwatch with a black leather band.

Nolan Capps hung his hooded jacket on the back of a chair and tried to look casual when he sat down beside her, but it was clear that he could eat her with a spoon.

I divested myself of coat and scarf and Kayra got up to help me put together salads.

"It's really nice of you and Dwight to talk to us," she said as I set out a bag of mixed greens and some bottled dressings. "This has to be a busy time for y'all. Grandma says the wedding's next Wednesday week?"

"That's okay." I quickly filled the bowls and she carried them over to the table. "I think everything's pretty much under control."

"That reminds me," Dwight said, pointing to a small box on the counter. "Is that what you've been waiting for?"

I examined the return address and tore it open as soon as I saw that it was from California. "Finally!"

Inside was the cake topper I'd ordered off the Internet, and I immediately excused myself to go call Dwight's sister-in-law and tell her to get out her brown paint.

"Oh, good," Kate said. "Bring it with you tomorrow night."

She must have heard my mental wheels spinning. "Don't tell me you've forgotten."

"Of course not," I lied, belatedly remembering that she and Dwight's two sisters were throwing a shower for me tomorrow night. "I was trying to think if I gave you a snippet of my dress so you could match the color."

"You did. And don't worry. I won't let anyone else see it."

When I returned to the dining area, the others were already transferring slices of pizza to their plates and I joined in after opening the tin of anchovies Dwight had picked up at the grocery for me. To his chagrin, both of the budding attorneys accepted my offer to share.

Conversation was general at first — schools, mutual acquaintances — but it soon got down to specifics about Martha Hurst. Nolan told Dwight about his mother's connection to the condemned woman and how he'd wheedled a promise out of Tracy to look up the case.

"She took you seriously enough to speak to an SBI agent," I said, and told them what Terry Wilson had told me last night about the phone call he'd gotten from her. "But he didn't really work the case except for interviewing a couple of the witnesses for the prosecution. Agent Scott Underhill was their lead investigator in conjunction with Sheriff Poole's department."

I had met Underhill four years ago when my nephew Stevie's girlfriend asked me to look into the unsolved murder of her mother. He seemed like a nice man, ethical and honest. "I don't know that he's necessarily the most effective investigator in the Bureau, though."

Dwight frowned. It's not that he's naive about the possibility of sloppy or unethical officers, but he thinks the public's too eager to blame the law whenever something goes wrong.

Kayra delicately lifted an anchovy filet from the flat tin and laid it across her slice of pizza. "You think he might have overlooked something?"

"Something that would prove who really did kill Roy Hurst and the killer shot Ms. Johnson to keep her from telling?" Nolan asked.

"Whoa, now," said Dwight. "That's a real stretch from your mama thinking Martha Hurst is innocent to Tracy Johnson fitting somebody else in the picture after all this time."

Kayra bit into the pointed end of her pizza slice and sighed. "I just wish we had more than your mother's intuition."

"It *is* more than intuition," Nolan protested. "He was killed with her good bat."

A collective "Huh?" went up from the other three of us.

"Maybe it's in the files Mr. Stephenson said we could look at."

Dwight looked at me. "Deb'rah?"

I licked tomato sauce from my fingers. "There was a list of items removed from the trailer in Brix Junior's discovery," I said, and went to see if I could find the file I remembered.

I had to rummage through two boxes before I found the right one. "Here it is." I ran my finger down the list. "A DeMarini aluminum softball bat."

Another item further down caught my eye — an Easton softball bat.

"Easton," I told Dwight. "Isn't that the brand your softball team uses?"

He nodded. "DeMarinis are way too expensive for us."

"That's what I mean." Nolan's dark face was eager and expressive and he gestured so forcibly with his slice of pizza that a mushroom went flying across the table. "If

Martha Hurst was like Mom, she had at least two or three bats, but the others would only be practice bats. The DeMarini would be her game bat. Mom said that Martha's had a monster sweet spot — it was the perfect length, the perfect weight, and had a sweet spot to die for. Everybody was jealous of it. I don't know what fastpitch DeMarinis cost back then — the company hadn't been in business very long — but two years ago I went in with my brother and sister to buy Mom a slowpitch DeMarini for Christmas and it was over two hundred dollars."

"Two hundred dollars!" I was incredulous. I hadn't bought a bat since Stevie was in Little League, but it never occurred to me that a bat of any description could cost more than forty or fifty.

"And you better believe that Mom would use a fence post before she'd take batting practice with that good bat and risk a dent."

Didn't seem like much of an argument to me, and Dwight was looking as skeptical as I felt. "Maybe not if she was thinking clearly," I said, "but Martha Hurst had a history of impulsive violence and I seriously doubt that she would've stopped to think about which bat she was going to smash somebody with. She would've just grabbed up the first one that came to hand."

"Mom wouldn't," Nolan said stubbornly. "She absolutely would *not* and she says Ms. Hurst wouldn't either."

He argued that this was proof enough for him, but finally had to admit that the choice of bats was a slender thread from which to try to weave a lifeline. While Dwight and I changed into old work clothes, he and Kayra cleared the table, stacked the dishwasher, and then spread Brix Junior's files on the table to read through everything themselves.

I brushed my teeth and rinsed away all traces of anchovies before joining Dwight in our new bedroom. April and the others had really knocked themselves out today. The bathroom was technically finished, although one of them had left a note warning us not to use the shower for two more days. In fact, all the construction work was finished. They had painted the walls a deep forest green like my old bedroom and the trim already had one coat of white enamel. The only thing lacking was the second coat, which Dwight and I eventually got around to. Being latex, the enamel dried so quickly that we got Nolan and Kayra to help us move in the bed and dresser so that we could begin refurbishing my old room for Cal.

I remade the bed while they brought in lamps and a blanket chest that doubled as a bench under the window. "What about her husband?" I asked.

"Gene Hurst? He had a stroke last year," said Nolan.

Kayra nodded. "Now he's in a nursing home over in Angier. We went to see him yesterday, but it was a waste of time. His mind's totally gone."

"But Mom says he stuck by Martha all through the trial. Never believed she did it."

"We're going to canvass the trailer park tomorrow," said Kayra. "See if anybody remembers the murder. In our law clinic, we learned that sometimes people will talk more freely after a few years have passed. They'll give up details and facts they wouldn't tell investigators the first time around."

The printer for my laptop doubles as a copier and they made copies of the witness lists and of the items removed from the Hurst trailer. I repeated my observation that none of the items seemed to include bloodstained clothing or footwear and they

immediately made the obvious specula-
tions I had made to Dwight earlier. No
bloody clothes was a talking point and
their optimism wasn't dimmed by
Dwight's suggestion that she could have
stepped out of the shower and then went
ballistic when she found her stepson/
former lover there again after she'd already
thrown him out.

I made a pot of coffee and we kicked it
around another half-hour till Dwight muf-
fled a yawn and Kayra announced that it
was time for them to leave.

"But could you let us look through any
of the records in your office?" she asked
him as they zipped up their jackets and
pulled on gloves.

"Sure, although everything that was presented at the trial will be in the clerk of
court's office," he replied.

"But wouldn't you have stuff that wasn't
used at the trial? Like a statement about
her bats?" asked Nolan, clinging to his
theory.

"Not that I know of, but I'll take a look
for you."

We walked out on the porch with them.
A frigid wind bit at our unprotected faces.
The rain had stopped and there were even
a few stars peeking through the broken

clouds, but the steps were so icy that Nolan's feet went out from under him and he would have fallen if Dwight hadn't grabbed him.

"You're not going to try to drive back to Widdington tonight, are you?" he asked.

"Don't worry," said Kayra. "Grandma's expecting us to spend the night with them."

We gave them directions for driving across the farm by back lanes and then on dirt roads so as to avoid most of the dangerously slick paved roads that lay between our farm and the Bryant farm.

Dwight made sure that they had our phone number in case they slid into a ditch along the way, but Nolan assured me they'd be fine. "I've got four-wheel drive on my Jeep."

"Four-wheel drive doesn't do a thing if all four wheels are on ice," I told him.

Kayra laughed and gave Dwight a good-bye hug. I got one, too.

"Nice kids," I said, leaning into Dwight's bulk for a windbreak as we watched the taillights from both cars disappear down the lane.

"Yeah," he said. "Too bad they're wasting their Christmas holidays on a wild-goose chase."

While he went to take a hot shower in the old bathroom, I gathered up spoons and coffee mugs and started the dishwasher. When I put Brix Junior's files back in the boxes, I noticed a scrap of paper on the floor under the table where it had fallen out of one of the folders. It was a short list of case law citations that Brix Junior probably intended to read up on. In the margin, he had scribbled a name followed by three question marks: "Deenie Gates???"

Deenie Gates.

Now why did that name sound familiar? It might have been a name out of the case law citings, but somehow I doubted it.

Then Dwight called to me from the bedroom. I slid the paper into the end folder and never gave it another thought that night.

Chapter 15

Never question the veracity of any statement made in general conversation.

Florence Hartley,
The Ladies' Book of Etiquette, 1873

Tuesday, December 14

When Mayleen Richards walked into the DA's suite of offices that morning, she learned that an SBI agent had been there the afternoon before and that Tracy Johnson's CPU tower was now at their Garner facility, undergoing a full lobotomy. Officially, the two agencies were cooperating fully, but Richards was competitive enough to want the Colleton County Sheriff's Department to get credit for bringing the killer to justice. And if she could be the one to actually crack the case, all the better. It would prove to Major Bryant that he'd been right in keeping her on the job.

"Not to worry," said Julie Walsh, who had blown in right behind her with an ornate Christmas wreath on her arm. Pink-cheeked from the icy December wind that whipped through the open parking lot on the north side of the courthouse, the young ADA hung her red wool coat and plaid scarf on the office coatrack and gave the detective a reassuring smile as she positioned the wreath on the wall above her desk, where its silver tinsel glittered with every stray current of air from the heating vents below. "Tracy was a suspenders-and-belt person. She backed up everything."

"Yeah, I noticed her box of floppies," Richards said glumly, looking at a now empty space on the desk, "but they must have taken those, too."

"I'm not talking about computer back-ups." Walsh opened the bottom two drawers of a four-drawer gray metal file cabinet that separated her desk from her murdered colleague's. "These were Tracy's. She preferred paper to a screen whenever she worked on something complicated."

"You show these to the state agents?"

"I wasn't here and I don't think they asked any of the others."

Richards quickly scanned the tabs on the manila folders tucked neatly into hanging files and pulled out random sheets. They seemed to be the personal notes and worksheets from past cases that Tracy Johnson had prosecuted during her time with Doug Woodall. The clerk of court's office said that Johnson had borrowed the trial documents on Martha Hurst, but she did not appear to have filed any notes on it here.

"What about her current cases?"

"Mr. Woodall's spreading them around to the rest of us till he can hire a replacement for her. Brandon Frazier and I are trying to reconstruct the game plan for a drug case coming up on Thursday, but if y'all can't find Don Whitley . . ."

"Yeah, I know," said Richards.

"Where you reckon he's gone?"

"Dammit all, Sheriff," said Doug Woodall.

The DA had found Dwight Bryant and Bowman Poole conferring in Poole's office and he was out for blood, waving aside their genial invitation to pull up a chair and how about a cup of coffee?

"We're pushing the limit now on the rules about speedy trials. Tracy already got three continuances and Judge O'Donnell says he won't grant another. We don't take this Ruiz to trial day after tomorrow, we're going to have to cut him loose. Let him walk. It's bad enough we have to proceed without her, but there's no point even starting without that deputy. We don't have him, we don't have linkage. So where the hell is he?"

Sheriff Poole paused on his way to refill his mug from the carafe atop a corner bookcase and drew himself up to his full five foot seven. Despite their difference in height, he somehow managed to make the taller man feel two inches shorter.

"You think we're waiting for him to phone in, Mr. Woodall? We put out an APB on him yesterday. We talked to his mama over in Widdington. We've got somebody watching his place here in Dobbs and we've just sent someone over there to search it. You got a suggestion what else we need to be doing, let's hear it."

"Now, Bo, don't get your back up," the DA said placatingly. Bo Poole's power base in the county was even stronger than his. Only a fool would alienate someone who could make the party give more than lip service when he ran for governor, and Doug Woodall was no fool. "I'm not trying to tell you how to do your job, but it's sure playing hell with mine."

"What about it, Dwight?" asked the sheriff. "What do the troopers say?"

"Wherever he is, he's not driving one of our units," said Dwight Bryant. "Ours are all accounted for. Nobody's seen him since he drove off alone from Jerry's night before last."

He raised a nearly imperceptible eyebrow to Bo Poole, who nodded and fixed their visitor with a stern look. "Dwight'll tell you what we've got, but it stays in this office for now," he warned as he stirred sugar into his mug and returned to the swivel chair behind the wide desk. "Agreed?"

"Your call," said Doug Woodall and leaned back against the doorjamb.

"Tracy Johnson was about six weeks pregnant," Dwight said tersely. "We're waiting on a DNA sample to see if Whitley's the father."

Woodall jerked upright. "The hell you say!"

"He was sucking down the beer at Jerry's pretty heavy, and when Deb'rah heard he'd gone missing, she remembered he seemed pretty cut up about Tracy. She thinks it's because they worked together on some recent cases and because Tracy had encouraged him to go for his associate degree."

"She know Whitley was balling her?"

"Not from me, she doesn't."

Bo Poole grinned and Woodall said, "Oh yeah, right. She told me about y'all's separation of powers."

"Anyhow, we don't know for a fact that he was. All we have are Tracy's cell phone records that show they talked to each other at least once a day and sometimes more. Best we can tell, the personal calls started last spring. End of May. That's when they spent a lot of time working together."

"End of May?" Woodall frowned and they could almost see the calendar pages turning in his head. "Oh yeah, that's when we went to trial on the Carson hit-and-run, right?"

"Right," said Dwight. "Whitley's testimony was key on that one, too. He was the arresting officer, the one who spotted the broken headlight before Carson could get off the interstate. When we first heard about Tracy Friday night, I did ask Deb'rah who she was with these days."

"I thought you said she doesn't know about Whitley."

"She doesn't. But Tracy dropped a hint that she *was* seeing somebody. Somebody she'd found — and I quote — right under her nose."

Woodall walked over to the coffee urn. "Maybe I'll take you up on that coffee now."

He inspected the inside of the extra mug on the bookcase, blew a speck of dust out of it and filled it with steaming hot coffee, then set it on the front corner of Bo's desk as he took one of the empty chairs.

"So you're thinking Whitley shot her Friday night?"

"Not necessarily. He was on duty then, though," Dwight said. "Supposedly working the south side of Makely, but there's nothing to show where he actually was."

"And his motive would be what? The baby?"

Dwight gave a palms-up gesture. "We're not that far along."

"What do the state guys say?"

"Well, now, Doug," said Bo, "we haven't exactly talked to them about this yet. Whitley's one of mine and I'm not gonna jump to any conclusions till I hear what he has to say."

Dwight nodded in agreement. "No point

limiting the investigation at this point. They've got better resources. Might as well see what they can turn up."

They discussed it a few minutes more, then Woodall sighed, drained his mug, and stood to go. "I just hope to hell Whitley turns up before Thursday."

As the door closed behind the DA, Dwight looked at his boss. "You didn't tell him about Whitley's e-mail."

"Did I tell him I might have a deputy who's gone somewhere to maybe kill himself? No." He set his mug on the shelf behind his desk. "Which is it, Dwight? A love affair gone sour or something to do with the job?"

Dwight shook his head. "Can't say, Bo. One thing we do know is that she was looking into the Martha Hurst conviction."

"Martha Hurst? Who the hell's that?"

"A Cotton Grove woman sitting on death row over in Raleigh. Due to take that gurney ride next month."

"Oh yeah. Beat the living hell out of her boyfriend with a baseball bat if I remember rightly?"

"Ex-boyfriend, current stepson," Dwight said. "And it was a softball bat."

"Baseball, softball, what's the connection with Tracy and Whitley? Neither one of them was around when that case went down."

"I don't know that there's a connection," Dwight admitted, "but just this past week, Tracy pulled the trial records and then she called over to Lee and Stephenson's and asked if she could go through Brix Junior's files. He was the one appointed to defend Hurst."

"Yeah, I remember now. It was a cake-walk."

"You work the investigation?" Dwight asked.

Bo Poole shook his head. "Just kept tabs on the reports. That was a hellacious summer. Four killings in a row. One right after another, and the worst was that little Langdon girl, remember? Oh, no, that's right. You weren't here then either."

"I heard about it though. A five-year-old? Went missing from her grandmother's backyard?"

"Yeah. Three weeks before we found her body. Tore everybody up something awful. We were stretched thinner than an ele-phant's rubber that summer." He sighed and leaned back in his leather chair. "You gonna look into this Hurst business?"

"I think we have to."

Faded blue eyes met dark brown ones in a long level gaze.

"This gonna come back and bite me in the ass, Dwight?"

"I hope not, Bo, but it's something we've got to do. If she's innocent —"

"My fault if that's how it turns out. I put Jones on it. I knew he was a screwup, but I couldn't spare anybody else right then. Thought it was so open and shut even he couldn't mess it up. 'Specially with the SBI looking over his shoulder. 'Course now, maybe they used a screwup on that case, too." He got up and poured himself another mug of black coffee, even though the ulcer that had started with his wife's losing fight with cancer already wrenched his belly. "Talk to them and keep me posted."

Out on the interstate, Deputy Silas Lee Jones pulled the earflaps of his wool cap down over his ears and watched sourly as Percy Denning, Mike Castleman, and Eddie Lloyd made like those forensic specialists on television. Cold enough to freeze the brass balls off a frigging monkey and they were pulling tape and punching numbers into a calculator and talking about trajectories when they didn't have a clue in hell where that slug had gone after it passed through Tracy Johnson's neck and shattered the window.

Yeah, they were starting from the new glass fragments they'd found by the edge of the outer northbound lane, fragments that came from the window of her car. Big damn deal.

But Major Bryant had ordered another sweep with the metal detectors, and another sweep he was going to get even if they all came down with flu for frigging Christmas. He stomped out his cigarette, pulled his gloves back on, and switched on the metal detector. Taking his own sweet time, he began to move it back and forth over the dry and brittle grass along the highway. The damn thing pinged every thirty seconds for stray bolts and screws, bits of chrome, bottle caps, a busted cell phone, even small rocks with traces of iron ore; and every ping meant he had to bend over and poke through the grass till he found the cause.

His ample paunch did not make for easy bending.

"Hey, Jones," Denning called from the west side of the northbound lanes. "We're gonna grid off a section up yonder."

"Up yonder" was on the southbound side of the four lanes, but several feet forward from where they had found the glass. They waited for traffic to clear, then darted across to a spot where they began to unwind yellow tape to grid off the area.

As the morning wore on, though, the only positive thing was the upward turn of the thermometer.

Back when Martha Hurst lived in Sandy Grove Mobile Estates, the trailer park was mostly white. These days it was thoroughly mixed — white, black, Latino, and even a few Asians for good measure, which meant that no one gave Kayra Stewart and Nolan Capps the racist attitude they might have received a few years earlier.

It was an older park, with towering pine trees and mature oaks that had dropped a thick layer of leaves and straw. Some of the dilapidated trailers had weathered to a dreary gray and several almost disappeared into the overgrown azalea bushes and head-high privet. The evergreen bushes gave the closely spaced dwellings an unexpected sense of privacy. Most of the small yards were unraked patches of wiregrass trampled bare by the eight or ten preschool children who seemed to romp unwatched by any adults. They darted in and out of the bushes like small winter finches and their knit hats and gloves were the only bright bits of color here, those and parts of broken plastic toys abandoned amid the leaves: a blue plastic trike with no wheels, a red sand pail, a turquoise-and-yellow Barbie dollhouse stained by rainwater that had dripped from the oaks.

Lot #81 was now occupied by a newish model. Strings of clear white lights turned the sheltering bushes into makeshift Christmas trees. A plastic snowman sat beside the steps and a wreath of artificial holly hung on the door. The shy young woman who answered their knock looked so pregnant that Nolan almost expected to see a donkey tied up by the deck, waiting to take her to a stable in Bethlehem.

Kayra launched into their spiel, but slowed as she realized the woman was shaking her head. "You don't speak English?"

"No hablo," she agreed with a regretful smile.

"Don't look at me," said Nolan. "I took French."

No one was home at 83 or 85, but at 82 they got lucky. "Naw, I've only been here four years," said the black man who opened the door. "Who you wanna try is Miz Apple, lives down there on the bend.

She's been here forever."

"Well, not forever, but surely the longest," said the elderly white woman when they repeated 82's recommendation. "But y'all come on in. It's too cold to stand here with the door open."

Inside was so warm that the kids immediately unwrapped their scarves, loosened their jackets, and stuffed their gloves in their pockets. The trailer was a single-wide and the tiny living room was crowded with a loveseat covered in colorful crocheted afghans, a red plush recliner, and a fifteen-inch portable television. A small artificial tree blinked cheerfully from atop the television and dozens of Christmas cards were clipped to tinsel garlands that hung across the window tops like multicolored valences.

Mrs. Apple gestured for them to take the loveseat, and as she sat down in the recliner, she adjusted the window curtain beside her chair so that she could keep an eye on the road, then picked up a crochet hook and resumed work on a pale pink crib blanket that was as soft and fluffy as her white hair. "For a neighbor's granddaughter," she murmured and looked at them expectantly.

"We were hoping you could tell us about

236

Martha Hurst," said Kayra.

"I was wondering what ya'll were wanting when I seen you going door to door like that. Martha Hurst! Now there's a name out of the past, idn it? Poor Martha. Did they kill her yet?"

"She's due to die next month. Did you know her?"

"Oh child, I know everybody," she said with a complacent glance at the many greeting cards that mutely testified to her gregariousness. "And I knowed that sorry Roy, too. No loss to the world that 'un was. Would you believe that he took a kittycat used to sit on my little porch here and throwed it through Martha's window one time?"

"Was it hurt?" asked Kayra in concern.

"Oh, it won't a real cat. Cement. Like a doorstop. But he sure did bust its head off."

As if summoned by memory, a gray cat strolled out of the kitchen, sniffed them both, and jumped up into Nolan's lap.

"Now that's not something he does with everybody comes in," said Mrs. Apple. "You must have cats yourself."

"No, ma'am," he said, "but I do like them."

"They always know." Her crochet hook

flashed in and out as the pink blanket grew beneath her fingers. "Now what was it y'all were wanting to hear about Martha?"

"The day Roy Hurst was killed," said Kayra. "Were you here then?"

Mrs. Apple beamed in anticipation of fresh ears for an old tale. "Oh yes. I'd just retired from my job with the county so I was still having fun doing nothing. I cooked for forty years out at the hospital where Martha used to work. Fact is, I put in a word for her when they won't gonna hire her on account of some trouble she got in back when she was younger. She was an aide and I was a cook. We used to ride in to work together sometimes. Anyhow, it was a real hot day and my air conditioner was broke so the windows was open and I heard some of the yelling. Iris — Iris Ford — she was the one lived next door to them. She was out watering her flowers and she said he was hot as fire 'cause Martha was telling him to get the rest of his mess out of their trailer 'cause she was gonna change the doorlocks soon as she got back from the beach. See, he used to live there with his daddy and she was one of the women he used to bring home with him, only after she met Gene, she didn't want to have nothing more to do with Roy.

He stayed on awhile after they was married, but they didn't get along. I don't know if he was jealous 'cause his daddy got her or if he just didn't want to have to pay rent on a place of his own. They had a knock-down-drag-out and he come screeching out in that raggedy ol' black car of his like a bat out of you-know-where. Almost hit some little girls playing jumprope right out here in front of my house. And that was the last time any of us ever seen him alive. About a hour later, she went off with her ballbats."

"Did he come back while Martha was at her ball game?"

"Not that anybody here seen. 'Course, Iris and me, we went for groceries about then, so I reckon he could've come and gone again."

"What about after?"

"I just told you, honey. Didn't nobody see him after he went tearing off like that on Saturday morning."

"But he was killed in the trailer."

"That's right, and me and Iris, we couldn't figure out when he got there less'n he sneaked in before she got home. See, after a game, she'd come home just long enough to tote her stuff in the house and get a shower and then go out drinking with her friends."

The old woman shook her head. "I went to bed at ten that night and I didn't see her come home, but Iris said it musta been around midnight. Not that she got up to look. She knowed the sound of Martha's car, though. If he was there and if they was fighting, they did it real quiet. Iris never heard a thing. 'Course now, she wouldn't, would she? She always took her hearing aid off when she went to bed. I remember one time —"

The trailer was so hot and airless that Nolan slipped off his jacket and wished he could crack open a window. He glanced at Kayra, who sat there with a frozen smile of politeness on her face while the torrent of words gushed over them.

"— so I said, if you'd've put on your hearing aid soon as you seen it, you'd've —"

"And nobody heard them fight that night?" he interrupted.

"Not a peep. Next morning, Martha was up early. Loaded up her car with stuff and took off. To the beach is what we heard, though how she could just walk away and leave him laying there's something I never could understand."

"When did you realize that Roy Hurst

was still in the trailer?"

"Didn't know for sure till the deputies come on Friday."

"But you thought — ?" Kayra prodded.

"Well, yeah, long about Wednesday, Iris noticed that his car was parked round back of the trailer where he used to park when he was living there. Them bushes used to be a little thinner back then. Now you could hide a herd of elephants behind Maria's place."

"The sheriff's department got an anonymous call that there was a dead man in the trailer. Who do you suppose made that call?"

"I don't know nothing about that," she said and her crochet hook flashed even faster, in and out of the intricate loops of pink yarn. The tree lights blinked on and off and the cat rearranged itself in Nolan's lap.

"I know I'd have been curious," Kayra said coaxingly.

The hooked needle slowed, then Mrs. Apple shrugged her stooped shoulders. "Reckon it won't do no harm to say now. It was Iris called 'em. The place'd been so still and quiet, which it wouldn't've been if he was crashing there. He'd've been in and out all hours, revving up that car motor,

241

but the car didn't move. Another thing — it was hot, hot, hot, and the windows was all closed up and her air conditioner won't running. Anyhow, Iris, she got me to go over with her and knock on the back door. And then we looked in the window and we could see him a-laying there."

By noontime, Deputy Jack Jamison felt as if he'd spent the day chasing his own tail around in circles.

First, he got a warrant from one of the magistrates, then he and Raeford McLamb drove out to Whitley's trailer to find some DNA samples. The patrol officer watching the place said there'd been no sign of the missing deputy. Inside, after bagging up Whitley's toothbrush, razor, and a comb with some hair still caught in the teeth, they did a quick-and-dirty. Tucked down in a drawerful of socks was an unmarked jeweler's box that held a gold-and-turquoise cuff bracelet that looked like the one in the sketch Mayleen Richards had shown them. They took it back to the courthouse with them and logged it in with the property clerk.

After that, while McLamb took the personal items over to the lab, Jamison went out to speak to Tracy Johnson's cleaning woman, a middle-aged white woman who'd been laid off from her clerical job when her company outsourced its routine data processing to New Delhi.

"Cleaning houses is harder, but it beats working at one of them big discount stores," she told Jamison. "I'm my own boss. Set my own hours. This way, I can at least help feed my kids and buy medical insurance. It's a high deductible but if anything really bad happens to me or my husband, we're covered. Besides, lessen you're management, them places won't give you any benefits either."

She told Jamison that Tracy was easy to work for. "I came in four hours a week. Dusted. Vacuumed. Mopped the floors. Changed the bed, cleaned the bathroom, did the laundry. Just her and the baby and she kept the place tidy. Some people, you wouldn't believe what pigs."

Her main complaint seemed to be that Tracy was too by-the-letter. "She could be a little tight-assed, if you'll pardon my French. Everybody else pays me off the books, in cash. She paid by check and she took out every penny of taxes and Social Security, too. Cost us both, but she said she was an officer of the court and she couldn't look the other way on it. Even preached me a little sermon about the obligations of citizenship and how taxes are like greens fees, only we get to play democracy instead of a round of golf. Like I've ever been on a golf course. Or had much democracy either for that matter."

She gave a sad smile. "And then she turned around and gave me a nice check for my birthday. For more than she'd withheld."

"What about men?" Jamison asked.

The woman shrugged. "Yeah, but don't ask me who. I never saw him. Just signs that somebody did stay over once in a while. He was always gone when I got there. Her, too, for that matter. Sometimes she'd get home before I left, but most times, I'd go a month or more without laying eyes on her or the baby either."

"What do you mean by signs?"

"Extra towels in the laundry. Whiskers in the sink where he'd shaved and then didn't wipe out the bowl. Beer cans in the garbage, and she drank wine. Condom wrappers in the bathroom wastebasket. Extra glasses in the dishwasher. Two coffee mugs left in the sink. The sheets. If you look, you can tell."

"Would you say he was here this week?"

She considered. "Maybe not Friday

morning. It was just the one cup and the bathroom sink was clean. And there weren't as many extra towels as there have been, but I did see a couple of beer cans and a condom wrapper, so yeah, I'd say he stayed overnight at least once."

"Thanks," said Jamison, closing his notebook as he stood to go. "You've been very helpful."

"Can't help myself from noticing things." Her face brightened. "Hey, maybe I ought to put in an application at the sheriff's department. I could be a detective, too. How good are the benefits?"

Jamison laughed. "Benefits are fine if you don't mind the shift changes."

He glanced at his watch as he left. He hadn't eaten lunch yet and his interview with the prisoner who'd sent Tracy a death threat wasn't for another hour. Plenty of time to swing by the house and grab a sandwich and maybe play with Jack Junior for a few minutes.

The receptionist at the pediatrician's office in Raleigh was properly solemn about the death of their small patient and the patient's mother, but she wanted to make it clear to Deputy Richards that Dr. Trogden was conferring an enormous favor by shortening his lunch hour in order to talk to her. "I hope you won't keep him longer than is strictly necessary."

"I'll try," Richards promised.

"Terrible thing," said the young doctor as he came around the desk to shake her hand. "Just terrible. But I don't see how I can help you. Mei was a normally healthy little girl. I saw her for her one-year checkup and everything was fine then. I was to have seen her for an ear infection late Friday afternoon, but as you know . . ."

"Yes," said Richards. "We were wondering if Ms. Johnson gave any indication when she called that she was worried about anything else."

"No, but ask my nurse. She took that call and then called back later after she checked my schedule and saw that we could squeeze Mei in."

"Sorry," said the nurse, reading from her notes in little Mei's file folder. "It really was a routine call. Ms. Johnson was upset that Mei was in pain, but that's normal for conscientious mothers. They'd rather hurt themselves than see their kids hurting. She said she had to be in court until around four, so I suggested a mild pain reliever and told her to bring the child in as soon before five as she could. There was absolutely nothing out of the ordinary about that call."

Struck by a sudden thought, Richards said, "Could you tell me who recommended Dr. Trogden to Ms. Johnson?"

The forms had two holes punched in the top margin and were held to the file by metal prongs that folded over each other. The nurse flipped to the bottom form that Tracy Johnson had filled out on Mei's first office visit. "Here it is. Dr. Grace Mac-Adams recommended us."

"MacAdams? She's ob-gyn, isn't she?"

"That's right. Her office is two blocks further down Blue Ridge Road."

"Sure," Terry Wilson had said when Dwight called him around noon. "Come on over now and I'll order another barbecue plate. You want potatoes or hushpuppies?"

"Neither. Just double slaw or string beans," Dwight told him.

"Deborah got you on a diet already?"

Dwight laughed and said he'd be there in twenty minutes. When he walked into the SBI facility on Old Garner Road, Terry met him at the entrance and whisked him past security down to his office, where two foam clamshells were giving off the appetizing smell of hickory-smoked barbecue and fried cornbread.

"I told you no hushpuppies," Dwight said.

"Think I don't remember the last time you said that? You wound up eating half of mine."

"Well, maybe just one," said Dwight, uncapping the plastic cup of dark and sweet iced tea.

As they opened their lunches, they were joined by an agent nearing retirement age.

"Hey there, Bryant," said Scott Underhill. He carried a bagel in one hand, a mug of coffee in the other, and a thick brown folder was tucked under one arm. "Terry tells me you got some questions about the Martha Hurst investigation?"

"Thank you for seeing me, Dr. Mac-Adams," Mayleen Richards said.

Dr. Grace MacAdams was tall and gray-haired with a firm handclasp and a slightly confused expression on her thin face. "I'm afraid I'm not completely clear on whether or not doctor-patient confidentiality survives the murder of a patient. I'm told that lawyer-client confidentiality can be breached, but —"

248

"Don't worry," said Richards. "I didn't bring a subpoena with me anyhow. This was spur of the moment. I was talking with the pediatric nurse where Ms. Johnson took Mei and she said you were the one that recommended him — Dr. Trogden."

"Oh yes." Dr. MacAdams wore no makeup, but her smile lit up her whole face. "His dad and I interned together. Lovely man. And so is his son."

"Anyhow," said Richards, "I was wondering if Ms. Johnson told you who the father of her baby was."

"The father? I don't understand. Mei was adopted from China. I don't think she knew who the parents were."

"No, I mean the baby she was carrying when she was shot."

Dr. MacAdams was clearly shocked. "She was pregnant?"

"The medical examiner puts it at about six weeks."

Sadness shadowed the doctor's eyes. "Did she know?"

"We aren't sure."

"I warned her that condoms weren't safe, but she was worried about the side effects of the pill." Dr. MacAdams opened the file on her desk. "She had an appointment to be fitted with a IUD last week, but she called and canceled it. And she was due for her yearly Pap smear in January. That's all I can tell you."

"Do you think she would have kept the baby? Carried it to term?"

"I really don't know, Deputy Richards, but she wasn't a schoolgirl, was she? If she was planning an abortion, I think she'd have kept last week's appointment, don't you?"

"Okay," said Denning as their shift ended. "Let's call it a day. We can finish it up here tomorrow morning."

"Maybe we ought to make just one more sweep around the outer perimeter?" Castleman suggested.

"Waste of frigging time," Jones grumbled.

"Not if everybody's careful," Castleman said pointedly.

"You saying I'm not checking every friggin' ping?" the older man snarled. Even though modern detectors are feather-weights compared to the originals, and even though he'd switched off with the others through the day, his shoulders still ached from carrying it so long.

"Look," said Denning, ever the peace-maker. "We're all bushed and getting sloppy. Two hours in the morning when we're fresh ought to do it."

"But another half-hour —"

"Give it a rest, Castleman," said Jones, perking up now that he was sure Denning was going to let them leave. "That damn slug's probably in the side of a car headed for Florida."

He spoke facetiously, but Denning glanced at Castleman in dawning surmise.

"Damned if that's not the smartest thing he's said all day," Denning muttered.

"No way," said Mike Castleman. "Somebody's car got hit, they'd be right on the phone to us. No, that slug's here. We've just got to find it."

Nevertheless, every local news channel carried the same story that evening: "And this update on that shooting death of a Colleton County DA last Friday: the sheriff's department has asked motorists to check their cars. If you or someone in your household drove south on the interstate between Dobbs and Makely around four o'clock last Friday, they're asking you to look and see if there is a bullet hole or a spot of freshly chipped paint on the driver's side of that car. If you find one, you should call the number you see at the bottom of your screen and report it."

Chapter 16

Amongst well-bred persons, every conversation is considered in a measure confidential. A lady or gentleman tacitly confides in you when he (or she) tells you an incident which may cause trouble if repeated, and you violate a confidence as much in such a repetition, as if you were bound over to secrecy.

Florence Hartley,
The Ladies' Book of Etiquette, 1873

Tuesday morning found me back in a courtroom in Dobbs for juvenile court, where I listened to a drugstore manager tell me how this was the second time this year that these two white teenage girls had shoplifted nail polish and lipsticks.

"The first time, they cried and said

they'd done it on a dare. I gave them a good talking-to and they swore they'd never do it again, so I didn't press charges. Now here they arc back and, Your Honor, you know they know better. They're in the school honor society. When I was in school, that meant something. We held ourselves to a higher standard."

The parents wanted to make restitution, but I wasn't having it. I fined the girls three times the value of what they stole and gave them suspended sentences on condition that they repay the store with money that came out of their own pockets, not their parents'. In addition, they were never again to enter that particular drugstore, and I gave them each twenty hours of community service. Finally, just so there was no misunderstanding on their part or their parents', I explained that "suspended" meant that failure to live up to any of the conditions I'd imposed could mean time in a juvenile facility.

After that, I dealt with two cases of truancy, three cases of vandalism, and a thirteen-year-old boy charged for the second time with being a Peeping Tom. The boy's father and I had known each other since grade school and my heart ached for him, but that didn't stop me from sending the kid for a mental evaluation before I passed final judgment.

By then it was heading for noon, so after signing all the necessary documents to set my rulings in motion, I recessed a little early for lunch. Portland Brewer had begun maternity leave this week, and to inaugurate her new leisure, she'd invited me over for soup and salad.

Not that I could see any sign of leisure when I got out of my car. A shiny white Chevy pickup sat in her driveway. It towed a familiar bright red trailer filled with ladders, paint buckets, and a tarp bin. Brack Johnson had been painting for my daddy for forty years and he painted my house when it was first built. He's choosy about who he paints for and he doesn't usually travel too far from Cotton Grove, but Portland's parents were old customers, too, so I guess he was willing to make an exception for her.

"What's up?" I asked when she opened the door.

"I'm having the nursery repainted. Peach. With lemon and orange trim."

"What was wrong with the — what was it? Key lime?"

"Lime was fine back in August, but it looks so cold now. And besides —" Her sudden smile was so bright it almost blinded me. "It's a girl!"

"A girl? That's wonderful!" I squeezed her hands. "But I thought you didn't want to know."

"I didn't, but you know how I was scheduled for a final sonogram yesterday? Well, the tech slipped and said 'she,' and then was so got away with herself that she couldn't pretend she hadn't said it."

"Does Avery know?"

"He was sitting right there. He never said anything before, but now he says he's sorta thought all along that it was a girl. He says he kept watching the screen the other two times and he didn't see any little peanut, so he was pretty sure."

I took off my coat and hung it over the bannister. "Are y'all pleased?"

"Thrilled. Want to know what we're naming her? Carolyn after my mother, Deborah after you."

As soon as she said Carolyn, I'd started to burble, but the Deborah so surprised me that for once I was speechless. I felt my eyes fill up with tears.

"Oh, Por," I whispered.

Her eyes were glistening, too. "Yeah, well don't get too sentimental about it, and you better hope she's more like my mother than you because we're going to expect lots of free babysitting out of you and Dwight."

"Anytime," I promised and cupped her swollen abdomen with my two hands. "Carolyn Deborah Brewer . . . Hey, did she just kick?"

"Knows her name already," Por laughed.

We went upstairs to see the fruit-colored nursery next to their bedroom. Brack had already capped the paint and was wrapping up his roller so it wouldn't dry out while he went to lunch. Although he'd been painting all morning, there wasn't a speck of peach-colored paint on the elderly painter's immaculate bib overalls.

"Looks good," I told him.

"Yeah, well, hit looked real good in that there green, too," he said, "but I reckon this color does look more like a little girl, don't you think? When I get this yellow and orange on the trimwork, hit'll really shine. Be so bright she won't have to cut on no lights till atter the sun goes down."

I love to listen to how country people of Brack's age talk. He sounds exactly like Daddy and Aunt Sister with their old-timey Colleton County accents and pronunciations that aren't going to last another generation.

We chatted a few minutes more. He asked about Daddy, I asked about his collards; then he left for lunch — "Reckon I'd better go git me some dinner 'fore they sell out of today's special" — and Por and I went down to her sunlit kitchen for canned lentil soup and salad-in-a-bag. Por's even less adept in a kitchen than me, but with us, talk has always come before food.

"What's this about a deputy gone missing?" she asked as she turned the burner on under the soup and pulled out bottles of dressing from the refrigerator.

"What've you heard?" I asked cautiously, trying to keep separate in my mind what was public knowledge and what Dwight might have confided. Not that he really had. Just mentioned that Don Whitley hadn't been seen since Sunday night.

"One of the troopers told Avery that there's an APB out on him. Is this anything to do with Tracy's death?"

"I don't know," I said slowly. "And Dwight didn't say when I asked him, but he was at Jerry's night before last at the dinner Bo's department gave for us and he seemed to be taking her shooting sort of personally."

I had said something along these same lines to Dwight yesterday when he told me about Whitley, but saying it again now to Por was like seeing an eye chart pop into focus the instant the optometrist slips the correct lens into the viewer. Once again I heard Tracy's words to me after court last week, but this time in the exact intonation she had used: *"I guess you've never worried about public opinion anyhow, have you?"*

Emphasis on the you.

As in, "you don't, but I do"?

"What?" asked Portland, who could always read me like a brief she'd just written. "You've thought of something. What?"

I told her of Tracy's last remarks. "What if she was talking about herself, not me? What if Don Whitley was the somebody right under her nose? He's sort of cute and nice and he's generated several drug cases for Doug's office this year, so they've been thrown together a lot, preparing for court."

"But didn't you say she made some snide remark about Dwight? About the disparity between an attorney with a law degree and a deputy with only a high school education?"

"That could've been about herself and Don Whitley, too."

I described Whitley's beery gloom at Jerry's, the last place he'd been seen. "He said that Tracy was the reason he was taking courses out at the community college. Maybe he was trying to improve himself for her."

Por snorted. "Like an associate degree in criminal justice would be enough for Tracy? I'm sorry she's dead and it's horrible that she was shot, but let's not forget that she could be a real snob at times."

"I know, but young as Whitley still is, he could go on for a regular BA. Hell, he could even go over to Eastern for a law degree. Hector Woodlief was almost fifty when he passed the bar."

"So if he was doing all that for her, would he've killed her?"

"Maybe she dumped him."

Unspoken came the thought that if he really was her lover and the father of her baby, maybe that's what they'd fought about. Maybe he wanted it and she didn't.

Or vice versa.

A lot of pregnant women have been killed by their husbands or mates these past few years.

I was dying to tell Por about Tracy's pregnancy so that we could thrash it out together. We've always bounced ideas and theories off each other, shared the good gossip, or asked for the other's take on something. It felt like a betrayal not to confide in her now the way I usually did, but a promise is a promise. To avoid temptation, I switched the subject to Cyl DeGraffenried and we spent the rest of our time together dishing about Cyl's sudden engagement, my wedding, and if Carolyn Deborah would arrive on her twenty-eighth due date in time to qualify as a tax deduction.

I left as Brack drove into Por's driveway and went straight back to the courthouse. If I couldn't talk to Portland, I could certainly talk to Dwight, right?

Wrong.

"Sorry, Judge, honey," said Bo Poole, who will never let me forget that someone once called me that my first year on the bench, "but he went to have lunch with Terry Wilson. Want to leave him a message?"

"That's okay. I'll see him tonight."

"Oh, yeah," he said with a knowing grin. "I bet you *will*."

Everybody's a comedian.

In a special hearing that afternoon, I was asked to terminate visitation rights for an allegedly abusive mother. What made it weird is that this wasn't an uneducated woman stressed out by a dead-end life with no options. This was the daughter of a fairly wealthy family with lots of resources. Indeed, it was the grandparents who were actually fighting the termination because the little three-year-old boy was their only grandbaby and they didn't want to be dependent on the goodwill of their former son-in-law for access to him. They had hired the best civil attorney in town, my cousin John Claude Lee, to defend against Millard King, attorney for the plaintiff.

Most times, small-town life can be as comforting as a woolly blanket on a cold winter night, the way it lets you snuggle down with people and places you've known forever.

It can also be as smothering as waking up with that blanket tangled around your restless body.

Whether personal or professional, I was beginning to feel as if every time I turned around these days, I was faced with a conflict of interest. It wasn't just the judgment I'd made this morning about a friend's son that troubled me. No, it was the way I had been less open with my oldest, dearest friend because of my promise to Dwight. It was having to deny my usual need to satisfy my admittedly nosy curiosity because of this new commitment to him. For the last two months, as old loyalties and old priorities shifted and realigned to accommodate the new, it felt to me like I was trying to cross the moving floor of a carnival funhouse.

And now here I was being asked once again to walk that tricky line between judicial objectivity and family ties.

I offered to recuse myself, but Millard King professed himself satisfied with my ability to judge fairly on the merits of the facts.

The father accused the mother of neglect and physical abuse and of putting the child in harm's way every time she was left alone with him.

While not specifically denying those allegations, John Claude argued that the grandparents would make sure their daughter was never alone with him and that any future visitations would take place in their home.

The father, an earnest young executive for Progress Energy, did not have his ex-in-laws' deep pockets, but he did have Dr. David Merten, a well-respected pediatric radiologist, whose show-and-tell consisted of a series of X-rays that documented at least three, and possibly five, separate fractures of the young child's bones. Dr. Merten had a well-timbred speaking voice and his vivid blue eyes flashed expressively as he laid out the dates for these X-rays and explained how unusual it was that an otherwise normal and healthy child should have so many greenstick fractures.

Pointing to faint shadows that may or may not have been earlier fractures and speaking in layman's terms, he said, "Children of this age heal so quickly that it's impossible to say for sure that some of these were indeed fractures, but here, here, and here, there can be no question that the bones were cracked. Fortunately, none of the boy's growth plates have yet been damaged, but should that occur, the bone might well stop growing so that the arm or leg would be shorter or would grow crookedly."

The X-rays of each undeniable fracture had been taken at the time the child suffered the "accidents," and those accidents corresponded to dates he had been in the custody of the sulky-looking woman who now sat beside John Claude at the defendant's table.

Despite my ties to John Claude, it was a no-brainer. The mother gave a "whatever" shrug when I ruled to terminate her visitation rights, but her parents, seated behind her, looked devastated.

I told the plaintiff, "I cannot order you to let your son's grandparents maintain contact with him, but I would strongly urge you to be compassionate to them. No child can have too many people loving him."

"Thank you, Your Honor," said John Claude, and I thought I heard a faint trace of genuine appreciation in his pro forma words. Not that he hadn't argued eloquently and diligently for his client. All the same, a little boy's well-being had been up for grabs here and John Claude Lee was a grandfather, too.

The rest of the afternoon session was filled by another truancy, a child who had taken his father's handgun to threaten another child who was bullying him, and a fourteen-year-old girl who wanted to go live with her father now that her mother had remarried.

Blessedly, I had no personal connection to a single one of the combatants.

Chapter 17

There is much that is exhilarating in the atmosphere of a ball room. The light, the music, and the company are all conducive to high spirits; be careful that this flow of spirits does not lead you into hoydenism.

Florence Hartley,
The Ladies' Book of Etiquette, 1873

On the way downstairs to meet Dwight shortly before five, I passed through the clerk of court's office to drop off some papers and found Kayra Stewart and Nolan Capps trying to persuade our clerk of court to let them borrow the file on Martha Hurst's trial.

Ellis Glover is tall and thin and completely bald except for a tonsure of straight white hair that circles a dome as shiny as any ivory billiard ball. Give him a monk's robe and he'd even look like one with his hooded eyes and ascetic straight lips. A kindly monk, but an implacable one who was unmoved by arguments to remove documents from his safekeeping.

"They're public records," Kayra said. "We have a right to see them."

"A right to see them," Ellis agreed. "Not a right to take them home with you."

"But you're getting ready to close."

"You can come back tomorrow," he told them firmly, reaching for the thick files they carried. "We open at eight o'clock."

As soon as they saw me, Nolan Capps put on that lost-puppy look he'd suckered me with last night. "Please, Judge Knott, couldn't you sign these files out?"

I shook my head. "No way do I want to be responsible for that much paper."

"Triage, then," said Kayra briskly. She shuffled through the folders as if picking out the kings and aces from a deck of playing cards. "We'll leave the trial transcript, the medical reports . . . take her deposition . . . take the witness statements . . . don't need the search warrants . . . initial statements of responding officers . . ."

Over Ellis's objections, she quickly win-

266

nowed the files down to a fraction of what they'd started with.

Ellis peered at me over his Ben Franklin half-glasses and his bald head gleamed in the ceiling lights. "Are you willing to be responsible for these?"

"It would appear so," I said and signed on his dotted line. "But they come home with me. And this time, you two can buy the pizza."

"Grandma and Miss Emily are making heavy hors d'oeuvres for tonight," Kayra said guilelessly.

"That'll take care of me, but what about you two and Dwight?"

"They told Nolan and me we could fix us a plate. We'll fix him one, too. Unless you think he'd rather have pizza than Grandma's sausage-and-rice balls or Miss Emily's angel salad?"

"Nobody likes a smartass," I told her. "See you out at my place."

Dwight was waiting for me down in his office since I'd driven in with him that morning. His shift was technically over at four and my workday didn't begin till nine, so each of us was inconvenienced by an hour, but somehow neither of us seemed to care.

"I forget," he said as we walked out to

his truck. "Your place or mine?"

"Mine," I answered.

The late afternoon air was milder than it'd been this morning, and predictions were that the warming trend would continue for the next few days. Jacket weather instead of heavy parkas and thick woolen scarves. As we circled the courthouse, the streetlights came on, along with the Christmas lights festooned down the length of Main Street's business district.

Dwight wasn't thrilled when I told him he was in for another session with Nolan and Kayra, but the promise of Bessie's sausage-and-rice balls mollified him a little. Even though he denigrates his mother's party salad as girly froufrou, I notice he always takes a second helping. We swung past his apartment so he could pick up fresh clothes, and I helped carry some more cartons down to the truck. We were hoping to repaint my old bedroom by the weekend, then move Dwight's bed in for Cal. When consulted the last time he was down, Cal had asked for "midnight blue," which was, according to him, a cool color.

On the drive out to the farm, I described my lunch with Portland and how the baby was a little girl who was going to carry my name.

"What about Tracy's baby?" I asked. "Was it Don Whitley's?"

"We still don't know. We sent his toothbrush and razor to the ME, but we don't have an answer yet." He glanced over at me. "Did you tell Portland Tracy was pregnant?"

"No."

"No?" I couldn't fault him for being skeptical. He knows how we confide in each other and he still turns slightly red every time he realizes she's heard how good he is in bed. "You tell her everything."

"Not when you specifically ask me not to. Besides, you threatened to put me on report."

He smiled and said, "So how come you're sitting way over there?"

I immediately slid over to his side of the truck and tucked myself under his arm.

"You really didn't tell her?"

"I really didn't. I wanted to, but didn't."

He slid his hand inside my sweater and I laid my head on his shoulder.

"Did Whitley shoot her, Dwight? Because of the baby?"

"I don't know, shug. We don't even know he's the father. Or that he and Tracy were hooked up."

"Portland doesn't think they were. She thinks Tracy was too much of a snob to go out with a sheriff's deputy."

The instant I said it, I wished I could take it back. Dwight and I had never discussed this aspect of our relationship.

"Officers don't fraternize with enlisted?"

"I guess."

"She think you were slumming?"

I pulled back indignantly, but his arm still curved around me.

"Oh, c'mon, Deb'rah. You know it's crossed a lot of minds. A college-educated judge marrying a dumb ex-Army cop?"

I heard the confident chuckle in his voice and relaxed against him again. "So you finally admit that I'm smarter than you?" I teased.

"Nope, just got more book learning. Take Andrew and April. She's a teacher, he dropped out of high school at sixteen, and look how good their marriage is. Look at my dad and mom. Hell, your own dad and mom."

"Mother didn't go to college."

"No, but she came from a solid middle-class family full of relatives who did, yet turned around and married a man who quit school in the sixth grade. If our mothers had been hung up on college degrees, you and I wouldn't be here."

Straight ahead of us, through the windshield, the new moon gleamed in the western sky like a shallow silver bowl. Dwight and I would be married before the bowl was full again.

The Christmas moon.

A honey-sweet moon, even if we weren't taking a proper wedding trip.

"Poor Tracy," I said. "And poor Don Whitley, too, if he loved her."

"If," Dwight said.

He and Portland could have their doubts. I kept remembering Sunday night and Whitley's sad eyes.

"I know you always say he's a good officer — all the arrests he's made, all the drug money he's confiscated — but he really doesn't seem like a cold-blooded killer."

"Not every killer's cold-blooded," he reminded me. "He may not look the type, but he sure was out working alone Friday night. No alibi. And taking off like this doesn't look good. We've searched his trailer. Doesn't look like he packed a bag or anything. Plus he hasn't used a credit card since Sunday morning. We've got a bad feeling about this."

"You think he's gone somewhere to kill himself?"

Dwight took a long deep breath. "He wouldn't be the first lawman to shoot his woman and then turn the gun on himself."

I put my hand on his leg and patted it consolingly. "If he killed Tracy and Mei, then maybe that's the best way out of this mess. Save the state a trial."

Kayra Stewart and Nolan Capps arrived as I finished freshening up for the shower. They were immediately followed by Dwight's younger brother, Rob.

Even looking closely, it would be hard for a stranger to tell that Rob and Dwight were related. He's a couple of inches shorter, thin and wiry, with their mother's bright red hair, grass green eyes, and pointed, almost foxlike features, while Dwight has their father's solid muscular build, thick brown hair, open face, and brown eyes.

Rob set a shopping bag filled with Tupperware boxes on the table. "Kate and Mother kicked me out, but Kayra and I managed to snitch this much food on our way out the back door."

"He lies," said Kayra. "Grandma and Miss Emily fixed this for us."

Dwight grinned. "All lawyers are liars, honey. Look at his nose. Yours'll start growing, too, the minute you pass the bar exam."

"We thought he could help us go through the files," said Nolan.

"I tried to tell them I know damn all about criminal law," Rob said. His was a wills and trusts practice in Raleigh's Cameron Village. "I haven't seen the inside of a courtroom in four or five years."

As they peeled off their jackets and sweaters, Kayra and Nolan reported on their day's activities and what they'd learned from a former neighbor of Martha Hurst's, a Mrs. Apple.

"You remember that anonymous phone call?"

"What about it?" asked Dwight.

"It came from her friend who lived next door. She noticed the guy's car parked behind the trailer after Martha left for the beach, but hot as it was, the air-conditioning stayed off and he wasn't in and out like usual."

Rob was barely listening. He lifted the lid on one of the plastic boxes and with his fingers fished out one of Bessie's famous sausage-and-rice balls. Dwight and Nolan were right behind him, ready to follow his lead.

"Could y'all please wait for plates and

273

forks?" asked Kayra, who had known Dwight and Rob for most of her young life. She rolled her eyes at me. "Men! Where are your plates?"

I pointed to the cupboard behind her.

"Omigod!" she said when she opened the doors and saw my mother's collection of Royal Doulton in all its service-for-twenty glory, from serving bowls and meat platters down to the bread-and-butter plates and nineteen delicate cups hanging from their little individual hooks. "Don't you have any everyday china? Or even paper plates?"

"Sorry."

Dwight paused with a pecan puff in his hand. "Want to let's bring my kitchen stuff over tomorrow?"

"Fine," I said. "There're still empty shelves in the kitchen."

"I wasn't paying attention last night." Kayra turned a saucer in her slender brown hands and read the maker's marks. "Is this what we ate pizza off of?"

I nodded.

"And you let us put these in your dishwasher?" She was clearly horrified.

"That's what a dishwasher's for."

"But they're Royal Doulton."

"They're dishes." I pulled four plates

from the shelves and handed them to her. "Dishes are meant to be used."

"But what if we break them?"

I laughed. "You sound like one of my sisters-in-law. My mother used this for every holiday in a household filled with roughneck boys and the only time anything got broke was when a preacher's wife knocked over a teacup. If it'll make you feel better, I do have regular mugs and glasses in that cupboard by the sink. Feel free to smash as many as you like."

I tucked the boxed cake topper in the shopping bag Rob had dropped on a chair and left them dividing the party food Bessie and Miss Emily had probably spent the day preparing.

Rob's wife, Kate, was a freelance fabric designer, who had inherited the old Honeycutt farm from her first husband. Although a New Yorker by birth, she had chosen to have Jake's posthumous baby here and then to stay on in the country to raise him. The Internet made it easy for her to work out of the farm's original packhouse, which she had remodeled for a studio. After she and Rob fell in love and married, they restored the old farmhouse far beyond its original state of utilitarian comfort. In addition to Jake's uncle, they had also taken in Mary Pat Carmichael, a young cousin of Kate's, who has grown into a protective older sister for little Jake Junior.

The Honeycutt farmhouse is only a few hundred feet down the road from the Bryant farm and actually touches at one corner, so I didn't have far to drive. When I got there, the circular drive in front of the house was lined with cars and trucks, but they had left me a space right in front of the door. The evening was now so mild that some of the guests lingered on the porch to greet one another before going inside.

Dwight's sisters stood in the doorway to welcome us and they made a big fuss over me as I came up the steps. Except for similar family mannerisms, Beth and Nancy Faye look no more alike than Dwight and Rob.

Beth took my shopping bag and promised to see that Kate got it. Then I was swept up into hugs by half a dozen of my female relatives who pulled me inside with boisterous cries of "She's here!"

The house could have served as an illustration of Christmas Past. Jugs of red-berried holly and nandina filled empty corners, while thick ropes of pine and cedar twined up the stair rails and filled the rooms with a woodsy aroma. Candlelight gleamed off the polished wood of antique tables and chests, and fires blazed in the hearths of the twin front parlors. A huge tree brushed the ceiling in one parlor and was decorated in dozens of old-fashioned glass ornaments and red velvet bows.

In the other parlor, some of my teenage nieces and a couple of my sisters-in-law had brought their instruments and were playing Christmas carols. As soon as Herman and Nadine's daughter Annie Sue spotted me, she snapped her fingers and they immediately swung into a chorus of "Here Comes the Bride."

Amid laughter and teasing, I was passed from hand to hand. Several of my in-state sisters-in-law and aunts were there, along with their daughters. Beth and Nancy Faye had teenage daughters, too. Aunt Zell had driven over from Dobbs with Nadine and Annie Sue, and Will's wife, Amy. Counting Miss Emily and Bessie, there were over thirty women flowing through the rooms. Someone handed me a cup of cherry-flavored punch laced with vodka.

And then another.

Just as I was beginning to feel like a cork

bobbing on the water at the end of a fishing line, Miss Emily and a heavily pregnant Kate led me to a couch seat near the Christmas tree. Paper and pencils were distributed for shower games that got funnier (and raunchier) with each cup of punch.

Eventually, it was time to open the many gifts. Minnie sat beside me with a legal pad to record who gave what — everything from one of Aunt Sister's patchwork quilts to everyday china for twelve from Kate, Miss Emily, Beth, and Nancy Faye.

Before refreshments were served, Kate called across the room, "Okay, Minnie. Tell us what Deborah's going to say to Dwight on their wedding night."

Minnie looked down at her legal pad and began to read off some of the remarks I'd made while opening the presents — "Look how big!" "Feel how soft!" — and so on amid raucous laughter.

Still joking, we moved into the dining room to fill our plates and refill our cups. Talk became more general as the party wound down. My nieces packed up the gifts and carried them out to April's car. She and Ruth had offered to drop them off on their way home through the back lanes.

Kate went up to make sure Jake and

Mary Pat were properly tucked in, and when Bessie and Miss Emily declared themselves ready for bed, too, I thanked them again for their part in the party.

"Well, now, I thank you for helping Kayra and her young man," said Bessie. "I know you don't really have time, but they sure do appreciate it."

"What are you helping them with?" Amy asked idly when I sat back down to wait for Kate to return.

"They've got their own private Actual Innocence project going," I explained. "They're trying to get a stay of execution for a woman who's due to die next month. Martha Hurst."

"Martha Hurst? Oh my Lord! I'd almost forgotten about her. Poor Martha."

I was surprised. "You know her?"

"She was an aide at the hospital when she killed that guy."

Amy has spent her whole working life in the hospital's human resources department. I should have remembered.

"What was she like?"

"Hard worker. Very nice. She did have a temper, but it blew over as quickly as it flared up. Underneath, she was a good-hearted woman and very detail-oriented. Nothing got by her. The patients loved her, and she never lost it with them."

"Were you surprised when you heard she'd killed her stepson?"

"Not really. Like I said, she really could fly off the handle, and he was such a bastard. Somebody needed to give him a taste of his own medicine and she was the one who could do it."

"What do you mean?"

"The way he beat up on his girlfriends. He broke Janella Hobson's nose and knocked out two of Deenie Gates's teeth and —"

"Deenie Gates?" In my mind's eye, I saw that scrap of paper in Brix Junior's hand-writing and again felt that sense of near familiarity. "Why do I know that name?"

Amy frowned. "Well, she did take the guy she was living with to court back in the summer. Would that have been you?"

"Domestic violence?" It was coming back to me. A skinny, defeated-looking white woman and a brawny Mexican without a green card. "He punched her in the ear? Burst her eardrum?"

Amy nodded. "That would be Deenie. She's bad for hooking up with guys who like to beat up on her."

"She works at the hospital, too?"

"Yep. Dropped out of school at sixteen

to come empty bedpans and scrub floors. She's a little slow. Not retarded exactly, just not the brightest bulb on the Christmas tree. Excellent, excellent worker. I wish we had a half-dozen more like her. Anyhow, Martha Hurst sort of took her under her wing. Unfortunately, she's the one who introduced Deenie to the Hurst guy. What was his name?"

"Roy," I said. "Roy Hurst."

"That's right. They broke up around the time Martha killed him. But not before he got her pregnant."

"What?"

"Oh yeah. She had an abortion, though. Said she wasn't ready to be a mother. Still isn't, if you ask me."

I would have pursued it, but Kate came down then and Aunt Zell and Nadine told Amy they were ready to go. We thanked Kate for a lovely evening.

"Tell Rob it's safe to come home," she called as I headed for my car.

Back at the house, Rob's car was still there and so was Nolan's, but the truck was gone.

"Where's Dwight?" I asked.

"He had to leave. Said to tell you not to wait up," said Rob. "Something about a missing deputy?"

Chapter 18

A lie is not locked up in a phrase, but must exist, if at all, in the mind of the speaker.

Florence Hartley,
The Ladies' Book of Etiquette, 1873

Tuesday night, December 14

"Damn, damn, damn!" said Bo Poole as he stared through the open door of the car.

"Yeah," Dwight agreed.

The night air was so mild that their words made no puffs of steam when they spoke.

The car, flooded with portable lights, brightened even more each time Percy Denning's camera flashed.

Inside the car, in the driver's seat, Don

Whitley lay with his head lolled back on the headrest. Except for the blood that had dried on his chin, his face didn't look that bad, but blood and brains and fragments of his skull spattered the car's headliner where the bullet had exited.

The gun itself had fallen between his legs. It was a .44 revolver that looked suspiciously like one of the old standard-issues before the department switched over to the newer automatics.

An open, half-empty fifth of bourbon had been carefully set in the well of the console between the two bucket seats. The cap lay on the dash. They watched as Denning's assistant slipped on a pair of latex gloves, then screwed the cap back on the bottle and bagged it.

"Came out here, drank himself stupid, then did it," Bo said.

"Out here" was a thick stand of trees and bushes along Ryder Creek, south of Dobbs. The rough trail that led in from the highway was used in summer by fishermen after sun perch and catfish, in the winter by occasional hunters. The four teenage boys and their coon dogs who had found Whitley were still over there by the creekbank. Their initial fear and excitement had begun to wear off now, and when one of the deputies came to ask if they could leave, Dwight nodded, having heard their story himself.

Denning finished bagging Whitley's hands and told the morgue attendant that they could take him.

Rigor had long since passed off, of course, so getting him onto a gurney and into the transport was no problem.

What was a problem was all the disturbance around the scene, and Dwight had already chewed chunks from the hides of the responding officers, who had thoughtlessly driven their units down the creek trail and right up to the car instead of walking in.

"Yeah, it looks like he shot himself," he told them, "but you didn't know that. What if this was a homicide? You'd've destroyed any tire tracks that might identify a perp. You walked all around the damn car so there's no way now to tell if a second person was here. First thing tomorrow, you get your dumb asses out to the community college and sign up for their elementary procedures class."

One of the officers made the mistake of saying he'd already taken that class.

"Then take it again," Dwight snarled. "And this time, it's on your own clock since you didn't learn squat the first time around."

He walked over to Mike Castleman, who had heard it on his radio. For more than four years, he and Whitley had worked drug interdiction together like a matched pair of hunting dogs, and now the deputy paced blindly around the clearing, oblivious to low-hanging branches that still had dried leaves clinging to the twigs.

"Why'd he do it, Major? Did he shoot Johnson? Is that why?"

"What do you know about him and Johnson?" Dwight asked.

"Nothing." With his back to the glare of the lights, Castleman's deep-set eyes were unreadable.

"Ditch the games, Mike. You were closest to him. Now he's dead, and I want the truth."

The deputy sighed and brushed dried leaves out of his curly black hair. "Ever since back in the spring, I had a feeling he was seeing somebody, but he would never say. Always claimed he was hitting the books when I tried to set him up with somebody. Then I happened to pass her place late one night about two weeks ago. His car was parked out front and there were no lights on inside. I wrote up a phony ticket and stuck it under his wiper. He was sore as hell with me next day. Made me promise not to say anything. And he wouldn't talk about her. Said she had some issues to work out."

"Issues?"

Castleman shrugged. "I don't know, Major, and that's the truth, but he was acting weird all last week. If I didn't know for a fact that he'd never touch the stuff, I'd've said he was dipping into some of the pharmaceuticals we confiscated."

"Weird how?"

"One minute he'd be fine-tuning ways to target drug runners, next minute he was talking about leaving the department, going back to school full-time. 'And live on what?' I asked him. He said money wasn't a problem, and hell, Major, you know what we make, so I figured she was going to support him. I said maybe you and he could have a double wedding, just joking, not meaning any disrespect, but he said they weren't to that stage yet. That she wouldn't even let him give her a bracelet, much less a ring. Then Thursday and Friday, he wouldn't talk to me. Acted like everybody pissed him off. And you saw how he was Sunday night. Sat off by himself. Hardly talked to anybody. I figured he was grieving, what with her getting killed like that and nobody knowing they'd been together. I told him I was there for him if he wanted to talk, but he told me to fuck off."

It was as if, having kept quiet for so long, Castleman had to let it all out. Dwight put his hand on the other man's shoulder.

"Damn it, Major! Why didn't he trust me? Talk to me? We were supposed to be friends."

He sounded so genuinely bewildered that Dwight could only give his shoulder another squeeze.

"We'll probably never know. That wasn't much of a suicide note he sent you and there was nothing more at his place or in the car."

Now that Whitley's body was gone, Castleman walked back over to the car with him and they watched as Denning finished lifting prints off the steering wheel and door handles.

"Here's part of the seal from the bottle," said his assistant from the backseat. She held up a small scrap of brown plastic in a pair of tweezers and Denning added it to his collection. "And here's another frag."

"Wait a sec." Denning found the bag in which he was gathering fragments of the bullet and she dropped in the bit of lead she had found.

"Too bad we couldn't find the slug that killed Ms. Johnson," he said. "Maybe we'll get lucky tomorrow."

"Where'd he get the .44?" Dwight asked Castleman. "And why you reckon he used it instead of his own gun?"

Castleman shook his head.

Silas Lee Jones walked up to them in time to hear Dwight's question. "Wadn't his daddy on the force down at Havelock? Maybe it was hisn's."

"If he did use it to kill Johnson," the sheriff mused, "it couldn't be traced back to him. Then when he decided to do this" — he gestured to the bloody interior of the car — "maybe it was his way of admitting guilt for her death."

It was well after midnight before Dwight got back to the farm. Deborah was asleep, but she had left a light on and the door unlocked. As he slipped into bed beside her, she stirred and came awake.

"Rob said they found Don Whitley. Does that mean — ?"

"Yeah." He wrapped his arms around her warm softness. She wasn't wearing a gown. Quietly, he described what Whitley

288

had done to himself and she listened without interrupting. "He was one of my first hires."

"Oh, Dwight. I'm so sorry, darling."

Even with everything else, that gave him pause. "That's the first time you've called me that."

"Is it? Are you sure?"

"I'm sure."

She touched his face in a gentle caress, and for a little space of time, he let himself forget what he had seen that night.

Wednesday morning, December 15

Before the sun edged over the treetops, Dwight was already dressed, and he was on his second cup of coffee by the time Deborah stumbled out. No lipstick, tangled hair, barefooted, and wearing one of his sweatshirts. She looked beautiful to him.

"You're going in this early?" she asked.

"Over to Chapel Hill." He filled a second mug and handed it to her. "Whitley's autopsy."

"But why? I thought you said it was suicide."

"It probably is. But I still want to be there. He was one of mine so I want to do it by the book."

"Okay. But don't forget Miss Sallie Anderson's dinner for us tonight."

She saw the look on his face and immediately said, "It's all right. You can skip it. I'll call and tell her you have to work. It's for some of her and Aunt Zell's neighbors that have known me since I was a kid. I'll probably be the only one there under sixty-five."

"You sure?"

"Absolutely."

"Thanks. And let's plan on my place tonight, okay? I'd like to be close to the office the next couple of days."

"Fine." She gestured to the files that Nolan Capps and Kayra Stewart had left stacked at the end of the table. "What about those? Did the kids finish with them?"

Dwight shrugged. "Probably, but I left first, so I don't know. I think they were going to stay the night with Bessie again, so you could call over and ask." He holstered his gun, grabbed his jacket, and opened the door. "See you tonight."

"Well, at least it's warmer today," said Deputy Silas Lee Jones as they returned to the scene of Tracy Johnson's death and unloaded the metal detectors. Denning had borrowed extras from neighboring jurisdictions so that the four officers could cover more ground faster.

Using cans of fluorescent spray paint, Tub Greene and Mike Castleman gridded off a section of the road bank along the southern and western perimeters of the area they'd searched the day before. In summer, this raised bank would be bright with golden daylilies or red poppies. Here in December, all the roots were dormant.

Denning had left his assistant processing the prints they'd lifted from Whitley's car and he was anxious to get back to Dobbs to finish the report on their colleague's suicide. They didn't have conclusive DNA proof yet, but his blood type matched the fetus Tracy Johnson had been carrying and it was beginning to look more and more like he'd shot her. Would've been nice to have the slug to prove it conclusively, but, "We don't find anything by lunchtime, we might as well hang it up," he said.

At the office, Mayleen Richards found Jack Jamison doggedly plowing through the bank records they'd brought from Johnson's house.

She hung her jacket on the back of her chair. "Finding anything?"

291

"She had the premium cable package," he said enviously. "HBO and all the rest."

"I don't suppose she wrote any checks to Don?"

"Nope." He ran his finger down her check register again. "Wonder what would've happened if he hadn't shot her? Reckon she'd've kept the baby?"

"Probably. Her doctor seemed to think so." Richards dipped into the box and pulled out utility bills neatly clipped together. Water, electricity, heating oil. "I'd hate for anybody to have to go through my bills. I just throw everything into a drawer and sort it all at the end of the year. By the way, how'd it go out at the prison farm? That guy that made the death threat?"

"Like we thought. Swore he was just mouthing off in the heat of the moment. Seemed surprised we even remembered." He paused to reach over and clear his computer screen. "The phone company said they'd forward a list of all her cell phone calls for this past month. Oh good. Here it is."

He followed the links the phone company had sent and soon his screen was filled with the minutes the slain ADA had used, from the end of the last bill until about a half-hour before she was shot. He printed it out and began by calling the last number.

Beneath the open Christmas cards and other papers in the box, Richards found three long yellow legal pads held together by a thick rubber band. They hadn't paid much attention because they looked new and unused. Indeed, the top two were, but the third . . . ? The first five or six pages were covered in writing that she now recognized as Tracy Johnson's.

"Hey, here's some notes she made," Richards told Jamison. "Wonder if it's for that drug case the DA's worried about."

There were Latino names and dates from back in the summer. Then, two pages over, at the bottom of a fresh page, "12 pkts (1gm ea) + \$120K > 10 & \$80K. \$40K????" The four question marks had been gone over several times till they were thick and black. In block letters were "DANNO R. a.k.a. DANIEL RUIZ" and the words "time served?" Beneath, Johnson had scribbled, "Talk to Don."

"What do you think?" she asked Jamison as he paused between calls.

"He looked at it a long moment, then said, "Same thing you're thinking. That he was sticking money from the drug stops into his own pocket and one of the perps has asked for a deal to help prove it. You need to show this to the major. This could be Don's real motive."

"Well, hot damn!" Deputy Jones yelled above the roar of morning traffic. "Looky what I just found!"

"Hey, way to go!" said Castleman, who'd been working the next box over.

The others crowded around to see the slug Jones had picked up.

"I was just taking it slow and easy, like you said, checking every damn ping. Not that there's as many up here as down closer to the road, and there it was on my first sweep of this box. Looks like a .44 to me, don't y'all think?"

The bullet was surprisingly undamaged.

"But then it wouldn't be banged up much, would it?" mused Percy Denning as he slid the slug into one of his small collection bags, then labeled and dated it. "It only passed through soft tissue and her side window before ending up here in the clay. If I'm lucky, I might even find some of her DNA material. Good work, Jones."

Silas Lee Jones stripped off his latex gloves and lit himself a cigarette. "And y'all thought I wadn't being careful," he said. "Reckon that shows *y'all*."

★ ★ ★

"So what were you hoping for?" asked the medical examiner as her diener began to empty out Don Whitley's digestive tract. "Bruises? Traces of tape on his wrists where he'd been constrained? Cut knuckles to show he'd tried to fight off somebody?"

Dwight gave a tired shrug.

"We'll run the gut just to cover all the bases," she said, "but I'm afraid that what you see is what you get. It's suicide, Major. Sorry."

Chapter 19

Avoid, at all times, mentioning subjects or incidents that can in any way disgust your hearers.

Florence Hartley,
The Ladies' Book of Etiquette, 1873

Although it was only seven-thirty when Dwight left, I knew Miss Sallie Anderson would be up. Indeed, she answered on the first ring. She was sorry to hear that Dwight wouldn't be with me that evening, "but I do understand. You knew them, didn't you, honey? That poor woman that got shot and her little girl, too? And then I heard on television about people needing to check their cars for bullet holes. What in the world is Colleton County coming to, Deborah?"

"Feels like the world is coming to Colleton County, doesn't it?" I said.

"Oh, honey, you know it!"

When I called over to the Stewart house, Bessie told me that Kayra was still asleep, but Nolan was up. I reckon he was if he'd slept on Bessie and Willie's couch. Even though this is the winter lull for farm chores, I doubt if either of them do much tiptoeing around once the sun is up.

Yes, he said, they'd finished with those files and they planned to sit and read the transcripts in Ellis Glover's file room today. No, they hadn't found any loose strings to pull on and help unravel the case against Martha Hurst.

"If you're still in the courthouse around noon, I'll take you to lunch," I offered.

I'd already hung up before I remembered Deenie Gates. It probably wouldn't help their cause to track her down, but then again, she might remember others with a better reason to kill her ex-boyfriend.

I showered and dried my hair, all the time wondering why Brix Junior had scribbled her name when there was nothing in his notes about her.

Eight-fifteen. Surely he wouldn't be on the golf course this early?

"Was just leaving for breakfast at the clubhouse," he told me when he answered the phone. "Baked cheese grits and the best link sausage I've had since your mama died."

The healthy bowl of cereal I was holding turned to sawdust in my mouth as I remembered the sausage Mother and Maidie used to make after hog-killing every winter. They would grind together just the right balance of fat and lean, season it with fresh sage, flecks of red pepper, salt and black pepper, mix it by hand in a large dishpan, then stuff it into the well-cleaned intestines.

Daddy and the boys continue to raise hogs for our own tables, but now those hogs are slaughtered at a nearby abattoir, and come back from the butcher as neatly packaged hams and chops and roasts, ready for the freezer. Maidie still gets fifty pounds of ground pork that she seasons herself. She takes down the old cast-iron sausage stuffer and makes long ropes of link sausage with commercial casings.

It tastes better than anything I can buy and I'm always grateful that she shares, yet it lacks something. Mother's strong and capable hands maybe? She died the summer I was eighteen, but as my wedding day gets closer and closer, I keep thinking of her. She had talked about my eventual marriage someday, had even said, "I wonder if you've met him yet?"

I wish she could have known it was Dwight.

"You want to speak to Jane?" Brix Junior said, bringing me back to the moment.

"No, I just had a quick question about your Martha Hurst file."

I heard his impatient huff, but I pressed on and asked him about the scrap of paper with Deenie Gates's name on it.

"Sorry. I have no idea who she is."

"Amy says she was hooked up with Roy Hurst at the time. That she was pregnant by him."

"Oh, yes . . . I do sort of remember now. They had a fight, right? 'Cause he'd moved on to somebody else?"

"Knocked out a couple of teeth is what Amy said."

"These people," Brix said, distaste in every syllable. "Not much better than cats in heat. I cannot tell you how glad I am to be through with them. Best I recall, though, she did have an alibi for the killing. Can't think what it was right now, but I'm pretty sure it was good or I'd've had her on the stand to cast doubt on Martha Hurst being the only one with a quick temper."

I thought of the drab, defeated-looking woman in my courtroom back in the summer. No quick temper there and hard to imagine that there'd ever been a time she stood up for herself. The only reason she was in court was because the State of North Carolina no longer allows the complainant in a domestic brawl to "take up the charges." If the cops get called in to break it up, somebody's going to come to court and answer for the disturbance. If I was remembering the right person, Deenie Gates would have dropped the charges if she could've because she was sure the man hadn't meant to hurt her, and besides, he had promised her he wouldn't ever hit her again. I forget what I'd decided. I'm sure I gave him some sort of penalty, but whether jail time had been involved, I couldn't say.

I thanked Brix for his time and he said he'd see me Wednesday.

Wednesday.

One week.

I dumped my cereal in the compost bin and looked over my to-do list. Everything that could be done ahead of time was already done except for the cake topper, which was now in Kate's clever hands.

Not knowing how long we'd stay at Dwight's apartment, I packed a case of lingerie and cosmetics, put a couple of extra outfits in a garment bag, and carried everything out to the car, including the files Kayra and Nolan had borrowed from Ellis Glover. As I left, I turned down the thermostat. No point paying for heat when the house would be empty.

Kayra and Nolan eased in and sat down at the back of my courtroom as I finished ruling on the last case of the morning, a judgment in a case of non-support — and good luck to the poor mother in finding the father, who had left the state without giving anyone a forwarding address. Surprise, surprise.

I recessed and motioned them back to chambers while I washed my hands and exchanged my robe for a deep blue wool blazer that I'd bought because it brought out the blue of my eyes. Forget-me-Knott blue, my mother used to say, because all of Daddy's children and most of his grandchildren have his eyes. Mother's were blue, too, but with a slight tinge of hazel, while Daddy's are the clear bright blue of a late summer sky just after sunset.

I usually grab lunch at a soup and sandwich place across the street. Today was so beautiful, though, that we walked three blocks to a new café that had recently opened. Taos Tacos is the first upscale Tex-Mex restaurant in Dobbs, and to help keep it in business, I try to go there at least twice a week. Kayra said she'd split a burrito sampler plate with me, and Nolan opted for the chicken fajitas.

The kids were in a glum mood. Last night, Rob had helped them get through the files I'd brought back to Ellis this morning. Today, they had skimmed through the trial transcript itself without finding any reversible errors.

"It doesn't seem real that she could've left a dead man on the floor of her trailer and then waltzed off to the beach for a week," said Nolan.

"Just because it's not something you could do doesn't mean she couldn't," Kayra told him.

I was learning that Kayra was the more cynical of the two and that she was only going through the motions because Nolan was such a believer. Or was it that she cared for him more than she might like to admit?

"But what about those two witnesses that Mr. Stephenson called to the stand?" he argued. "They said that she seemed perfectly normal the whole time she was there and was really surprised when the police showed up at their door to tell her about Roy Hurst. Doesn't that tell you something?"

"Tells me some people are good liars?"

I took a sip of my iced tea — in the South, iced tea is like champagne: goes with any kind of food any time of the year — and told them about Deenie Gates. "My cousin thinks he remembers that she had a solid alibi for that time period, but maybe she could come up with other suspects. Too bad you can't find someone who actually saw him alive after Sunday morning."

"But that couldn't be, could it?" asked Nolan. "That's when he was dead."

"No," I corrected. "According to the medical examiner's report, his death occurred sometime between Saturday afternoon and Tuesday. Unless the body's still warm, MEs usually begin by asking when the decedent was last seen alive. After that, the deterioration of the body helps calculate what was the latest he could have been killed."

"So technically, he could have been killed as late as Tuesday?"

"Exactly. Not to get gross while we're

eating shredded meat, but you're familiar with dating time of death by maggot growth?"

"Sure," Kayra said cheerfully. "Isn't there a formula for calculating the blow-fly's larval stages depending on the temperature?"

I nodded, and Nolan stopped loading his tortilla with the strips of pale white chicken. "Could we please change the subject?"

"Hey, remember the Gell case?" Kayra said excitedly. "The medical examiner wasn't told that there were witnesses who swore they'd seen the victim alive at a time when Gell was in jail."

Alan Gell had been a big story here in North Carolina when his murder conviction was overturned after he'd spent four years on death row. The prosecution said it had relied on SBI statements to build its case against Gell, and the ME's office had based the time of death on a range of data that began with the last credible witness to see the victim alive. The earliest date within that time frame happened to be the only day Gell could have done it since he was in jail on an unrelated matter the rest of that time. He was tried and convicted and sentenced to death. Later, it was determined that the SBI had withheld the statements of several witnesses who swore the victim was still alive after that date. His attorneys managed to win a new trial, the original verdict was overturned, and there was much talk about prosecutorial misconduct. As a result, North Carolina law now requires prosecutors to share their entire file with the defense before a felony trial.

"Maybe that happened here, too." Nolan's face brightened up and he went back to his food, all thought of insect evidence momentarily banished. "Maybe this Deenie Gates actually saw him after Martha left for the beach. Another case of the prosecution withholding evidence illegally."

"Not illegally," I said. "Gell's case changed the law, but back then there was no legal compulsion to tell his defense everything, only an ethical one."

"All the same . . ." Nolan said stubbornly. "There has to be a reason this woman's not in any of the files."

"Where can we find her?" asked Kayra.

"Someone in Mr. Glover's office could probably pull a home address up for you," I said. "If you haven't worn out your welcome with them. Or you could try out at the hospital."

Chapter 20

A phrase may, by the addition or omission of one word, or by the alteration of one punctuation mark, convey to the reader an entirely different idea from that intended by the writer.

Florence Hartley,
The Ladies' Book of Etiquette, 1873

Wednesday, December 15

Driving back to Dobbs after the autopsy, Dwight swung by the SBI facility on Old Garner Road. Security greeted him by name at the door and waved him past with only a perfunctory glance at his shield.

"Agent Wilson's in his office, Major. Want me to buzz him?"

"That's okay. I know where it is."

He turned down the hall to Terry Wilson's office and saw that Terry's door wasn't fully latched. As he pushed it open and stuck his head in, he found Terry and K. C. Massengill locked in each other's arms. They jerked apart as the door nudged K.C.

Terry scowled at him. "Hey, don't you know how to knock?"

"Not when the door's open." Dwight grinned. "What if I'd been your boss?"

K.C. smoothed her blond hair and tugged her sweater down around her shapely hips. "We were just saying good-bye."

"That's a lot of serious good-bye for somebody who only works two halls over," Dwight observed.

"I have to go to Charlotte for a couple of days."

"And don't tell me you and Deborah don't ever mess around in chambers," said Terry, beginning their usual banter. "Even when she's not going somewhere."

But K.C. saw the weariness in his eyes and put out her hand to him. "I'm sorry about your deputy, Dwight."

"Yeah," said Terry. "That sucks, man. They sure it's suicide?"

"I just came from his autopsy."

"Bummer. This anything to do with

Tracy Johnson's shooting?"

"Probably."

"Y'all talk. I'm gone," K.C. said. "Don't forget the cat food, hon, okay?"

"Gotcha," said Terry. "Drive carefully."

"Y'all have a cat?" Dwight asked when the door closed behind K.C.

"Part of the package. For some reason, every woman I fall for has a damn cat. Deborah was the only one didn't. Probably why it didn't work out for us."

Dwight smiled at his sour tone. "Lucky for me."

"You didn't come by to talk about cats, though, did you?" Terry sat down behind his desk and gestured for Dwight to take a chair.

"Nope. Just tying off loose ends. Seeing if Tracy Johnson had any real reason to pursue this Hurst business so Bessie's granddaughter'll stop bird-dogging Deb'rah and me every night."

"Well, ol' son, I went through everything we have on it. I even read Scotty's field notes. He might not've pushed as hard as you or me, but this is no Gell case, Dwight. Not a single person he interviewed saw Hurst alive after Saturday evening."

"As he was leaving the trailer park, right?"

"Well, naw, he pawned a couple of rings belonged to his stepmother around four o'clock, then went next door to the Fliptop Grill for a couple of beers, caught the end of a Braves game, and left around six. That was the last anybody says they saw him till that anonymous call a week later."

"Kayra persuaded an old woman who still lives there to admit it was the next-door neighbor who called it in. She also told them that the nosy neighbor didn't notice his car parked in the bushes around back till long about Wednesday."

"Anybody see him drive in?"

"The old lady says not."

"That's still in line with the prosecution. They argued that Martha came home that night, found him there, and just let him have it for stealing her rings."

"And took off for the beach the next morning, leaving him there to rot in the August heat?"

"You're not going to start expecting logic from the criminal mind at this late date, are you?"

"What can I tell you?" said Dwight. "I still believe in Santa Claus."

When he got back to the courthouse and parked, Percy Denning, Mike Castleman, and Eddie Lloyd were crossing the street, heading out for lunch.

"We got lucky, Major," said Denning. "Silas Lee found the slug that killed her."

"Really?"

He hadn't meant to sound so surprised, and the others grinned.

"I've already put it under the microscope," Denning said. "It came from Whitley's .44, all right."

So that was that, thought Dwight as he continued on to his office. Whitley and Johnson and an affair that went sour. Because she was a snob like Deborah thought? Too concerned with class differences to be seen with him openly? Or did the baby she carried complicate things? They would probably never know. But at least it cleared Tracy's murder off his plate, and if the citizenry would just behave themselves between now and next Wednesday, maybe he and Deborah could get married in peace.

As he approached his office, a uniformed officer passed him in the hall with an armload of brightly colored boxes and a "Joy to the World" smile on his face. "Toy drive's picking up, Major!"

Every year the department collected toys for needy children, which reminded him that he still hadn't shopped for Cal. He couldn't decide between a dirt bike for the farm or a ten-speed for the town up in Virginia. His thoughts were interrupted by Mayleen Richards, who came down the hall with a yellow legal pad in her hand.

"Um, Major Bryant? I think you need to take a look at this."

She laid the pad on his desk, the pages curled back on themselves to show a page six or eight sheets down. "We found this at Ms. Johnson's house. That's her handwriting."

He studied the figures with a sinking heart. "Shit!"

"Yes, sir."

"Okay, Richards. I'll take it from here," he said.

She hesitated, then accepted the dismissal.

Dwight lifted his phone and called the DA's number. "Miss Helen? Dwight Bryant. Is Mr. Woodall in the courthouse today?"

"Sorry, honey," came the voice of Doug Woodall's longtime secretary. "He's in superior court in Makely. Won't be in till tomorrow morning."

"Do you know if the Ruiz trial's still on the calendar for tomorrow?"

"Well, such as it is without that deputy that went and killed himself. Brandon Frazier's going to handle it best he can, but just between you and me and the doorknob, honey, that guy's gonna walk."

Dwight read over Tracy's notes again. "Time served?" she'd written. Sure looked like she was getting ready to cut a deal with this Danno R. He was evidently claiming that he'd had twelve packets of drugs and a hundred twenty thousand in cash when Don Whitley stopped him. By the time it got to the property clerk, the twelve packets had dwindled to ten and the cash was down to eighty thou. If he was reading her notes correctly, she was willing to deal; to let Ruiz off with time served if he could prove that Don Whitley had skimmed his stash. Which the guy would no doubt be able to do. Civilians were always surprised to hear how often drug runners gave one another countersigned receipts — so many grams received, so much cash to make more buys — like a handshake ought to mean more in that world than it did in the straight world these days.

"12 pkts (1 gm ea) > 10"?

He called the DA's office and got Brandon Frazier, who told him that the drug found in Ruiz's car was cocaine. "Why?"

"No reason. Just doing some paperwork over here," Dwight said, unwilling to let the word out about Whitley just yet.

Had his deputy been a user or had he been dealing on the side himself?

He called the ME's office, and after the phone rang six times for the doctor doing Whitley's autopsy, her voice mail kicked in. "Dwight Bryant here," he said. "Do me a favor and run a tox screen on Whitley. See if he was doing coke."

After that, he carried Tracy's legal pad across the hall to show Bo Poole.

"He shot her with the gun he used on himself, but it wasn't about love or sex," he told his boss. "She was going to put him in prison."

"Whitley was dirty?" the sheriff asked.

"How else would you read her notes? It was his testimony that was going to put Ruiz away, so Ruiz decides to take a plea and turn it back on Whitley."

"Then Tracy tells him what she has planned for him: 'No more pattycake, buster, you're going down.' So he shoots her, hears she's pregnant, then kills himself in remorse?"

Dwight nodded. "So what do you think,

Bo? Do I try to make this Ruiz guy confirm what Tracy knew or do we just let the law play out in the courtroom tomorrow?"

"Either way, he was going to walk, right?"

"If he could help her build a case against Whitley, she was probably going to cut him loose. He's been a guest in our jail since July. Five months. Almost what he'll wind up serving if convicted."

"Which Doug don't think's gonna happen if we believe all his pissing and moaning yesterday." Poole leaned back in his chair. "You can talk with Ruiz, but what the hell's the point? He's not going to plead now that Tracy and Whitley are both dead. Not when he can walk out a free man tomorrow with no record. Any chance of recovering the money?"

"I doubt it. Jamison and Richards searched his place when they picked up his DNA samples. They flipped through his bank statements, but didn't see anything out of the ordinary. I'll have 'em take a closer look. They did find an expensive gold bracelet that he gave Tracy and she gave back to him. What happened to the rest of the money, though . . ." Dwight gave a palms-up shrug. "He told Castleman that money wouldn't be a problem if he quit the department."

"Oh, hell, let it go," said Bo. "Even if you found a pot of cash sitting in his checking account, without Ruiz, you couldn't prove he didn't save it clipping grocery coupons out of the *Ledger*."

Out at the hospital, Deenie Gates had positioned the folding yellow plastic board beside the door to the second-floor men's room. It read, CAUTION — WET FLOOR, although she hadn't yet begun to mop.

"Why you here wanting to know about Roy Hurst?" she asked, giving Kayra and Nolan deeply suspicious looks.

"Because Martha Hurst is about to be put to death for killing him, and we thought you might have remembered something after all these years," they explained. "Something that could help her."

"I don't remember nothing." The woman was so bone thin that her shoulder blades were sharply outlined beneath the dark red uniform shirt she wore, but she wielded the heavy mop and bucket with surprising strength. Kayra found it impossible to guess her age. There was no visible gray in her lanky brown hair, but from the wear and tear on her face, she could have been anywhere from thirty to sixty.

"Did you see him at all that Saturday?" Kayra persisted. "Y'all were together back then, right?"

"No."

"We heard you were going to have his baby."

"You heard wrong."

"He didn't get you pregnant?"

"You people cops or something?"

She sloshed her mop up and down in the bucket of disinfectant, then plopped it out on the tiles. Nolan had to step back smartly to avoid getting his sneakers wet as she pushed it back and forth.

"We're not cops," he said. "My mom was a friend of Martha's. We heard she was your friend, too."

"I got nothing against Martha," said Deenie Gates, and her mouth tightened in a grim line. "But I don't know nothing about her killing Roy and that's all I got to say. I got work to do."

Again the passive aggression of her dripping wet mop threatened their shoes and they retreated.

That afternoon, Dwight had Daniel Ruiz brought into an interrogation room. Ruiz was early thirties, with a chubby face and brown eyes that, at first glance, appeared sleepy and relaxed. It was only later that one noticed how wary and alert they were beneath those drooping eyelids. His English was good and, unlike other Latinos caught in this situation, he did not pretend he needed an interpreter. Nevertheless, for all the comprehension he showed to Dwight's questions, Dwight might as well have been speaking Russian.

No, he hadn't been offered a deal. How could there be a deal when he was innocent? Oh, and he was truly sorry to hear about the beautiful ADA's death, but there had been no understanding between them.

Missing drugs and money? But he'd known nothing about the drugs and money in that car. It wasn't even his car, merely one he was driving down to Florida as a personal favor to an elderly friend who was spending the winter there.

Don Whitley? Was that the officer who shot the lady DA? Sorry. He had been treated courteously by the officers who arrested and booked him, but they hadn't exchanged business cards and he didn't know their names.

"Yeah, right," said Dwight and signaled to the bailiff to take Ruiz back to his cell.

He hadn't been back in his own office

ten minutes when Doug Woodall appeared in his doorway.

"I thought you were down in Makely."

"Miss Helen said you called about the Ruiz case? I hope to hell you've got something we can use on that slick bastard."

"Sorry," said Dwight and told him about Whitley and the deal it appeared that Tracy was making with Ruiz. "Did you authorize it?"

"Hell, no! Not that I wouldn't have if she'd asked me. A dirty officer's worth ten Ruizes and you know it, Bryant. Damn!" Doug Woodall was far too political not to consider the lost enhancement for his tough-on-all-crime reputation.

"Well, well, well," he said as he continued to put all the pieces together. "Little Tracy was fixing to grab herself some headlines, wasn't she? Taking down a crooked officer? Puts her name right out there as the defender of truth, justice, and the American way."

"Worked for you, didn't it?" Dwight asked sardonically. "Getting the death penalty for a white woman?"

Doug grinned. "Martha Hurst? Hell yes. And if I decide not to run for DA next time, Tracy would've been nicely positioned for the job. Nobody else on my staff has her combination of smarts and ambition."

"Maybe she planned to run next election no matter what you decided," Dwight said.

Doug's face relaxed into a confident smile. "She try that and I'd've had her for breakfast."

"Yeah? Seems to me that prosecutorial misconduct's as good an issue to run on as crooked officers skimming drug money. How'd you feel about her looking into the Hurst trial?"

"Didn't bother me a bit. That was an open-and-shut case based on solid facts provided by this office and the SBI. She could look from now to election day and not find a damn thing." But as he considered Tracy's ulterior motives for questioning the Hurst trial, his indignation grew. "Well, damn! You think she was going to try to take *me* down?"

After Woodall left, Dwight called a meeting of the detective and drug interdiction squads and they exchanged reports of the day's findings, from the slug that Jones had picked up this morning to the notes on Tracy Johnson's legal pad.

"Hey, no fuckin' way!" said Eddie Lloyd when told that Whitley had been pocketing cash and drugs from some of the stops. His brown eyes flashed angrily. "He kill her because she was going to dump him, that's one thing. But kill her and the baby because one scumbag said he was dirty? Shit, Major. That don't fly."

Mike Castleman sat silently with the same sick look on his handsome face that he got every time he was forcibly reminded of little Mei's death.

"Mike?"

"I never saw him take a dime, Major," he said, but his eyes dropped almost immediately and Dwight knew what he was thinking, what they all were thinking.

Rivers of money flowed up and down the interstate. Whenever these three stopped a likely car, they'd call one of the others on patrol as backup. The goods were usually hidden in the trunk. While one officer moved on to search the front of the car, it would be so easy for someone like Whitley to slide a packet of drugs or bills into a breast pocket before sealing the briefcase or box that held all the cash, cash that wouldn't actually be counted till it was turned in to the property clerk. Sooner or later, though, they'd be tripped up by a smartass like Daniel Ruiz, who was sharp enough to know that the DA's office would turn him loose in a heartbeat if he could prove that he'd been skimmed by an officer. It had happened in other jurisdictions and only the most naive would think that it wouldn't happen here, too.

They kicked it around another ten minutes, then Dwight said, "Okay. Jack, you and Mayleen go through his place one more time. See what you can find, then everybody turn in your reports. Let's wrap this up today."

Chapter 21

The trials of married life are such, —
its temptations to irritability and con-
tention are so manifold, its anxieties so
unforseen and so complicated, that
few can steer their difficult course
safely and happily, unless there be a
deep and true attachment.

Florence Hartley,
The Ladies' Book of Etiquette, 1873

When I finished court that Wednesday afternoon, I checked by Dwight's office, but
it was empty and an officer said that he was
in a meeting, so I drove over to Aunt Zell's
and freshened up there. Uncle Ash fixed us
drinks and they wanted to know if what
they'd heard about one of Dwight's deputies was true — that he'd killed Tracy
Johnson and then himself?

I said it seemed to be true, but I hadn't talked to Dwight since this morning and so I didn't really know any of the details other than where he'd been found on the bank of Ryder Creek, which reminded Uncle Ash of camping there as a boy to catfish all night.

Talk circled back to the wedding and I went up to the closet at the head of the stairs in my old apartment so that I could check again for the tenth time that I had every item laid out on the bed to go with the dress I had found in a shop over in Fuquay, of all places. My bouquet and Portland's would be delivered to the church next Wednesday, along with boutonnieres for the men.

"Daddy offered to rent a tux," I said, "but I just couldn't picture him in one, could you?"

"Actually, I can," she said. "Kezzie Knott's always been a fine-looking man from the first time I saw him, way back when my grandfather was still practicing law."

I knew from family lore that Daddy had retained Brix Senior the first time he was charged with possession of untaxed liquor, but I hadn't realized that this was where he and Mother first saw each other.

"Oh, Sue didn't see him then," said

Aunt Zell. "She was in school. I was five and Grandmother had baked a fresh coconut cake and she had me take a piece over to the courthouse for Granddad's lunch. Everybody knew me, of course, and the bailiff let me sit next to him in the jury box till Granddad finished arguing his case. It was your father he was defending. Got him off, too. Not that I understood what was actually going on, but Granddad introduced me to him out in the hall and I remember thinking those were the bluest eyes I'd ever seen."

"Forget-me-Knott blue," I murmured and Aunt Zell smiled.

"That's what Sue always said. Come with me, honey."

I followed her down the hallway to the master bedroom and sat on the edge of their bed to watch as she took two white boxes from the drawer of her dressing table. Handing me the smaller box, she said, "This is the last one. I brought a handful home from England years ago to give to family brides and I was down to two when Minnie married Seth. I was saving this one for you, but I almost gave it to Portland when she and Avery got married."

"Didn't think I'd ever make it to an altar?" I teased.

"That did cross my mind," she said dryly.

I opened the box and there was a little silver sixpence, the face of King George V engraved on the front and crisp oak leaves and acorns on the back, just as I remembered. "I can't believe you still have this. Didn't you lend it to Portland?"

She nodded.

"That makes it even more special," I said. I'm not superstitious, but this coin that Portland had worn in her shoe on her wedding day felt like an omen that maybe Dwight and I really could build a marriage as strong as hers and Avery's.

"And this is something else I've been keeping for the right moment," said Aunt Zell.

Inside the second box was a flat black velvet jeweler's box that bore the name of a store that had gone out of business several years ago. I lifted the hinged lid and found the most beautiful bracelet I'd ever seen. Each delicate gold link was a small blue enameled flower no bigger than the nail on my little finger, and each five-petaled flower was centered with a tiny drop of shining gold. "Oh, Aunt Zell! How long have you had it and why haven't I ever seen you wear it?"

"It was never mine to wear," she said gently. "Sue had it made up when she knew she was dying. She told me to keep it for you till the time was right. She said I'd know. 'If nothing else, it can be her something blue,' she told me."

We sat there on the edge of the bed with tears rolling down our faces as she fastened the bracelet on my wrist.

Forget-me-nots.

As if I ever could.

"I meant what I said Sunday," she said. "She would have been so happy that you were marrying Dwight."

"Here, now," said Uncle Ash, who had come to see what we were up to. "What's all this sniffling about? Dwight hasn't run off with a dancing girl, has he?"

I jumped up to show him my bracelet and he gave a nod of bittersweet recognition. "I remember the day you came back from Sue's with that and put it in that drawer, Miss Ozella."

I waited for him to elaborate as their eyes locked in wordless communication, but all he said was "That was a sad time all right, but this is supposed to be a happy one. Come on, ladies, shake a leg! Sallie's expecting us."

I put the little box with the sixpence beside the satin slippers I would wear next week and joined them downstairs to walk the half-block to Miss Sallie's house.

Despite my missing groom, ten of us sat down to dinner — the Reverend Carlyle Yelvington, the minister of First Baptist and the man who was going to perform the ceremony Wednesday, had been pressed into service to balance the table. As expected, the others were Aunt Zell and Uncle Ash's age, men and women who had known me since I was a scabby-kneed tomboy whose mother despaired of ever turning her into a proper young Stephenson lady.

"Not that your mother was much of one either," Miss Sallie said tartly as her part-time cook and housekeeper brought in an elaborate crown roast of pork filled with a flavorful concoction of tender shrimp and creamy grits. "Marrying a scalawag like Kezzie Knott. Broke your grandmother's heart when she announced their engagement. She cried for a week."

"Broke more than just Catherine's heart," said David Smith, Uncle Ash's brother and Portland's father. "Half the boys in this county went into mourning, too."

"Oh it was a seven-day wonder all right,"

said Miss Abby Jernigan, who had given me her late husband's robe when I was first elected. "Richard Stephenson's granddaughter marrying a moonshiner with a houseful of motherless boys?"

I didn't take offense. Their smiles were too indulgent and reminiscent of bygone youth and high romance. I've always loved hearing how people met and fell in love, and I made each of them tell me their stories, from the Smiths, who literally ran into each other when she was learning to roller-skate, to Bonnie and Ken Knowles, who met when they both signed up for flying lessons from the same instructor back in the late sixties. Even after all these years, there was wonder in their voices at the miracle of finding each other out of all the whole world over. I just wished Dwight could have been there to hear.

One of the benefits of dining with a bunch of very senior citizens is that everyone's ready to go home to bed by nine-thirty. When I got to Dwight's apartment, he was in bed himself, watching an old World War II comedy on television.

I dropped my clothes on the nearest chair and snuggled in beside him.

He noticed my new bracelet right away

and was touched by the story that went with it. "You're a lot like her, you know."

"Am I?" I asked, pleased.

"Why do you think I fell in love with you?"

"Tell me," I said.

Chapter 22

The pleasure of your guests, as well as the beauty of the rooms, will be increased by the elegance of your arrangements; and by the judicious management of wreaths, bouquets, baskets, and flowering plants in moss-covered pots, a scene of fairy-like illusion may be produced.

Florence Hartley,
The Ladies' Book of Etiquette, 1873

Now that we were into single digits — seven days and counting — the next three days passed in a blur. Two luncheons and another dinner. Friday was my last day of court until after the Christmas break; and with the investigation of Tracy's death and Don Whitley's suicide winding down, Dwight, too, was finally able to give more attention to our wedding. It hurt him to know that one of his deputies had fallen to the same temptation of easy money that had overtaken one of my own colleagues, a temptation coupled with the rationalization that drug money, like insurance money, was there for the taking and therefore wasn't quite like stealing.

Now Russell Moore was disbarred and sentenced to three years of hard time, and Don Whitley was dead by his own hand.

The only bright spot for the sheriff's department was that the media, ignorant of any subtext, were treating Whitley's acts as motivated solely by passion. Unfortunately, men killing their women and then themselves is so commonplace these days that the story barely made it through a full news cycle.

Dwight and Bo planned to reorganize the drug interdiction procedures after the first of the year, but for now, Bo had told Dwight to go act like a man who's getting married.

Accordingly, Seth, Reese, and Andrew drove their pickups over to Dobbs Friday evening to finish moving him out to the farm — lock, stock, and nice leather furniture that would replace the ratty castoffs

April had given me when I first moved into my new house.

I drove on ahead to clear space in the garage for his boxes. The temperature had dropped again and the house was like ice when I got there. I quickly pushed the thermostat up, built a fire in the living room, and sprinkled cinnamon, cloves, and nutmeg into a small pan of hot water, then turned the flame on low so that it would simmer and fill the house with a spicy aroma. Yeah, yeah, I know that's cheating, but I wanted it to smell like home to Dwight and I really did plan to bake next week.

Honest.

Maidie and Miss Emily had both sent over enough casseroles to get us through these last few hectic days and I slid a chicken pot pie into the oven with silent gratitude. Wineglasses and matching towel sets and steak knives are all well and good, and I knew we would enjoy them for years, but a freezer full of casseroles when there's no time to cook? Now that's a truly inspired wedding gift.

We still hadn't painted my old bedroom, but the paint was there in the empty room, the cans turned upside down so the color would stay mixed. I changed into jeans and a paint-speckled sweatshirt, spread out tarps to protect the carpet, and used a brush to cut in the corners and around the molding. The white paint on the ceiling still looked fresh and clean, and we'd agreed to finesse it till the next time. Midnight blue might be Cal's idea of a cool color, but using it on four walls and the ceiling, too, would turn the room into a black hole. Or maybe that was the whole idea? Dwight keeps saying that Cal's fine with the wedding. He was so young when Dwight and Jonna split that he really doesn't remember when they were a family, but I still worry.

By the time the caravan pulled into the yard, I was almost ready to start rolling the walls. Seth and Andrew quickly unloaded their trucks, then reloaded them with the old couch and chairs for one of Robert's grandsons, who was setting up his first apartment. They declined my invitation to supper, but Reese had no one waiting for him at his trailer so he volunteered to stay and help paint.

It was heading for one in the morning before they finished the last bit of trim. I had hung all of Dwight's clothes in his side of our big new walk-in closet, and his socks and underwear were now neatly tucked away in dresser drawers.

Saturday was spent rearranging cupboards, cabinets, drawers, and bookshelves to accommodate Dwight's things. We both culled ruthlessly and wound up with several large boxes to donate to various charities.

I'm always amazed by how much you can get done if you just keep doing, and we emptied his last box shortly before eight.

Dwight put a fresh log on the fire and sank wearily onto the couch. "We're not supposed to be anyplace tonight, are we?"

"Tomorrow night's your mother, and Monday is Daddy's, but nothing tonight." I loaded the CD player with Christmas music and turned the volume down low. "Are you hungry?"

"Not really. Let's just sit a minute."

He stretched out, with his head in my lap, and I leaned back. The house felt warm and cozy and, all things considered, was amazingly tidy. The fire crackled and shot bright sparks up the chimney and an English boy choir sang ancient carols.

"Yeah," Dwight murmured. "I could get used to this."

"Ummm," I agreed.

I only meant to rest my eyes for a minute. The next thing I knew Dwight was tugging at my hand. "C'mon," he said sleepily. "It's after midnight. Time for bed."

I didn't argue.

Sunday morning dawned crisp and clear. A beautiful high-pressure day of frosty crystalline air, blue skies, and brilliant sunshine. We decided it might be politic to show up for Mr. Yelvington's sermon since he was going to marry us in three days, so we drove over to Dobbs and slipped into a back pew at First Baptist just as the choir was entering. Portland and Avery were across the aisle, two rows forward, and when she spotted us, she made a sad face and shook her head. I gave her my "What?" look, but before I could make out what it was she was commiserating with me about, Dwight nudged me to pay attention to the minister.

Despite being Baptist, the Reverend Carlyle Yelvington was less a hellfire-and-brimstone preacher and more of a come-let-us-reason-together mediator. The subject of the day's sermon was gratitude — to live in the moment, to be grateful for what we had instead of pining for what we did not have. My eyes met Dwight's and happiness flooded my soul like the morning sunlight that streamed through the stained-glass windows. From that moment on, I promised myself, I would truly try to live in every moment with a grateful heart.

That promise lasted about thirty-eight seconds after Mr. Yelvington pronounced the final "Amen," when Portland hurried over to grab me and wail, "Oh, Deborah! What are y'all going to *do?*"

"About what?" I asked her.

"You didn't hear?"

"Hear what?"

"The country club had a fire last night."

"What?"

"A short in the dining room Christmas tree. They put the fire out before it spread to the rest of the building but the dining room's a mess. Smoke and water damage everywhere. It'll be at least six weeks before they can reopen it."

Aunt Zell and Uncle Ash always sit near the front of the church, so it took them a few minutes longer to reach us. Aunt Zell was even more upset than Portland. "Oh, honey, I don't know what can be done at this late date. Everything's booked through New Year's."

"What about the fellowship hall here?" I asked. The hall was gloomy, its kitchen outdated, and no champagne would be allowed, but at least it was convenient.

It was also taken.

"The Hardisons are celebrating their fiftieth anniversary then," said Aunt Zell. "I called around this morning and everything's taken."

Before I could go into a meltdown, Dwight put his arm around me. "It's okay," he said. "We'll figure out something. It's not the end of the world."

Uncle Ash and Avery rumbled male agreement, while Portland and Aunt Zell and I rolled our eyes at one another. You don't invite two hundred and fifty of your closest friends and relatives to a champagne reception and then say, "Sorry, folks. No champagne. No wedding cake. Check back in six weeks."

But when we drove out to the country club, Job's comfort was all we found. Ours was not the only event planned for the holidays, of course, and some of the county's most prominent citizens were milling around the vestibule in anger and dismay. The club manager had barricaded himself in his office with insurance adjusters, but he had posted a large, hastily composed sign that apologized for any inconvenience and promised that all deposits would be promptly refunded.

"I'm sorry about your reception, Deborah," said Mary Jess Woodall, not sounding very sorry at all, "but Doug and I had a charity auction scheduled for tomorrow night to raise money for the battered women's shelter. We usually clear about eight thousand dollars so those women and their children can have a decent Christmas."

"What'll you do?" I asked.

"Tents," she said succinctly.

"Tents? Mary Jess, it's December."

"That's why they invented portable heaters, sugar. I'm having one set up around on the side there. The kitchen wasn't damaged and they can still serve out of it."

"Tents," I told Dwight, charmed by the idea of a big white one.

"Better start calling right now," said Mary Jess. "I rented the last one in Raleigh that's available for tomorrow night. And that reminds me. Did I get your check yet?"

"In the mail tomorrow," I promised and pulled Dwight out of there to go find the nearest phone book.

"How about my office?" he suggested.

Ten minutes later, I was seated at his desk, walking my fingers through the yellow pages.

Forty minutes later, I had exhausted all

the places open on Sunday in a forty-mile radius. Who would have thought so many Christmas parties were held under canvas? Oh, there were a couple of tents available for other nights, but for Wednesday afternoon? Three days before Christmas?

"I can give you a green one, but it doesn't have sidewalls," said one hopeful entrepreneur. "I'm pretty sure there's no bad weather predicted before Christmas."

I told him to hold that thought and called Minnie, who had already heard about the fire and who was properly sympathetic. "We've got the potato house half cleared out for Christmas dinner," she said. "We could go ahead and clear even more space. It's not very elegant, but it *will* hold two hundred and fifty people and if you don't have any other choice . . ."

With its concrete floors and exposed rafters, the tin-sided potato house is fine for square dances, pig-pickings, and big family reunions, but for a champagne reception? Minnie was right, though. How much choice did I have?

"It's so much extra work for y'all," I said weakly.

"So? School's out and the farm is full of kids who can help shift potatoes and string up greenery."

"Today's our last day of work, so Dwight and I can help, too," I promised.

"We'll see," she said. "Let me call around to the others."

"Thanks, Minnie," I said glumly.

"Don't forget tomorrow night at Mr. Kezzie's," she reminded. "Adam and Frank are getting in this evening if that snowstorm in Chicago doesn't hold them up."

I told her we'd be there and wandered out in the hall to look for Dwight.

Onc of Bo's officers came by with a large black plastic garbage bag over his shoulder.

"You look like Santa Claus," I said.

The man laughed. "Feel like him, too." He opened his bag and showed me the pile of toys it held. "Gonna be a good Christmas for a lot of kids who have nothing. It hurts to know how many are out there, doesn't it?"

As he continued on down the hall with his sack of goodies, my internal preacher said, *"And you're annoyed because you're going to have to drink champagne and cut a cake in a potato house?"*

The pragmatist nodded, in complete agreement for once.

I thought about living in the moment.

I thought about gratitude.

"Hey, shug," said Dwight when I found him down in the squad room. "Any luck?"

"Tons of it," I said and told him what my family were going to do for us.

"Then let's go Christmas shopping."

"I've already done mine," I said smugly, "but I'm always happy to help spend somebody else's money."

The family dinner at Miss Emily's that night was made even more special by the eight-year-old towhead Velcroed to Dwight's side.

Rob had driven to Virginia that morning and picked him up, a ten-hour round trip that would've taken Dwight fifteen hours, slow as he drives.

Cal and Kate's young cousin, Mary Pat, were longtime pals. She was nearly six months older, but because of how their birthdays fell, they were at the same grade level. Four-year-old Jake was big enough to hold his own with them, so there were plenty of giggles and easy chatter around the table. Although Cal and I had been comfortable with each other back when Dwight was still acting like just another brother, he was wary of me now and I didn't try to force it or play up to him. Eventually, he relaxed enough that I could throw in an occasional remark or question and he could respond normally.

The others had heard about the country club fire. "Minnie already called me," Kate said. "I told her I'd help with the decorations."

"Me too," said Mary Pat.

"Such a shame," Miss Emily commiserated, but Dwight shrugged and said, "I have to admit I'm not real sorry about the way it's working out."

I looked at him inquiringly.

"Sorry, shug, but I'm not really the country club type."

"As if she hasn't noticed," his sister Beth sighed with a shake of her head.

Even though we had moved furniture back into the room that would be Cal's, Dwight had decided that the two of them would sleep over at Miss Emily's till after the wedding.

He walked me out to my car afterwards.

"You sure you don't mind?" he asked.

"I don't mind."

"We'll be over first thing tomorrow with a tree."

"Fine," I said. "I'll go to bed early and dream girlish, virginal dreams."

"Not too virginal, I hope," he said, and gave me a very experienced kiss.

Chapter 23

If a lady's domestic duties require her attention for several hours in the morning, whilst her list of acquaintances is large, and she has frequent morning calls, it is best to dress for callers before breakfast.

Florence Hartley,
The Ladies' Book of Etiquette, 1873

Dwight hadn't been kidding when he said "first thing tomorrow." I was still in my robe and gown and had barely plugged in the coffeemaker when he drove into the yard. The back of his truck was filled with greenery and three red-cheeked children.

I poured coffee for both of us and tried not to show my dismay when he brought in the pine tree. It was tall enough, it was wide enough, but when he set it up in the cast-iron stand his mother had provided, I could see right through it.

"Nice," I said bravely and handed him a steaming mug.

"Oh, we're just getting started." He glanced at his ragtag crew. "I did sort of promise them hot chocolate, though."

"Three hot chocolates coming right up." I pulled milk from the refrigerator and packets of cocoa mix from the cabinet. "And how about some waffles?"

While I puttered in the kitchen, Dwight and the kids transformed the tree. He had brought along the thickest pine branches he could find. The cut ends went down into the stand's reservoir of water and were held in place with picture wire guyed out from the trunk of the tree. The boys went back and forth lugging in more branches, and Mary Pat washed her grubby little hands in the kitchen sink to set the table for me. By the time I put waffles, syrup, and a half-pound of bacon on the table, the "tree" was almost as thick and full as anything you could buy at a farmer's market, and the room smelled like a pine grove.

"You really did build a tree," I marveled.

After breakfast, we strung the lights and loaded the branches with all the ornaments the bar association had given us.

"Miss Deborah, what does *Kama Sutra* mean?" asked Mary Pat, holding up the angel my cousin Reid had embellished.

"It's Hindu for 'Merry Christmas,' " I said.

Dwight laughed and Mary Pat gave him a suspicious look.

I hastily asked Cal, "Did you see your room yet?"

"No," he said, wary again.

Pointing toward the hallway, I said, "It's down there at the end. The midnight blue one. Go see how you like it."

I deliberately stayed where I was so that they could explore without self-consciousness. A few minutes later, we heard laughter and tumbling.

"Y'all better not be bouncing on that bed," Dwight called.

Silence. Then giggles and the thumps began again.

"Thanks," Dwight said.

"For what?"

He waved his hand across the messy table and the needle-strewn floor. "For all this. For making it easy for Cal."

"He's an easy kid to like," I said lightly. "And the broom and dustpan are in the pantry there."

I had loaded the dishwasher and the floor was free of woodsy pine litter when the children came back down the hall.

"It's very nice," Cal said politely.

"But there aren't any sheets or blankets on his bed," said Mary Pat.

"I know. I thought we could drive over to Dobbs and let you pick them out," I told Cal.

"Can Mary Pat and Jake come, too?"

"If it's okay with Miss Kate," I said.

"And you come, too, Dad?"

"If it's okay with Miss Deb'rah," said Dwight.

Kate was over at Minnie's when I chased her down by phone, and she was more than willing for me to take the kids off her hands so that she and Minnie and April could work out logistics for the reception.

"And don't worry about helping us this morning," she said. "We've got a crew here ready to go."

Ninety minutes later, we stood in the bed linen section of a huge outlet store on the edge of Dobbs. We had looked at a dozen different sets of kid-friendly designs and Cal had narrowed his choices to either dinosaurs or footballs when Dwight's pager went off. It was work, of course.

"Sorry," he said when he'd called in, "but I'm going to have to go see what this is about."

Since we'd driven over in my car, we all went out and piled in and Dwight drove to the courthouse.

Several officers were milling around a white SUV in the courthouse parking lot when we got there.

"It's the damnedest thing," said the middle-aged black man who owned the car. "I drove down to Georgia Friday night to see about my mother. She had a heart attack and was in the hospital. When it hit, I thought maybe it was a little rock thrown up from the road, but my brother took one look and said, 'Uh-uh.' Then I got back to Raleigh last night and my wife told me they were asking on TV if anybody's car got shot about then, and — well, take a look."

There in the left rear window was a neat bullet hole. All the other windows were intact.

Dwight looked at Mayleen Richards. "Get Denning out here," he told her.

A few minutes later, Percy Denning hurried out to join us while his assistant drove the crime scene van over to the SUV.

"This is probably going to take a while,"

said Dwight. "If you want to go on back to the farm, I'll have someone drive me out."

"Da-ad!" Cal protested.

"Sorry, buddy, but I have to stay."

"It's okay," I said quickly. "We'll go back and finish deciding which sheets, maybe do a little Christmas shopping and grab some lunch, then we'll swing back here before we head home. If you can turn loose earlier, call me."

"I really like Chinese," said Mary Pat.

"Me too!" said Jake.

"Okay," said Cal.

Chapter 24

Be assured of this — little can you know of the moral conduct of another; little is it desirable that you should know. But whenever improprieties are so flagrant as to be matters of conversation; when the good shun, and the pitying forbear to excuse; be assured some deeper cause than you can divine exists for the opprobrium.

Florence Hartley,
The Ladies' Book of Etiquette, 1873

Monday morning, December 20

While Percy Denning worked inside the SUV, Dwight questioned the man, a Mr. Harper, himself.

"Do you remember what time it was on Friday?"

"Probably between four-fifteen and a quarter to five? Late afternoon, but not dark yet. I wasn't paying attention to the time and I didn't have the radio on. I was thinking about my mother. Remembering how hard she and my dad worked to get us all through school. The kind of thing you think about at a time like that. Your mother still young and healthy?"

Dwight nodded.

"Then you don't know yet how it feels to think you might lose her."

"Is she okay now?"

"Thanks be to God. They put in a pacemaker and she's doing fine, all praise to His name."

With his assistant's camera documenting every stage of the search, it took Percy Denning less than fifteen minutes to find where the slug had ricocheted off a metal seat-belt buckle and buried itself in the upholstered rear seat.

"Weird," he said, holding the little clear plastic evidence bag up to the sunlight, "but it sure does look like another .44. Let me go run it under my microscope."

"We'll be in my office," said Dwight. "If you'll step this way, Mr. Harper?"

"This isn't going to take too long, is it? My wife wanted to go Christmas shopping this afternoon."

"We just need to get your address and phone number and have your statement typed up," Dwight assured him.

"Give me a keyboard and I'll type it myself," said the man. "I'm an insurance adjuster and I spend half my life typing up reports."

Twenty minutes later, Denning walked into Dwight's office.

"It's a match, Major. And there's a tiny, tiny fleck of dried blood. I don't know if it's enough for a DNA match, but I'll send it in." He hesitated.

"Something else, Denning?"

"I didn't say anything Friday because it didn't seem important, but Whitley's liquor bottle . . ."

"What about it?"

"It might not mean a thing, but his were the only prints on the bottle."

"So?"

"The *only* prints, Major."

"Oh," said Dwight in dawning comprehension. "No smears, no blurs?"

"No, sir."

"I see. And Whitley's prints?"

"One perfect set. It's like he picked up this pristine bottle one time and never changed the position of his fingers."

"So somebody got cute."

"Not cute enough. That little strip of plastic off the cap that we found under the seat? There's a partial thumbprint and it's not Whitley's. I don't know if there's enough to get a hit, but I'll run it through AFIS."

After Denning left, Dwight placed a call to Chapel Hill. As he hung up, Bo Poole came back from lunch and did an exaggerated double take upon seeing him behind the desk. "I thought I told you not to come back till you were married."

"Sorry, Bo, but we've got a little problem."

"Let me get this straight," said the sheriff when Dwight finished explaining. "A bullet that was fired the same night Tracy Johnson died, a bullet that may have killed her if that's her fleck of blood, wound up in a car headed to Georgia?"

"That's right."

"It's from the same gun Don Whitley used to shoot himself Sunday night?"

"That's what Denning says."

"And the slug Silas Lee found on Wednesday morning? It's from the same damn gun?"

"Denning says it wasn't even messed up

much, so it was easy to match it up."

"Real convenient, won't it?" said Bo. The faster his mind worked, the slower his folksy drawl. "Wanted to make sure we'd tie the gun to both deaths, didn' he?"

Dwight nodded. "We've talked about how Tracy was backtracking on the Martha Hurst case and we all know that Silas Lee was in charge of that investigation. Tracy gets shot and when the metal detectors don't turn up the slug right away, guess who just happens to finds it?"

"A little extra insurance," said Bo. "Slick."

"Not really," Dwight said and told him about the extremely clean bourbon bottle. "No prints from the ABC clerk that sold it to him and bagged it up. None of Whitley's prints when he took it out of the bag or put it in his car or picked it up more than once when he was working up the nerve to shoot himself. I just talked to the ME who did his autopsy. They found a huge amount of sleeping pills in his bloodstream."

"In the bourbon?"

"Maybe. Denning's going to check it."

"How you want to handle it?" asked Bo when they had discussed all the probabilities.

"First I need to make one more phone

call and then I thought I'd get the whole search team in here, see if any of them saw him plant the slug."

Eddie Lloyd and Mike Castleman were out on the interstate, Silas Lee was in court upstairs, and both uniforms were on patrol. It took a good hour to call them all back in, and Dwight used that hour to put some pressure on Daniel Ruiz's attorney, who blustered and squirmed and talked about client confidentiality and eventually told him what he needed to know.

"Let's go into the conference room," said Dwight when Mayleen Richards came to tell him they were all there. "Leave your guns out here."

That startled them into uneasiness. Except for Denning, they were unaware of why they'd been summoned for this meeting, and they looked at one anther in puzzlement, but did as ordered, then filed into the conference room and took chairs around the table.

Richards remained standing by the open door with her own weapon visible.

Dwight quickly laid it out for them, beginning with the discovery of a third matching bullet less than two hours earlier. "Except that it appears to be the first one, the one that killed Tracy Johnson and caused the car crash that then killed her little girl. The third slug is what killed Don Whitley. The second one is the one that you found in the road bank, Jones."

"Yeah," said Sheriff Poole. "Want to tell us again exactly how that happened, Detective Jones?" His tone made a sarcasm out of Silas Lee's title.

Jones might not have been the sharpest detective on the squad, but he was not a complete idiot either. "Hey, you saying I planted it? That I killed Whitley? That's crazy! I wasn't even the one that laid off that part of the grid."

"Who was?" asked Dwight.

"It was Castleman. And he kept bugging me to go slower, be more careful."

All eyes turned to Mike Castleman.

The deputy brushed back a black curl from his forehead and gave a deprecating smile. "Hey, now, guys. Wait just a damn minute here. Yeah, I may have gridded off where the trajectory could have gone, but Denning and Lloyd were the ones who figured out the perimeters."

"But we didn't work that part of the bank at all," Denning said quietly. "Only you and Jones here."

Silas Lee Jones was still working it out on his fingers. "One of us killed Ms.

Johnson and then shot Whitley, too? Why?"

"Yeah, why?" asked Eddie Lloyd, leaning in on Castleman, his wiry body as tight as a coiled spring.

"Not you, too, Eddie? Why would I shoot him?" said Castleman. "We were partners, friends."

"And it's because you were friends that you could get him to meet you at Ryder Creek after you read that e-mail he sent you Sunday night," Dwight said inexorably. "That wasn't a suicide note. That was a heads-up from a colleague who was going to turn you in. What'd you do? Tell him you could show him proof that it was Lloyd who was dirty and that he was the one shot Tracy?"

Castleman's handsome face had gone pasty.

"You were in court with her that morning. Something she said about Ruiz must have tipped you off that there was a deal in the works and what it was. You heard her say she was driving back early, so you waited out there on the interstate for her, shot her, and then pretended you were on a regular patrol. Immediately after the crash, her cell phone was seen in its holder, yet by the time Denning got there, it had disappeared. It and her Palm Pilot, too. And you were first officer on the scene."

"You were skimming the take?" Eddie Lloyd exclaimed.

Dwight nodded. "I talked to Ruiz's defense attorney. We thought it was Whitley he was going to finger. It wasn't. It was you, Castleman."

"No!" Mike Castleman stood up so abruptly that Richards's hand went for her gun as his chair crashed to the floor behind him.

"I'm a father." He looked at them beseechingly. "I have a daughter. I wouldn't have killed a little girl. I wouldn't. I *couldn't*."

"Maybe not if you'd known she was in the car," Dwight said. "That's what you said at Jerry's Sunday night. You didn't notice the car seat. You were concentrating on the driver."

"Michael Castleman," said Bo Poole, "you're under arrest for the murders of Tracy Johnson, Mei Johnson, and Donald Whitley."

As they slipped the handcuffs on, Dwight motioned to Richards. "You and Jamison. Get a search warrant and turn his place inside out. Look for her cell phone and Palm Pilot and find out what he did with the money."

"We'll look," said Richards, "but I bet he was using it to pay his daughter's tuition. And he said he was getting her a new car for Christmas."

Dwight reached for his phone and dialed Deborah's number. When she answered, he said, "Ready to go home?"

"I'm at the hospital," she told him.

"Huh?"

"It's okay. Nobody's hurt, but see if you can find Kayra and Nolan and tell them to meet us in your office. His mother was right. Martha Hurst didn't kill her stepson."

"What's the matter?" asked Bo, who'd been watching his face. "She's not leaving you at the altar, is she?"

Chapter 25

A lady who has children, or one accustomed to perform for herself light household duties, will soon find the advantage of wearing materials that will wash.

Florence Hartley,
The Ladies' Book of Etiquette, 1873

Told by an impatient Mary Pat that he needed to choose between dinosaurs and footballs *now!,* Cal picked a dark blue set printed in stars and planets, only to learn that kid prints didn't come queen size. Happily, almost as soon as we got to the larger sizes, he spotted white wolves howling to a midnight Arctic sky. "Look at the paw prints on the sheets," he told Jake and Mary Pat.

We bought sheets, pillowcases, and comforter and a couple of goose-down pillows for Cal, and as we passed a machine on the way out of the store, I gave them quarters for jawbreaker bubble gum.

After linens came toys. We crossed the half-mile-long parking lot to the other side of the outlet mall and descended upon Mertz's, one of those big-box chain stores that sell everything from shoes and clothes to upholstered furniture and garden supplies. The kids looked at bicycles and skateboards and I made mental notes of the things that seemed to interest Cal so that I could tell Dwight.

When she turns twenty-five, Mary Pat is due to inherit an enormous trust fund, but for now, she was anxiously worried that her allowance wouldn't stretch to cover a stuffed dog she wanted to get for Kate's new baby next month.

"Everybody have all your Christmas presents wrapped and hidden?" I asked.

"I don't," said Cal. "I don't know what to get you and Dad."

"Me? I'm easy. Anything chocolate works for me. When I was a little girl, Santa Claus always brought me a box of chocolate-covered cherries. The dark ones. Not milk chocolate. It hasn't felt like a real Christmas since I grew up because nobody ever gives them to me anymore and I can't buy them for myself."

"You can't?" They were intrigued by the notion of forbidden sweets.

"Well, I could, I suppose, but that would be like cheating. No, I guess I'll have to spend the rest of my Christmases without them. Besides, they probably don't even make the bittersweet kind these days." I gave a dramatic sigh as Mary Pat and Cal exchanged significant glances. "But for your dad? He's really hard. Let me think."

"Not clothes."

"Not clothes," I agreed, thinking of the beautiful brown sweater I'd bought Dwight when I held court up in the mountains in October. Normally I wait till the last minute to go Christmas shopping. I love the crowds, the decorated stores, the sales. This year, though, as soon as I knew what our Christmas was going to entail, I'd begun picking up gifts. Now they were squirreled away in my garage like a stash of acorns against a winter storm. "So how much were you thinking to spend?"

"Well, I have twenty-seven dollars and eighty-nine cents, but I still need to get something for Grandma." Cal looked up at me in hopeful earnestness and I wanted so badly to hug him. He was going to be built like Dwight and he had Dwight's brown eyes, with a light sprinkle of Rob and Beth's freckles across his little nose.

"I know! How about something for his beer-making? When he was moving the other night, somebody stepped on his measuring scale, so he certainly does need another one and there's a kitchen supply store just two doors down from here."

Soon we were discussing the merits of the different scales for weighing quarter-ounces of hops or flavorings and settled on one that had a small removable aluminum pan.

Best of all, it cost less than fifteen dollars.

By now it was lunchtime, as Jake had reminded us ever since we left the toy department at Mertz's, so it was back over to the food court beside the linen store for egg rolls all around and a communal carton of shrimp fried rice. The place featured stainless steel tables and chairs and was jammed with Christmas shoppers. At the next table, two young women were showing each other their finds while their toddlers played around their feet.

"I've been wanting linen napkins forever," I heard one of them say. "And these were such a good buy, I decided the hell with it."

"Good for you. You know, I've never re-gretted the things I've bought for myself," the other one said solemnly. "Only the things I didn't buy."

At that moment, the first woman's little girl tripped and fell and split her lip on the edge of the stroller.

Blood streamed from the cut. The mother instantly scooped up the wailing child and started to dip one of her new napkins into her cup of ice water. At the last second, though, she pushed the cloth napkins aside, grabbed one of the used paper ones littering the table, and held it to the child's mouth while she darted to the counter for more. The other woman brought another handful back to the table and they applied ice and cold wet napkins until the bleeding stopped, all the time worrying aloud whether or not the child would need stitches. The young mother was almost in tears herself. By the time they'd decided it should be looked at, I had heard enough to realize they were sisters, wayfarers off the interstate, who hadn't a clue as to where the nearest emergency room was.

"Excuse me," I said, "but if you're wanting a hospital, you're only about two minutes away."

"Oh, thank you," they said, gathering up their belongings.

I gave them directions and they hurried out.

"I hate stitches," Cal said darkly and the other two nodded in total agreement.

As they compared their various scars and told one another horror stories about hospital emergency rooms, I started thinking about the implications of what I'd just seen. That was a distraught protective mother, no question of her maternal concern, yet she had unconsciously rejected the option of using one of her new linen napkins to stop the blood, had even wasted a precious extra second or two to go fetch paper ones.

I remembered Herman bitching at us the other day for using his good screwdriver to open a paint can.

So why, given her choice of three softball bats, would Martha Hurst have smashed her stepson/ex-lover with her good game bat?

Maybe Nolan's mother was right after all. Maybe she really hadn't.

But Roy Hurst had died in her trailer on the only day Martha could have killed him.

Or did he?

I thought about all the literature I'd read

on forensic entomology and the graphic discussion Kayra and Nolan and I had about blowfly larvae at the Taos Tacos. No way would the ME have made a mistake about counting the stages.

Unless — ? What was it that old woman at the trailer park had told them?

Kayra and Nolan had struck out with Deenie Gates, but I was a judge. And what's the good of having the office if you can't take advantage of it once in a while?

"Come on," I told the children. "Let's go visit Miss Amy."

"Who's Miss Amy?" they asked.

"My brother Will's wife."

"You have an awful lot of brothers, don't you?" asked Cal.

"Don't worry," I said. "There won't be a test till next Christmas."

I called ahead and gave Amy a sketchy idea of what I wanted without going into too much detail — too many little big-eared pitchers in the car with me — and when we got to the hospital, she pointed me to a meeting room off the lobby where Deenie Gates was waiting and whisked the three kids off to check out the games in the children's lounge on the third floor.

I had expected the same sullen reaction

that Kayra and Nolan said they'd received from the woman and had thought I might have to trick her into talking. Instead, I got a shy smile of genuine warmth when I sat down at the table across from her. Now that I saw her again, I began to remember. Lank blond hair, the muddy skin tones of a recovering alcoholic, and eyes that kept glancing away, unable to maintain steady contact. She was still prematurely stoop-shouldered as if expecting a blow, but there were no visible bruises today.

"How's it going, Ms. Gates?"

"Going good, Judge Knott. Real good," she said. "I been doing what you told me to — making up my own mind, not waiting for some man to make it up for me. You were right. I won't really getting nothing from none of 'em 'cepting their fists and more stuff on my charge cards. I'm the one going out to work every day while they lay around and watch the sports channel and drink my beer. I'm the one putting food on the table. How come I need to take their shit? That talking-to you give me was the best thing ever happened to me. I mean, I know some of the others tried to tell me, but something about seeing you were there in that black robe? I only come up before men judges before and you talked to me

366

like you knew I could do it."

I was profoundly surprised. I had evidently given Deenie Gates my standard battered-woman talk, but for once it hadn't fallen on deaf ears. I barely remembered her, yet she remembered me and what I'd said to her.

"Ms. Gates —"

"No, call me Deenie. It's okay."

"Deenie, then. You know that Mrs. Knott in human resources is my sister-in-law, right?"

"She is? No, ma'am, I didn't know that."

"Well, she is. And she tells me you're one of her best workers."

"I am," she said, pride in her voice. "You could eat off'n my floors."

"She also told me that Martha Hurst was once a good friend to you back before she went to prison."

"Yes." Her eyes met mine with less frequency.

"She's going to die for something she didn't do, Deenie, unless you speak up to help her."

Silence. Her shoulders hunched in on themselves more than ever.

"I know she didn't kill Roy, Deenie, and you do, too."

"You do?" Her head was down but she

didn't sound belligerent, only curious.

"I do. But I can't prove it. You can, though, can't you? Roy was your boyfriend. You were seeing him. You saw him after that Sunday, didn't you?"

"No, ma'am!" Her head came up and her eyes met mine. "No, ma'am, I didn't. Honest."

"But you know who did, don't you?"

Her head went down again.

I waited quietly and she shifted uneasily in her chair.

At last she said, "I'm not saying I know anything about how Roy got hisself killed, but if I *did* know, I'd get in trouble, wouldn't I? 'Cause I didn't tell before? Maybe go to jail myself?"

"For telling the truth and saving Martha's life? Oh, no, Deenie. Nothing like that would happen. Not if you didn't have anything to do with Roy's death. Did you?"

She shook her head vigorously and her hair swung back and forth like a curtain in front of her lowered face.

Again I waited quietly until she couldn't bear the silence any longer.

"You gotta promise he won't hurt me."

"He who, Deenie?"

"I don't know why he had to go and get so mad about it. I was growed. I was sixteen. Already working here. Mom won't but fourteen when I was born. He ain't my real daddy anyhow."

"Who?" I asked again.

"Pa. He's the one killed Roy 'cause Roy got me pregnant and won't going to marry me like he promised. He come home that night with blood all over his shirt. On the front of his pants. On his shoes. He throwed the shirt away and made Mom wash his pants. She liked to never got all the blood out of 'em. He said I'd brought shame on him and Mom, and after they went to bed, I sneaked out and got the shirt out of the garbage bag. I thought I was going to keep the baby and I thought that would be all he'd ever have of his daddy. His daddy's blood. But then later, everybody said so much, and with Martha and all? So I got the doctor to take it."

"What night did this happen, Deenie?"

"It was a Monday. Pa'd worked late and was coming home and he seen Roy's car and followed him out to Martha's trailer. I think he just walked in behind him, grabbed up one of Martha's bats, and never even gave him a chance to talk. He said he smashed his privates to mashed potatoes so he couldn't never do to another girl what he done to me. And he said he'd do the same to Mom and me if we told anybody. Well, Mom's dead now and he's took up with another woman and I ain't seen him in I reckon two years. Good riddance, I say."

Even after all her emotional outpouring, it still took me several minutes to convince Deenie to come with me to the sheriff's department. "No charges will be filed against you," I said. "You'll even be a hero for getting Martha out of prison."

A split second after she agreed, Dwight called.

"You ready to go home?"

"I'm at the hospital," I told him.

"Huh?"

"It's okay," I said. "Nobody's hurt, but see if you can find Kayra and Nolan and tell them to meet us in your office. His mother was right. Martha Hurst didn't kill her stepson."

"I can't go now," said Deenie when I ended the call. "My shift's not over."

"That's okay, Mrs. Knott will make it right with your supervisor."

"Well, let me go get my coat and pocketbook out of my locker."

We went out into the hallway and I told her I'd meet her in the front lobby as soon as I found Amy and the children.

As we parted at the elevator, she hesitated. "Should I bring the shirt?"

"Shirt?"

"Pa's shirt with the blood. Should I bring it?"

I couldn't believe what I was hearing. "You still have it after all these years?"

She shrugged her rounded shoulders. "I couldn't leave it at home. Mom would've found it. So I brought it here and stuck it up on the top shelf in my locker and then I didn't know what else to do with it, so I just left it there. Should I bring it?"

"Oh, yes, indeed!" I said.

Chapter 26

I know not a more cruel situation than that when the heart is bestowed on one whom the judgment could not approve. I would impress on every young lady how much she may prove the best guardian of her own happiness.

Florence Hartley,
The Ladies' Book of Etiquette, 1873

Things got a little hectic after that.

Dwight met us at the courthouse door and sent the children home to his mother in a prowl car. Kayra and Nolan pulled up as they were getting into it and Mary Pat immediately clamored to stay. Kayra had often babysat Kate's two, and they looked upon her as just another kid. If she could stay, why couldn't they?

"Get in the car," Dwight said mildly.

Mary Pat's bottom lip was out, but she followed the boys into the backseat and even helped Jake with his seat-belt buckle.

Dwight leaned in at the open window. "This is Deputy Maynes. If you're good, when you get outside of town, he'll put on his blue lights and siren for you."

As we walked down to Dwight's office, he hit the high spots of his last three hours for me. I was stunned to hear that it was actually Mike Castleman who had killed Tracy and Mei and then staged a phony suicide for Don Whitley.

He didn't give me time to dwell on it, though, because Bo Poole and Doug Woodall were waiting for Deenie Gates's show-and-tell.

That her stepfather's bloody shirt had been in her locker all these years astounded everyone, but, as Percy Denning later said, what better place to store it? "And thank God she put it in a paper bag rather than plastic. It got enough air to dry out instead of rotting or molding."

The summer shirt was one issued by a local bakery to their deliverymen. It was a light gray cotton blend, and although at first it simply looked like a gory mess, Denning read it like a child's primer and pointed out the sequence of details: "See this spurt of blood? That happened with the first blow to the head. This area here is splashback from when he was pounding the victim on the floor. Here's where he wiped off his hands and here's where he pulled out his shirttail and wiped down the bat."

He folded it up lovingly. "It's a petri dish of DNA. There'll probably be hairs, and look at those beautiful sweat stains under the arms. If the guy's a secreter, we'll have him nailed six ways to Sunday."

Doug Woodall wasn't looking at all happy. He had prosecuted Martha Hurst originally and he was already thinking of how this was going to impact on his race for governor. A human witness could be mistaken or lying. A bloody shirt was irrefutable.

"Okay," he said at last. "Maybe this is how it went down and maybe it isn't, but how did the ME miss the time of death by two whole days?"

"I think I can answer that," I said. "You still have Brix Junior's files here, Dwight?"

He did and I pulled out the packet of photos taken in the trailer that Friday morning all those years ago. "Just this past week, I knew I wasn't going to be out at the farm for a few days, so I turned down the thermostat when I left to save energy, and the place was chilly when I got back." I turned to our two law students. "Kayra, you said the former neighbor told you and Nolan that one of the reasons they snooped around Martha Hurst's trailer after they realized Roy's car had been parked there for several days was because the air-conditioning unit wasn't running even though the windows were closed and it was very hot that week."

"Hey, that's right!" said Nolan. "I bet Martha turned it off when she left for the beach."

"But look at this picture," I told them. It was as I'd remembered even though the significance hadn't registered on me at the time. The picture was a close-up of a bloody dent in the wall. It was also a close-up of the light switch and the thermostat. "See? The lever's been pushed down to its coldest setting."

Percy Denning immediately caught the implications. "The blowflies would have started laying eggs on the body almost immediately," he said. "If the trailer was warm — and without air-conditioning, those things heat up quick in the summer — you'd start seeing successive larval stages pretty quick."

"But if the trailer then became cold?" Doug asked.

"If the ME was given the colder temperature as what the body had experienced since death, it would make it appear as if the maggots had begun growing sooner in order for that many stages to have developed, so that would push back the supposed time of death."

Bo gave a long-suffering sigh of exasperation. "We didn't have a crime scene van back then. Silas Lee Jones was the lead detective on this case. He'd have been one of the first ones out there, right behind the responding officers. And Silas Lee has never liked summer heat and humidity."

"Shit!" said Doug.

To do Doug credit, he had learned from the mistakes of other DAs around the state. He did not stonewall, he did not try to cover it up. Once the DNA tests came back proving exactly what Percy Denning had postulated, Deenie Gates's stepfather was arrested and Doug petitioned the governor for a stay of Martha Hurst's execution and either an unconditional pardon or a new trial. He took full responsibility for the flawed evidence that had convicted her, although he took it in such a way that voters could assume that he was being noble and that his zeal for capital punishment had nothing to do with it. He even gave generous credit to Kayra and Nolan for their "selfless dedication to truth, thus proving yet again that there is no need to abolish the death penalty in North Carolina because the system does work."

With an ADA, her child, and one of his own deputies murdered by another deputy, Bo Poole had a harder row to hoe, but he's political to his toenails and the whole tragic episode with Mike Castleman was structured as an example of how rigorously the Colleton County Sheriff's Department policed itself.

Buried somewhere near the bottom of the story was the announcement that Deputy Detective Silas Lee Jones would be retiring, effective January the first.

Chapter 27

It requires the exercise of some judgment to decide how far an individual may follow the dictates of fashion, in order to avoid the appearance of eccentricity, and yet wear what is peculiarly becoming to her own face and figure.

Florence Hartley,
The Ladies' Book of Etiquette, 1873

Doug's press conference didn't take place till the day after Christmas, four days after our wedding. Nevertheless, there was so much fallout from Monday that it made our wedding on Wednesday feel almost anticlimactic.

For a while, that was all anyone could talk about at Daddy's Monday night, but the novelty of being together soon took over.

Most of our family dinners are big,

sprawling, multigenerational affairs and Christmas dinner would certainly be that, but for Monday night, Daddy had asked that it be only his eleven sons and their wives, Dwight, and me. Any grandchild who wanted to come help Maidie would be welcomed, but they were to keep quiet while serving and otherwise stay in the kitchen until supper was over.

All the leaves were added to the big dining room table and the doors to the front parlor were folded back so that a second table could be added, yet even then it was a tight squeeze to get twenty-five of us seated.

It was the first time in years that all of us had sat down together under the same roof at the same time. Adam, Frank, Benjamin, and Jack and their families had flown in yesterday or today and were bedded down in spare rooms all around the farm. The deaths of people they didn't know could not hold their attention long, and dinner soon turned into a rowdy retelling of old family stories.

"Hey, Frank, remember when you figured out how to coil a piece of copper tubing without crimping it?"

"Y'all remember the licking we got when we parachuted Deborah off the packhouse and tore a big hole in Mother's brand-new umbrella?"

"What was the name of that sexy little cheerleader you and Haywood got in a fight over in high school?"

"Smokey Johnson's a granddaddy now? You know not! He's younger than me."

"— and believe it or not, I've still got them antlers! Where are they, honey? She's always putting my stuff out in the barn and I keep bringing it back in just like that cat we had, remember? Kept bringing Mama Sue lizards and mice, like we'd bring her birds and rabbits."

"Hey, Ben? You recall the time you and Andrew and Robert tried to teach that last mule how to jump fences?"

" 'Course you don't remember, Deb'rah, but Mama Sue thought you won't never gonna learn to walk because one of us was always toting you on our shoulders. For about six months there, every time she turned around, she'd say, 'Put that child down and let her walk.' Remember, Dwight?"

And Dwight was right there with us, laughing and remembering and not having to be brought up to speed because he knew the punch lines and the in-jokes and the subtexts.

"What I remember," I said, "is how y'all used to tease me that Mother and Daddy were going to trade me in when my five-year warranty expired. That was you, Will! You and Adam told me not to say anything to them about it and maybe they'd forget. I couldn't talk about turning five and going to kindergarten until Seth finally told me the truth because I was afraid they'd trade me in."

Taking his prerogative as my oldest brother, Robert lifted his glass to propose the first toast. "And now you're marrying ol' Dwight. Here's luck to you both, honey."

All down the table, glasses were raised to our health and happiness.

"Speech! Speech!" they called.

I shook my head. "Dwight can make a speech if he wants to. All I can say is how much it's meant to me to be a part of this family, to know that you were always here for me. And not just you brothers, but you sisters-in-law, too."

"Your turn, Dwight," they said.

"I'm not going to get sloppy," he said. "But I do thank you for everything, especially for Deb'rah, and I promise that I'll do my best to make her happy."

"I gotta be honest with you, son," Daddy

said as a mischievous smile twitched his lips. "You marry her on Wednesday and it's a 'as is' deal. She don't come with no warranties this time around."

"I'll take my chances," Dwight said. "I know the manufacturer."

Tuesday was so busy for all of us that Dwight and I didn't get to have the quiet time with Cal that we had planned. DNA tests confirmed that Whitley was the father of Tracy's unborn child and Dwight had to go into work to check up on the details. Minnie called first thing to say that she had phoned a fabric shop in the edge of Cary and they were holding several bolts of white cheesecloth for me to pick up this morning. "And what about rice bags?"

I confessed that I had totally forgotten about them. I hadn't realized that Nadine was on an extension till I heard her say, "Rice isn't good for birds. People use birdseeds these days."

"I thought rice was for fertility," I said innocently. "What do you get with birdseeds, Nadine? Eggs?"

"You laugh, but Nadine's right," said Doris, who had found Minnie's third extension. "People are going to want to throw something at you and Dwight when y'all leave. It's traditional. Get some extra-fine netting and a few yards of narrow white ribbon and a five-pound bag of bird-seeds. Cal and Mary Pat and Jake can help you tie them up in little pouches. I've got a big white wicker basket I'll send over to put them in. It'll be real pretty."

The children thought that making rice bags would be fun so I took them with me to Cary, and after we dropped off the bolts of cheesecloth at April's house, we went back to mine and started an assembly line. I cut the white netting into five-inch squares, and laid them out on the table. Using a measuring spoon, Jake carefully put a tablespoon of birdseeds in the center of each, Cal gathered up the edges and twisted it to make a little pouch, then Mary Pat tied them shut with a bow.

They told me I didn't really need to pay them for their help, but I explained that I was an officer of the court and I had to be careful about violating child labor laws. We agreed that ten bucks apiece was a fair price. It took us till lunchtime, but in the end we had over two hundred "rice" bags finished when Haywood and Isabel's daughter Jane Ann came to collect them with Doris's white wicker basket.

"Wait till you see what we've done with

the potato house," she said happily.

"I can take a break now," I said, reaching for my car keys.

"No!" she exclaimed. "Aunt Minnie and Aunt April said to tell you to stay away. They want to surprise you."

"What about us?" asked Mary Pat.

"It's okay if y'all three come back with me," she said. "Miss Kate's gone to get barbecue for our lunch."

They rushed to put on their jackets and follow her out to the car.

The house seemed so quiet after they left that I put on Christmas carols, then washed and dried Cal's new sheets and pillowcases and made up his bed. The sheets were white with dark blue and black paw prints. The comforter and pillows were dark blue at the top with a border of white snowbanks and white wolves, which helped lighten the room a little, as did the white shade on his nightstand lamp. I hung crisp white curtains at the windows and white towels in his bath. The books and toys would have to come item by item as needed.

In the late afternoon, I lay down for an hour, then took a long hot shower and got dressed.

The rehearsal went off smoothly that

night and the church looked lovely, dressed in its Christmas greens interspersed with masses of bright red poinsettias and tall white candles.

On Wednesday morning I had my hair done in nearby Cotton Grove, then Daddy drove me over to Aunt Zell's in his battered old red pickup. He had bought a new suit for the occasion and Aunt Zell was right. He still is one fine-looking man.

He was in a reminiscent mood, and as we drove, he kept coming back to various family ceremonies — Andrew's first shotgun wedding as compared to the one with April, Zach and Barbara's big outdoor extravaganza at the farm that went on for three days and included a pig-picking and fireworks, Frank's hasty marriage to Mae a whole continent away.

As we neared Dobbs, I said, "Tell me about yours and Mother's."

"Ain't much to tell," he said. "Won't what I was brought up to, that's for sure. Me and Annie Ruth, we just stood up together in the preacher's front parlor in our Sunday clothes, sorta like Adam and Karen done. Your mama, though, she had to get married at First Baptist, same church as you and Dwight."

"Had to?" I asked.

"Had to," he said with a nod. "First, we was just gonna run off to South Carolina, but it was near 'bout killing her mother that she was gonna marry me, and Sue said the least she could do was let Miz Stephenson give her the fancy wedding she'd always planned on. The church was packed. Half of 'em was there to see what sort of roughneck I was, half of 'em was there 'cause they loved your mama, and the other half was there 'cause they was Knotts."

I had to laugh. "Half the church will be family today, too."

"Yeah, well, there was right much talk when Sister come in with all my boys and her gang, too."

"You didn't have a honeymoon either, did you?"

"Well, naw. In the first place, I didn't have no extra money for a wedding trip, and Sue, she wanted to start being a mama to the boys right away. Like you with Cal."

"Cal has a mother," I said.

"Yeah, but you're marrying his daddy."

"Yes."

"It'll be easier on you than it was for your mama. Some of 'em — Andrew and Robert and Frank — they was still sorrowing for Annie Ruth and they sort of blamed Sue for not being her. It took her a while but she gentled them all. Even Andrew. She wouldn't never give up on him, even after he got the Hatcher girl pregnant."

"I know," I said. When Mother was dying, Andrew was one of the most grief-stricken. And the most guilt-ridden for the hostility he'd shown her when she first came to the farm.

"Yeah, I reckon you could say our only honeymoon was our wedding night. Sister kept the boys for me and next day we went and brung 'em home."

"Well, one night's enough, I guess, if you're in love."

"No it ain't," he said brusquely, as we pulled into Aunt Zell's driveway. "And twenty-six years ain't enough either. Was all we got, though, and I reckon we made the most of it."

"You lived in the moment," I said, squeezing his hand.

"I don't know about that. I'm just saying we knowed what we had and we was grateful for having it."

Portland and Aunt Zell were waiting for me on the side porch.

"Happy is the bride the sun shines on," Uncle Ash said, giving me a kiss. He clasped Daddy's hand in both of his. "How you holding up, bro?"

Daddy just smiled. "Reckon I'll be fine once you pour me some of whatever that is you're having."

Uncle Ash laughed and took him on out to the sunroom to join Avery, who was tending bar this afternoon.

"Pour one for us, too," Aunt Zell called after them.

"Not me," I said. Butterflies were starting a fly-in through my stomach and I felt hollow inside.

"Did you eat anything today?" asked Aunt Zell.

I shook my head. "I couldn't."

"Yes you can. You girls get started. I'll be right back."

"Let her feed you," Portland advised. "You really do need something in your stomach besides butterflies, and that drink won't hurt either."

We went up to my old bedroom. I helped her on with her red velvet dress first. We had decided against the white fur trim after all. It had a high empire waistline that flattered her fuller breasts and minimized her bulging abdomen. The color was wonderful with her dark hair and eyes and her skin had that creamy glow that only pregnant women seem to get.

Aunt Zell returned with a loaded tray — peanut butter on plain saltines, with a shot of bourbon for us and a glass of diet cola for Portland.

"You look beautiful, honey," she told Portland. Then, casting a practiced eye at her midsection, she said, "How do you feel?"

"Wonderful! I finished putting everything back in the baby's room yesterday, then did two loads of laundry, and yet I don't feel one bit tired today."

"You've lightened," Aunt Zell said sagely. "Won't be long now. Today or tomorrow at the latest."

"Huh?" we said.

"The baby's dropped. Took some pressure off your lungs. No wonder you feel so good. Well, let's just hope you don't drop it the rest of the way when you're walking up the aisle."

Then it was time for my dress, a sheath of reembroidered silk brocade the color of pale champagne. The top did offer the option of spaghetti straps, but after trying it both ways we decided to go strapless for the ceremony.

"I'll help you hook them on when we get to the reception," said Portland.

A fitted long-sleeved jacket with a cropped waist went with the dress. I had planned to wear my red velvet cloak to the church if the weather had been cold or rainy, but with the sun shining and the air mild, I put on the jacket instead and fastened the two buttons.

Gold drop earrings that had belonged to my mother for the something old, Portland had lent me the small gold sunburst pinned to my jacket collar, and for blue, of course, the bracelet that Mother had sent to me down the years.

"I wrapped the sixpence in a little cotton and stuffed it way in the tip of your shoe," said Aunt Zell, handing me a satin pump that had been dyed to match my dress. "See how it feels."

I slipped it on and couldn't feel a thing.

I had done my makeup before I left home and Portland gave my hair a final spritz of spray.

"Oh, my!" said Aunt Zell, and her eyes were suspiciously bright.

"Hey, no crying till we get to the church," I told her.

Portland gave an unladylike sniffle and I handed her a tissue, too.

"Y'all about ready?" Uncle Ash called up the stairs.

I took a deep breath and looked at myself in the mirror. I seemed to be moving in a golden haze.

"Ready," I said.

As the opening notes of the wedding march sounded and Portland took her first step down the aisle, Daddy kissed my cheek. "They always say you take more atter me than your mama, but today, daughter, you look just like her."

Then we were moving down the aisle ourselves and there was Dwight, looking incredibly handsome in his brown dress uniform. It was only when I got closer that I saw how white he was.

"Dearly beloved," the Reverend Carlyle Yelvington began solemnly. He paused and smiled broadly at the congregation. "As you know, this ceremony was to have been followed by a reception at the country club. Because of the fire, that has been changed to the Knott family farm. For those of you unfamiliar with the area, there are maps in the vestibule."

He smiled again, and this time his smile was for Dwight and me as he began to speak those old familiar words. "We are gathered here today to join this man and this woman in holy matrimony . . ."

I handed my bouquet of yellow roses and baby's breath to Portland, and after that, everything blurred — the vows, the exchange of rings, even our brief kiss to seal the ceremony felt as if it were happening in alternate universes, as if the ceremony itself were in ultra slow motion while the world and all that was in it swirled around us in high speed.

("I told you you should have eaten something," Aunt Zell said, when I tried to describe the feeling afterwards.)

Then suddenly we were out of the church and into cars for the drive back to the farm. It was a ragtag caravan: Rob's luxurious Cadillac followed Seth and Minnie's Honda through the shortcuts across the farm so we could get there first and set up a receiving line. Behind us came Daddy's Chevy pickup, Uncle Ash's Lincoln, and Dr. Yelvington's Volvo, with Miss Emily and the children bringing up the rear in Portland and Avery's SUV.

When we walked into the potato house, I was dumbfounded by its transformation.

"Wow!" said Dwight.

The walls were so thickly lined with young pine trees that it was impossible to see the stud framing. Small clear lights twinkled through the branches. Overhead, more strings of the clear lights had been laid across the rafters, then billowy white cheesecloth had been tacked to the underside and looped and draped so lavishly that the effect was like stars shining through soft white clouds.

A dozen or more round tables, covered in white cloths and centered with pots of poinsettias, circled an area for dancing, and guitar and fiddle cases were stacked waiting for their owners at one end. Reese and Stevie were already standing behind a long white table that held trays of stemmed glassware from the country club and tubs of champagne and nonalcoholic sparkling cider. The cake, topped with a perfectly detailed bride and groom in pale gold and formal brown, was presided over by several of my nieces and Dwight's.

"And look on the tables," said Jane Ann. "Emma did them for you."

On the tables, each pot of poinsettias bristled with those plastic card holders that come with florist flowers, and each held a playing-card-sized photograph of various brides and grooms. I looked closely and recognized Seth and Minnie, Frank and Mae, Rob and Kate, Maidie and Cletus,

Portland and Avery, Aunt Sister and Uncle Rufus. On the back of each card was the date they had married and some comment from the couple themselves:

"Don't laugh at my hair. Beehives were stylish then."

"The first time we met was in kindergarten. He broke my red crayon and I told him I hated him."

"This was taken ten minutes after we walked out of the wedding chapel down in Dillon. Everybody said it wouldn't last three months."

"He's been gone eight years, but in my heart, he's still the gawky kid who brought me daisies when we were courting."

"I wanted to go to Hawaii for our honeymoon. He wanted to take his bluetick to a field trial in Pennsylvania. Marriage is a compromise. We went to the beach with my cocker spaniel."

I was ready to go around the room and read every one of them, but Minnie pulled us into a reception line at the door as friends and family streamed in with hugs and kisses.

Haywood held up the line to tell Portland, "You just cost me five dollars, missy. I was sure that baby would be here today."

"Hang on to your money, sweetie," she

said. "The day's not over yet." She laughed at my look of concern. "Don't worry. I'm fine. I just need to sit down a few minutes."

That was all Avery had to hear. He immediately brought a chair.

We hadn't bothered with a professional photographer, but Zach and Barbara's Emma had begun an online album for us with her digital camera, and she snapped several candid shots.

"Come here and let me hug you," I said. "I love the photo cards you made. Do we get to keep them?"

Dressed in their Sunday best, Cal, Mary Kate, and Jake darted in and out with some of my older brothers' grandchildren.

Nadine and Doris both told me I looked beautiful and — a slight surprise in their tones here — that my dress was perfect, "even though that side slit does show right much leg, don't it?"

I hugged them both.

"You're a brave man, Dwight Bryant," said Adam when he and Karen came through. "If this family gets to be too much, you can always come join us out in California."

As the arrivals thinned, Aunt Sister opened her fiddle case, tuned up, and began to play a familiar melody. Haywood and Herman and Will joined her with their instruments, then Annie Sue began to sing in her high sweet voice.

It's a dumb song. It's corny. It's sentimental. It's the cliché of clichés and I usually roll my eyes and snicker every time it's played.

Today though, my eyes began to puddle as Daddy took me by the hand and led me to the center of the floor.

I buried my face against his chest as we moved to the music, and he said, "Here, now, it's gonna be fine."

"I know," I said.

"He's been loving you a long time, shug."

"Yes."

"And you been loving him, too. The only difference is that he knowed it and you didn't."

I lifted my eyes to his and smiled. "I wish you'd told me sooner."

He gave a soft snort of laughter. "And since when did you ever listen to me?"

"You'd be surprised," I said.

Dwight and Miss Emily joined us on the floor, and after one circuit we changed partners and I went into his arms. Other couples followed, the music became more lively, and the party took off.

"Husband and wife," I said as the floor became crowded with so many of the people we both love.

"For better or worse," he agreed.

"In sickness and in health."

"Maybe even in anchovies." His arms tightened around me.

For one brief instant, I thought of Tracy Johnson. If she hadn't been too status-conscious to stand before the world with a sheriff's deputy, would she still be alive?

Then Dwight kissed me and champagne corks began to pop as I entered fully into the moment.

"Thank you," I said to Whoever might be listening.

"My pleasure," said Dwight and kissed me again.

We hope you have enjoyed this Large Print book. Other Thorndike, Wheeler or Chivers Press Large Print books are available at your library or directly from the publishers.

For more information about current and upcoming titles, please call or write, without obligation, to:

Publisher
Thorndike Press
295 Kennedy Memorial Drive
Waterville, ME 04901
Tel. (800) 223-1244

Or visit our Web site at:
www.gale.com/thorndike
www.gale.com/wheeler

OR

Chivers Large Print
published by BBC Audiobooks Ltd
St James House, The Square
Lower Bristol Road
Bath BA2 3BH
England
Tel. +44(0) 800 136919
email: bbcaudiobooks@bbc.co.uk
www.bbcaudiobooks.co.uk

All our Large Print titles are designed for easy reading, and all our books are made to last.